LIGHT
from
DISTANT
STARS

Center Point
Large Print

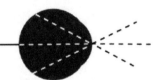

**This Large Print Book carries the
Seal of Approval of N.A.V.H.**

LIGHT
from
DISTANT
STARS

SHAWN SMUCKER

CENTER POINT LARGE PRINT
THORNDIKE, MAINE

The Library of Congress has cataloged this record
under Library of Congress Control Number: 2019944732

For Linda
(1968–2016)

What chance did we have?
We are the children of our father.

John Steinbeck

I talk to God, but the sky is empty.

Sylvia Plath

Love is not consolation. It is light.

Simone Weil

LIGHT
from
DISTANT
STARS

PART ONE

Monday,
March 16, 2015

*Darkness was upon
the face of the deep.*

Genesis 1:2

one

The Body

Cohen Marah clears his throat quietly, more out of discomfort than the presence of any particular thing that needs clearing, and attempts to step over the body for a second time. His heel no more than lightens its weight on the earth before he puts his foot back down and sighs. He tilts his head and purses his lips, as if preparing to give a talk to an unruly child. He does not take his hands out of his pockets, worried that he will taint the scene, which in the next moment he realizes is ridiculous. This is where he works. This is where he works with his father, Calvin. His fingerprints are everywhere.

He stares down at the body again, and sadness keeps him leaning to one side. It's the physical weight of emotion, and that weight is not centered inside of him but skewed, imbalanced. It is not his father's slightly opened eyes looking up at him from the floor that bring down the heaviness, and it is not his father's cleanly shaven cheeks, haggard and old. It is not the way the tangled arms rest on his chest, or the way his one leg is still bent and propped up against the examination table.

No, the thing that weighs Cohen down is the shiny baldness of his father's head, the way the light reflects from it the same way it did when he was alive. The light should dim, he thinks. It should flatten out, and the glare should fade. There should be no light, not anymore.

two

The Preacher

When Cohen was a small boy, lying on the floor under the church pews on a humid summer Sunday night, the bright ceiling lights shone. He listened to his father's voice boom through the quiet, the heavy pauses filled with scattershot responses. "Amen!" and "Preach!" and semi-whispered versions of "Hallelujah!" so hushed and sincere they sent goose bumps racing up his skinny arms.

Under the pews, on the deep red carpet, drowning in the hot, stuffy air, young Cohen drifted in and out of sleep. It was as if he had descended beneath some holy canopy and settled into the plush red carpet surrounded by a rain forest full of trees, which were actually the legs of pews and the legs of people and women's dresses draped all the way to the floor, rustling ever so slightly with the sermon. He could smell the hairspray and the cologne and the sweat mingling like incense, a pleasing offering to the Lord.

Far above him, like branches moving under the weight of resettling birds, people waved paper fans created out of their Sunday evening bulletins,

15

folded an inch this way, an inch that way, stirring the air. But to no avail. Sweat came out of their pores. Sweat welled up in droplets like water on a glass. Sweat trickled down, always down. And even there, from the floor, Cohen could imagine it: the sweat that darkened the underarms of Mr. Pugitt's light blue collared shirt, the sweat Mrs. Fisher blotted from her powdery temples, the sweat that made his father's bald head shine like a beacon, and the sweat that sweetened the nape of Miss Flynne's slender neck.

Ah, his Sunday school teacher, Miss Flynne! Cohen was only nine years old in 1984, but he could tell that something about Miss Flynne opened doors into rooms where he had never wandered. Why couldn't he speak when she looked at him? Why did the lines of her body push his heart into his throat? She was all bright white smiles and straight posture and something lovely, budding.

His mother was not all smiles, not in 1984 and never before that and never since. Sometimes, from his place of repose under the church bench, he could peek out and see his mother's stern face, eyes never leaving his father. The intensity with which she followed his father's sermon was the only thing that could distract her enough to allow him to slip down onto the floor. No one else seemed to notice her lips, but Cohen did, the way she mouthed every single word to every single one of his father's sermons, as if she had written them herself. Which she had.

Sometimes, when Cohen's father said a word that didn't synchronize with his mother's mouth, she would pause, her eyes those of a scorned prophet, one not welcomed in her own town. Cohen could tell it took everything in her not to stand up and interrupt his father, correct him, set him back in the record's groove. But she would shake her head as if clearing away a gnat and find the cadence again. Somehow their words rediscovered each other there in the holy air, hers silent and hidden, his shouted, and Cohen's mind drifted away.

If Cohen rolled over or made too much noise or in any way reminded his mother of his existence there beneath the canopy, she hauled him back up by his upper arm or his ear or his hair, whatever she could reach, hissing admonitions, hoisting him back to the pew. He felt the eyes of the hundreds of other people on the back of his own neck, sitting there like drops of sweat, their glances grazing off his ears, skimming the top of his head, weighing down his shoulders. There was a certain weight that came with being the only son of a popular country preacher. There were certain expectations.

His sister Kaye was always there, waiting for him in the canopy, only four years older than him and sitting completely still. She had an unnatural

17

ability to weather even the longest of sermons without so much as twitching, without moving a single muscle. Sometimes she didn't even blink for long minutes at a time. He knew. He watched her, counting the seconds. When they got older, she told him her secret to this, the things she thought about to keep her in that central spot, the stories she made up. She told him about the things in the church she would count: the wooden slats on the ceiling, the imperfections in the wooden pew, the number of pores on the back of the person's neck in front of her and how those tiny hairs became an endless forest through which she embarked on an adventure.

When Cohen became bored contemplating his sister's stillness, which took only moments, his gaze joined with those hundreds of other gazes, the way small streams drown into bigger ones, and he stared at his father on the stage. Cohen was transfixed by what he saw. His father reached up with his long, slender fingers and loosened his tie. He raised a pointed finger to the heavens and made a desperate plea, his voice a cadence, a rhythm, a kind of calling out, and the congregation heaved with emotion. People shouted. Women's shoulders shook with poorly suppressed sobs. Men leaned forward, their faces in their hands, as if scorched by Isaiah's coal.

Cohen's father pulled a pure white handkerchief from his pocket and wiped his bald head dry, and the lights shone. An usher opened the windows that ran along the east side of the building, and a cool night breeze blew through, leaking in and spreading along the floor, gathering in pools that Cohen slipped into when his mother had been taken up again by the words of her own sermon.

three

The Sycamore

Cohen steps over his father's body, finally, reaching with his toe for the far side like a burglar in a black-and-white movie, movement exaggerated, each step a gigantic cursive letter. But even with that large first step, even after reaching as far into the future as his leg will allow, Cohen's heel comes down and touches the edge of the pool of blood, the mercury-red puddle that leaks out from under his father's neck and outlines his head like a saint's halo in stained glass.

Cohen hisses at himself for his clumsiness. He pulls his hands out of his pockets and holds on to the examination table with one hand for support, leaving a neat line of fingerprints all in a row. Each one is like the labyrinth behind Saint Thomas Church, the slowing curves circling back in on themselves, each with a middle that is never the end. He lifts his heel, contorts his body to try to examine the back of his foot, and there it is, a small dash of blackish red, like the sticky remains of a lollipop. He rubs his finger tightly along the heel of his shoe, transferring most of the blood from the back of his foot to his index finger. He stares at it, not knowing what to do next.

It is the blood of his father, the life that has pumped through him all these years. The blood that turned his father's face red when he shouted from the front of the church, the blood that fled and left his father's face white when he realized he had been found out, when Cohen's mother stormed out onto the baseball field, when he was told to leave the church. It is his father's blood, the same blood that in many ways is all wrapped up inside of him, pumping through his own body, circling his own maze of veins and arteries and capillaries that his teachers said could reach to the moon and back.

He sighs.

He walks through the basement holding his bloodied finger out to the side, as if it is someone else's hand entirely, as if he is looking for a trash can to put it in. His feet are still heavy as he walks a straight line past the bodies on the stainless-steel tables, past the various coffins, some open, some standing up and leaning against the wall, others closed. He feels a twinge of guilt that one of their employees will have to be the first to find his father, and for a moment that is nearly enough to send him off track. Poor Beth, if she comes back this afternoon, before anyone else. What will she do when she finds Cohen's father on the floor? Call the police? The ambulance?

Cohen? Marcus, on the other hand, might faint. It would be like him to do that, to see the blood or the partially opened eyes of his already dead employer and drop over. The fainting funeral worker.

But Cohen does not want to be the one to find his father, not now. Did the neighbors hear the long and loud argument he had with his father last night? Did they see Cohen storm out, angry, muttering to himself? No, it would be simpler if he was not the one to find the body, if this accident was brought into the light by someone else.

It was an accident, wasn't it? He looks closer at his father, at the scene. His father wouldn't have done this to himself.

Would he?

With a deep breath, Cohen walks up the basement steps and out of the funeral home. He touches nothing on his way except the doorknob, and that he opens with his coat pulled down over his left hand.

Emotion catches him again, and his eyes well. He will never see his father again, not his smile or the tired lines of his face or his strong hands flexing away some phantom pain. Cohen wipes his eyes and clears his throat.

Outside, the city streets are quiet. It's a small, vibrant city, drifting from north to south, down toward the river. It's a quiet place in the middle of the afternoon before the children are released from school. It's a green city, cement and macadam and asphalt sharing space with sycamores and oaks and maples.

Cohen feels better. It's easy to begin to pretend he has not yet seen the body of his father when he is standing under that sky stretched tight, a sheet once white but now washed into a shade of gray. The early spring day carries a bite of winter that awakens him to his life. The air smells one moment of warm, earthy spring and the next of low, frozen, gray clouds. The air sneaks in around the edges of his overcoat, soaking in through his thin, worn suit, and he wonders if he has time to run home and change before going to his nephew's baseball game.

He looks at his watch. He doesn't have time. He remembers the blood on his index finger. He scans his suit, his coat, anywhere he might have accidentally rubbed his finger, anywhere he might have marked himself with his father's blood, but he doesn't see anything.

He looks up and down the sidewalk before squatting like a catcher beside one of the city's new trees growing in front of him. It is no more than three or four inches thick, a sapling. But he thinks it would be better to clean off his finger farther from the funeral home, so he stands and walks another block on Queen Street to a larger tree, a sycamore with its winter skin peeling into spring. He wipes his finger on a piece of rolled-back bark, and it is a relief, removing his father's blood from his hands. He wonders why he didn't simply wash his hands in the sink. Was he worried Beth would return? Or was he simply not thinking clearly? He feels muddled, confused, the shock of finding his father mingling with the approach of grief.

It is a relief to him that spring is coming.

Cohen looks up and down the street again. He glances at all the windows, all the dozens of windows in the dozens of houses, afraid he'll see someone looking out at him, someone watching him wipe his bloody finger on the rolled-up parchment of sycamore bark.

He feels a sob rise in his throat, thick with sadness and anger and regret. His father is dead.

four
The Teacher

In 1984, on bleary-eyed Sunday mornings, when the Holy Spirit was less of a shout and more of a whisper, there was Sunday school with Miss Flynne. Ah, Miss Flynne, the slight young woman barely escaped from girlhood who stood meekly at the front of their chaos. She would raise her hand halfway, then use that hand to adjust her glasses, as if she had never intended to quiet them. She would clear her throat gently, then louder. She was pretty when she stood at the edge of anger, her cheeks flushed, her soft mouth a firm line.

Miss Flynne sometimes took off her shoes and socks in those moments when it seemed the chaos could never be put back inside the box, and Cohen always marveled at the exquisite whiteness of her feet, the slenderness of her toes, the bright glossy green of her toenail polish. It seemed rather fancy to him, and also a bit strange. Weren't her feet cold? His own mother rarely took off her socks in their house. It seemed like something the people in his church would not approve of if they knew about it.

But who in the church besides her Sunday

school class would ever see her bare feet? Who would ever see her as he did in that moment, removing her shoes, her socks? She moved slowly, and he could tell she no longer heard the children but had become completely engrossed in that small unwrapping. She draped the bright whiteness of her socks over a chair at the front of the room, and that was when he saw her initials close to the top, almost hidden under a frill of lace.

HMF.

He knew the *F* stood for Flynne, but what of the *H*? The *M*? He spent those first chaotic moments of Sunday school trying to guess Miss Flynne's first and middle names.

Heather Madeline?

Harriet Madison?

Holly Miriam?

He sighed. It seemed a nice thing to contemplate on a dreary Sunday morning while the anarchy of the class boiled around him. But a certain kind of stillness settled in the room as Miss Flynne took advantage of the greatest weakness of any nine-year-old: curiosity.

At the front of the class, she situated a felt board with felt Bible characters that somehow stuck, and they stared out at Cohen. Without saying a word, Miss Flynne went about arranging the flat people on the pale blue board, and that quieted some of the Sunday school students.

They wanted to see what the morning's story would be. She moved slowly, either out of great concern for the careful placement of the flannel people or because she was delaying the moment she would have to confront the children. When the scene was set, she lifted her Bible up in front of her bright green eyes and spoke, and when she read the Bible, she became a proclaiming angel, and no volume level was unattainable. She was transformed from a timid mouse to some kind of powerful cherub. The children froze in place, waiting for their imminent demise.

Belshazzar the king made a great feast to a thousand of his lords, and drank wine before the thousand. Belshazzar, whiles he tasted the wine, commanded to bring the golden and silver vessels which his father Nebuchadnezzar had taken out of the temple which was in Jerusalem; that the king, and his princes, his wives, and his concubines, might drink therein. Then they brought the golden vessels that were taken out of the temple of the house of God which was at Jerusalem; and the king, and his princes, his wives, and his concubines, drank in them. They drank wine, and praised the gods of gold, and of silver, of brass, of iron, of wood, and of stone. In the same hour came forth fingers of a man's hand, and wrote over against the candlestick upon the plaister of the wall of the king's palace: and the king saw the part of the hand that wrote. Then the king's countenance was changed, and his thoughts troubled him, so that the joints of his loins were loosed, and his knees smote one against another.

At the words "came forth fingers of a man's hand," every child finally went silent, imagining a bodiless hand carving lines in a plaster wall, frightening the most powerful man in the world. Jared Simms, sitting at the back of the class, sucked in his breath and held it. Little Mary Everett, the same age as Cohen but the height and weight of a five-year-old, peed in her chair. Cohen knew because she did it often and he expected it in moments like that. He saw the drops begin to drip from the metal folding seat.

The vision of a bodiless hand haunted Cohen's dreams for three solid nights, so that sometimes, even when he was awake, he thought he could see the hand coming toward him through the reflection in his window, index finger extended, preparing to write some portentous message on his own wall. Or perhaps directly on him, the way God had marked Cain.

What would that hand have written? What

message could have possibly prepared nine-year-old Cohen for the future of his childhood, the crumbling of his family, or the arrival of the Beast?

He was so young. He knew nothing of messages that could terrify a king. He knew nothing of a lions' den or the heady aroma of red wine when a person's nose was deep inside the stemmed glass. He knew only of hot summer nights, lying on the sanctuary floor, listening to his father's voice rain down, or cool Sunday mornings in the basement of the church, staring from Miss Flynne's green eyes to her green toenail polish to her white socks still perched on the chair.

HMF.

five
The Phone Call

Cohen drives into the VFW parking lot a few miles outside the city. If he keeps going for another ninety minutes, he would lose himself in Philadelphia, those endless streets and back alleys, those cratered avenues and narrow passages, the place where his mother and sister fled when he was a child. Only his sister came back. On his days off he sometimes drives into that city, vast and imposing. He likes that the streets there don't recognize him.

A few lonely cars are parked in front of the VFW, but it is a quiet building lost in between towns. He doesn't remember at any point in his entire life actually seeing anyone coming out of or going into the building. The sign out front is always changing, from "VFW Bingo Tonight" to "Oyster Soup Night" to "Pancake Breakfast This Saturday." But he has never seen anyone standing at the sign, arranging the letters. He smiles to himself, imagining a mysterious, bodiless hand forming the messages.

Cohen pulls around behind the VFW and follows a stone lane that leads down the hill. He can see the baseball field from there, nestled in a flat space at the bottom. A train track lines the first-base side of the diamond, and beyond that, farmers' fields go on for miles, stretching out to forest-covered hills. It's sometimes hard to imagine the city is only a few miles away, all concrete and intersections and traffic lights.

The flurries stopped at some point during the drive, as if they suddenly remembered it's March and there is no real place for them. The sky is low and cold. A sporadic breeze whips the treetops before fading to nothing.

Back when he was nine years old and his parents were still together and they all lived happily in the country, he rode his bike all over this area, where the air smelled like hay or manure or spring mud depending on the day, and where you could tell the month by what was growing in the fields or how tall the corn was. He'd wandered the wide creek beds, forded every stream, fished in every bend. Sometimes, like today, it feels almost unbearable, the presence of his past.

He gets out of the car and walks gingerly through the soggy grass, the earth giving way beneath him. He sees three small children squatting close to the train tracks. Each of them is in their own world, digging into an old sandpile with small sticks, ignoring the cold day, the low clouds, the expansive fields that threaten to engulf them. They seem completely fine with their own smallness, and they go on poking the earth like tiny mosquitoes on the back of an elephant.

The flurries come down again, and they provide a stark contrast to the boys playing baseball, one team wearing candy-green uniforms, the other in stop-sign red. Both teams are sponsored by local businesses, the names of which are emblazoned in large, all-capital letters across the front of the uniforms. Parents offer up encouragement, then silence swells as each pitch spins toward the catcher.

Cohen played on this field when he was young, on a team sponsored by a local business, Lengacher's Cheese. Their hats and uniforms were a pumpkin orange with white letters. He remembers the adjustable bands on the hats with their small line of tabs that fit neatly into the line of holes. He remembers how the leather glove felt on his hand, smooth and worn and essential, as if he had managed to love baseball enough that his own hand had grown, expanded, and padded itself. But not all of it is the same: the old chain-link fences have been replaced with new ones, and the bases actually attach to the field—when he was young, they were rubber mats you threw down and tried not to slip on.

Cohen drifts in behind his sister—she stands on the ground beyond the end of the aluminum bleachers, eyes intent on the field. He stops and stares at the back of her for a moment. Everything seems forced now that he knows what he knows about their father. How should he approach her? How should he talk to her? He is nervous that he'll slip up, say something he shouldn't yet know. He takes a deep breath and smiles and wraps his arms around her from behind, pinning her arms to her side. He picks her up a few inches off the ground.

"Whoa!" he exclaims. "You *are* heavy with child."

She pushes at his arms and he lowers her back to the ground. She shakes her head. "Always tactful, my brother," she says in her scratchy voice, and Cohen thinks again that if someone didn't know her, they'd assume she was a smoker. She rolls her eyes. "Besides, as you well know, it's 'heavy with children.' " She cups her hands around her mouth and shouts, "Let's go, Johnny!"

She turns to Cohen and puts one arm around his shoulders in a side hug, as if trying to make up for implying he isn't tactful. He recognizes the gesture. She is so kind she can't even pretend to insult without immediately apologizing.

He nudges up against her. "Still two babies in there, huh?"

She rolls her eyes again, doesn't even dignify his question with a response.

"Where's he playing? I can't see him."

"He's on first," she says.

"That's where all the action is."

"Yep."

"C'mon, Johnny!" Cohen shouts, wanting to make sure his nephew knows he's there. The boy is ten and in a phase where all he talks about is baseball. Well, he's also in an astronomy phase, so it's mostly baseball and outer space.

Cohen remembers those days—the crack of the bat, the feel of the ball nestling into his glove, the smacking sound of a tight catch. These memories of childhood baseball are almost primitive. They awaken something instinctual in him, something basic. These feelings are connected to his father, and a deep sadness returns, weighs him down, always flanked with anger and regret.

He remembers baseball with his father. The ball floated through the air, red seams spinning like the rings around a planet. There was always the smell of cut grass, the clippings gathering on his white shoes. He reached up and caught the ball, and his father shouted something encouraging so that he swelled from the deepest part of his chest. He smiled and yet always tried to hide his smile—it seemed unmanly to be affected by praise. It seemed one should take it in stride, as if it was expected. He threw the ball back to his father, harder this time, and again he watched the spinning seams, again he heard the ball smack deep into the leather.

He feels for his phone, deep in his overcoat pocket. A wave of guilt washes over him as he looks at the screen. No one has called. How long would it take for someone to find his father? Would they call him first, or would they call the police? It would be so much easier if they called him first—he could go to the funeral home, he could be the second one there. This would excuse the presence of anything out of the ordinary: his fingerprints, or that thin slice of a mark in the otherwise perfectly round puddle of blood. He begins to doubt his decision not to call the police.

"Hello. Earth to Cohen," Kaye says playfully.

"Sorry."

"I said, have you talked to Dad this afternoon?"

He swallows hard. "Nah. No. I've been out and about."

She nods. "Strange," she says, more to herself than to Cohen. "I don't know why he's not answering his phone."

It's Cohen's turn to nod. He tries to shout for his nephew again, tries to cheer him on, but there's a strange obstruction in his throat, like a kink in a hose, and he stops halfway through, coughs.

"Are you sick?" she asks without looking at him.

"Allergies, I think."

She nods again, stepping to the side and trying to see around a newcomer who has stopped directly in front of them. "This weather's been crazy. Makes my skin ache. Does Dad need one of us? Didn't two come in last night?" She hugs her round stomach close, shivering as another burst of wind sweeps down the hill.

"Say I should be there, Kaye. You don't have to beat around the bush."

"Well," she says, casting him a glance, "I can't do everything around here. I am growing humans, after all."

He loves her. Without his father, she will be all he has left. She and Johnny. And the twins, whoever they end up being. He doubts his resolve for a moment. She means more to him than every other person in his life combined. Why shouldn't he tell her he found their father? Why didn't he call someone? What good was this deception?

He wraps an arm around Kaye's shoulders. "I hear you. Yeah, okay, I'll make my way over there. I planned on working all night tonight anyway. Are you coming in tomorrow?"

She's not listening. She's looking back at the field and hopping up and down. "Yes!" she screams. "Nice catch, Johnny!" She looks at Cohen and punches him proudly in the shoulder. Her eyes say, *Did you see that?*

"Do they always play in this weather?" he asks, catching snowflakes as the flurries turn into a legitimate snow, the kind that sticks to the grass and the leaves and coats the tops of people's heads, the slopes of their shoulders.

She shrugs. "It's rare to have this kind of weather during baseball season. But they do seem to start earlier every year."

Cohen looks over his shoulder and can no longer see the faraway hills beyond the train tracks. The wind picks up, driving the snow in horizontal lines, and everyone in the bleachers pulls their coats closer or plunges their hands into their pockets. The boys look like turtles, all of them pulling their heads down inside their collarbones, their shoulders rising against the weather. They blow into their hands, and their breath clouds out in bursts of white.

Many things happen at once. The umpire, dressed in black and wearing a black face mask, stands up and waves both arms back and forth like a man on the tarmac waving off an airplane, calling off the game. The snow falls harder and mixes with sleet, stinging the skin. The train whistle sounds from far off, a distant warning.

And Cohen's phone rings. He feels it buzz in his pocket, like a lost bee.

But he's caught up in the mass movement of the fleeing crowd shielding themselves from the sleet and the snow, everyone trying to find their child so they can move to the shelter of their car. There is the sound of aluminum baseball bats being thrown into a canvas bag, the clanging of soles banging their way down the wet aluminum bleachers. The coaches' sons have been charged with retrieving the bases, and they disappear into the whiteout. The sleet taps against the chain-link fence posts with the lightest of pings.

Cohen reaches into his pocket and pulls out his phone. "Hello? Beth?" he shouts into the phone, the wind crackling the sound in his receiver. He cannot hear her over the sound of the baseball bats and the shouting and the snowstorm and the sleet on metal. And the train whistle again, closer.

"Wait a minute," he says without waiting for a reply. He looks up. He remembers the children playing beside the train tracks, but he can't see the tracks anymore through the heavy snow, so he veers over in that direction. The train whistle sounds again, and he feels panic rising, a sickening sense of being too slow to stop a future he can nearly see. Once, he had to work with a body hit by a train. He had to walk parents in to view their teenage child, pieced back together with what had been found.

"Hey!" he shouts blindly into the storm, holding his phone at his side, getting closer to the tracks. "Where are you kids at? Get out of here!" The train approaches, only a few hundred yards away, a single bright light pointing the way. "Hey!"

He pushes his way through the snow like someone lost among a clothesline of drying sheets. He arrives at the sandpile. The children are gone. They've fled the storm too.

When the train passes, it brings a sense of anger with it, and those far-off hidden fields roil in its wake. Its whistle blast fills Cohen—in that second, it is everything. He waits fifteen seconds, thirty seconds, and the train passes.

He turns and tries to find Kaye, sees she is already in her car, and remembers Beth is on the phone. Beth, who thinks she is delivering the most horrible news she could possibly bear. Beth, who must have walked into the funeral home basement and found his father.

Cohen crosses the parking lot. Headlights and brake lights are everywhere as the teams disperse, and car exhaust belches out into the early spring parking lot.

Where is the sun? he wonders. *Where is the sun?*

"Beth, are you still there?" he says into the phone while jogging toward Kaye's car. He holds up one finger to Kaye, asking her to wait.

"Cohen, what are you doing? Are you listening to me? Did you hear what I said?" Beth asks. Her voice sounds drawn out, like a long string of sap about to break under its own weight.

"No," he says. "It's snowing here. It's windy. I can't hear anything. I'm with Kaye."

"Cohen," Beth says. "It's your father. It's Calvin."

Cohen nods, and relief rushes over him. Finally this part will be over. Finally someone has found his father and has reported it and he can be brought into the situation naturally. Finally he is allowed to know what he already knows.

"What?" Cohen asks, trying to sound surprised. "What about him?" It's very difficult sounding surprised when you know what's coming. You have to be a fine actor to pull that one off, and Cohen is no actor. In fact, he's a terrible liar. He walks up to Kaye's car and motions for her to roll the window down. He wants to be able to tell her as soon as he gets the news from Beth.

Kaye rolls down her window, and the swirling snow blows inside. "Goodness, it's cold, Cohen. What's wrong?" she asks, shielding her eyes against the bright white outside the car.

"It's Dad," Cohen says, holding his hand over the phone.

"What do you mean, it's Dad?" Kaye asks, going from annoyed to concerned in the space of two seconds flat. Suddenly the snow does not bother her. Suddenly the sleet rat-tat-tapping on the glass windshield and bouncing into the car and glancing off the steering wheel is nothing. The tiny white particles cling to her sweater, her eyelashes, lodging themselves in the space between her fingers.

Cohen holds up a finger again, and the snowflakes and sleet continue to fill his hair, ricochet off his face. "Beth, what's wrong?" he asks, waiting for the words, "Your father is dead" or "Your father has died" or "There's been a terrible accident." He's eager for those words so that he can stop pretending. So that he can know, legitimately, what has happened.

"Cohen, what's wrong with you?" Beth shouts. "Why won't you listen to me? Your father is on his way to the hospital! You and Kaye need to go there right away!"

"Wait," Cohen says. His face feels suddenly numb. He wonders if this is what it feels like to have a stroke. "Dad's not—wait. What?"

"Something happened," Beth says, and she starts to cry. Her words come out an octave higher. "There was an accident. Or someone did something. No one's telling me anything. But your dad. He's . . . You need to get over here. Both of you."

"He's not—dead? Is he?" Cohen asks, and he cannot hide the complete disbelief in his voice.

"Not yet," Beth says, taking a deep breath. "Please, Cohen. Please come to the hospital. Hurry."

six

The Old House

Cohen drives to Saint Mary's Hospital using back roads to reenter the city, and it's a draw, really—the time difference between shooting straight into town and winding around the traffic. The fields are cold and wet and seem somehow betrayed by the weather.

He is driving past the house he grew up in, the house he lived in with his mother and father and sister before things fell apart, and he wonders if maybe this is why he came this way. That was house number one, and the majority of his memories of that house are peaceful, straightforward. There were four of them around the dinner table, four of them waking up in the morning, grumbling and quiet and arguing over cereal or the last piece of toast. Everything was as it should be.

He slows down, amazed that it still stands alone, that no other houses have been built around it. He glances at the upstairs windows, one of which was his bedroom. He wonders who lives there, if the inside is still the same. Had anyone ever found the treasures he had hidden in the heat registers or retrieved the baseballs accidentally lodged in the second-story gutters?

His phone rings and he answers. It's Kaye, driving behind him.

"What are you doing?" Kaye asks. "Why are you driving so slow?"

He can tell by the sound of her voice that she's been crying. "Sorry. I got caught up looking at the old house, to be honest. Sorry."

She is silent, and in his rearview mirror he can see her looking off to the side, taking in the old house, wiping tears from her cheeks. When she talks, a deep hesitation pulls on her words, and there is a ready-made apology in case the words are not accepted. "Do you think"—she pauses—"one of us should call Mother?"

He has to bite his lip to avoid laughing, but it is not a humorous laugh trying to escape. Rather, it is a laugh born of disbelief or cynicism. "No," he says, and his voice catches. He clears his throat again, coughs. "Not yet. Let's wait until we know what's going on."

"What will we do without him?" Kaye asks, and her voice disintegrates.

"Listen," he says, surprised at how convincing he can be. He nearly believes himself. "It's going to be okay. It is. No matter what. You have to be strong, Kaye, for Johnny and for me. I need you to be strong for me. Do you hear me? I can't do this. Not alone."

She doesn't say anything, but he looks at her

again in his rearview mirror and can see her head moving straight up and down, up and down.

"Okay." She sniffs loudly, taking a deep breath. He wonders if she's looking for that same place inside of herself, the place she used to go during their father's long and heavy summer sermons, the place where time could not wear her down.

"Okay," she says again.

He edges his car forward, and his mind wanders elsewhere, and soon he's approaching the funeral home in the small city, the funeral home their family owns, only a few blocks from the hospital. He thinks about finding his father in the basement, now hours in the past. It's hard to believe all these things have happened today. And so much more to come. He wants it all to be over. He wants to be three months from now, or six, when everything is sorted out and life is swinging back into something like normal, and the pit of anxiety in his stomach is gone.

He stops the car again, this time at the red light beside the apartment and funeral home, where he and his father lived after his mother left with Kaye, where his father still lives. He can see the window that looks out from what had been his bedroom.

He notices the street corner with the navy-blue postbox standing in the narrow grass strip separating the street from the sidewalk. It is directly opposite the funeral home, and it stands there like an old watchman, some kind of sentry. It's like the guard who never leaves the tomb of the unknown soldier.

That was it.

That was the very spot where he first saw the Beast, where it crawled out from under those nighttime shadows and came at their apartment, furtive and floating and dark, the stuff of childhood nightmares.

Only, it hadn't been a nightmare. It had been real.

seven

The Detective

His phone rings again. Kaye blows her horn.

"I'm sorry." He winces, cutting off Kaye's pleading. "I'm sorry. I got distracted again. I'll drive. I'm driving."

He pulls away from the traffic light by the funeral home, but he can't help looking in the rearview mirror at the spot where he first saw that thing, that darkness. It looks so normal, the grass frosted by the earlier snow, the blue United States Postal Service box standing there, unassuming. There's a boy pushing his bike along the sidewalk, taking his time. The boy reminds Cohen of himself at that age.

Cohen parks across the street from the hospital and realizes he will need to act urgently now. He will need to present the world with a Cohen who knows nothing, a Cohen who wants to know as quickly as possible what has happened to his father.

"You are an impossible driver, do you know that?" Kaye blurts, pulling out a handkerchief and blowing her nose before crossing the street with Cohen, pulling Johnny behind her. The boy takes fast steps in order to keep up, still in his baseball uniform with a borrowed coat that has sleeves reaching down past his fingertips. His cleats make a clacking sound on the wet street.

Cohen doesn't answer. They all walk through the emergency entrance, skimming the ground, barely touching the shining floors of the hospital.

"I'm sure he's okay, right? Don't you think so, Cohen?"

Cohen walks straight to the receptionist, still not looking at Kaye. "We're here to see my father," he says. "Calvin Marah?"

The woman says his father's room number. Cohen, Kaye, and Johnny stand beside the elevator, wait impatiently, and consider the stairs. Just as they decide to take the steps, the elevator dings and the doors slide open. On the way up, Kaye paces in the tight space, her right arm resting on her large stomach, her left hand cupped over her mouth. Two steps this way, that way, this way.

"What could possibly have happened?" she asks herself, pacing and talking, her voice muffled by her fingers. "Beth didn't tell you anything? Nothing? Did he have a heart attack? Stroke?" Two steps this way, two steps that way.

Johnny stares at her as if waiting for her to explode. Cohen reaches over and puts his hand on the boy's shoulder. "It's okay, Johnny. It's going to be okay."

Will it though? he wonders. *Will it?*

There's a reason hospital descriptions are cliché, and that's because they all really do smell the same, sound the same, look the same. There is the neatness of a nice hotel but overlaid with a kind of sterility. The lights are a shade brighter than anyone would like. All shoes squeak on the shining floors.

Cohen feels like he shouldn't be there—he always feels that way in hospitals, even though he spends more time there than most people. Usually, though, he is in the morgue, in the basement with the dead, not on the floors with the nearly dead or dying or recovering. A hospital seems too important a place for someone to simply walk in and out as they wish. He would have felt better if there was a metal detector to go through or if a security guard gave him a quick pat down. In a place where people die or are brought back from death or walk along the line between life and death, it seemed to him that you couldn't be too careful. There should be some kind of protocol. There should be standards for who is allowed in.

An image flashes through his mind of his father's bald head resting on the funeral home basement floor. He squeezes his eyes shut, feeling like he might pass out. He wonders if that would be good, if that would demonstrate some kind of emotion consistent with these events. Kaye reaches up and puts her arm around his shoulders, and he can tell that she, too, is struggling. She's leaning on him. They're leaning on each other.

They walk out of the elevator and find their father's room. Johnny has drifted into the wake behind them. Cohen and Kaye stand there for a moment, staring at the closed door that leads into their father's hospital room.

"Should we go in, Co?" she asks, looking up into his face. He looks down into hers, finds the face of his big sister at the end of one of her weekend visits from Mom's house, asking him if he was doing okay—*no, really, are you doing okay? You can always come home with us, you know?* And he has the same old feeling he always had with her: a strong desire to tell her the truth about what was really going on in his life, yet always coupled with a complete inability to do so.

A rustle of movement on the other side of Kaye catches his attention. But why? Nurses move here and there, pulling carts and pushing IV trolleys. Doctors go from room to room. The red second hand on the otherwise black-and-white clock slides in a gliding motion around the circle. There is plenty of movement on that floor, outside of his father's room. So why does one particular rising catch his attention?

The movement is that of a woman standing up from a waiting room seat, part of a row of chairs against the wall. She wears a long black trench coat that reaches to her calves, and under that a professional outfit—slacks and a button-down shirt. Her fingers are laced together in front of her, and she wrings them tighter together as if she's nervous, as if her hands need to be drained dry. She nods at Cohen. He has a strange feeling that she expects him to recognize her, and even more odd, he does recognize her. He nods back, thinking hard.

"Cohen Marah?" Her voice is smooth and kind, and it catches in the middle of his last name. She has a pretty nose and wide-set eyes and short brown hair.

Cohen nods. "Yeah, that's me."

"C'mon, Co," Kaye says. "We have to go in. We have to see Dad."

He nods to her, and he is aware of how much nodding he does, how much acquiescing. "Sure. Let's go." He turns back to the woman he knows he should know. "I'll just be a second."

"I'll be waiting," she says. "I have a few questions for you, if that's okay?"

And even though the woman's last sentence comes out like a question, Cohen senses it's not a question. In fact, it is the opposite of a question. It's a demand. The way the woman says "I have a few questions for you" sends a jolt through Cohen's body. All at once he realizes what the woman does, and it takes everything in him not to run. She's a detective, he realizes, or a police officer.

He's like a deer when a twig breaks in the

undergrowth. He takes a deliberate, steady breath, tries to slow the blinking of his eyes. He becomes very aware of every muscle in his face, his swallowing, his breathing. Breathing. He realizes he isn't breathing. He takes a deep breath, sighs, hoping that it sounds like the sad sigh of a man going in to see his father for the last time. What if she has already spoken to the neighbors, and they've told her about the loud fight between him and his father? What if she noticed the sliver missing from the round pool of blood and tracked it to his shoe?

Why does he feel so guilty?

It comes to him the way a star first appears in the darkening sky.

"Ava?" Cohen asks quietly, and he says the name the same way you say a new word in a different language, a word you've never said before. And when he says her name he speaks a million things into existence: memories and emotions and regrets. It's all there around his head, a cloud, a nebula. All issuing forth with the speaking of a name.

The woman nods, smiling, and for a moment she seems genuinely happy to see Cohen, or perhaps she's surprised that he recognizes her. But her face changes as she remembers the circumstances, the dying man in the room, and her smile dwindles into sympathy and something else. Something else.

"Can we grab a coffee later?" Ava asks.

"Okay. Sure," Cohen mumbles, feeling himself veer off track. "I'll only be a moment. I need to find out about my father." His voice trembles. He turns away from Ava, puts his hand on the latch that opens the door, and pushes. He enters the room with Kaye looking up at him, her eyes asking questions. Johnny is right behind them, looking over his shoulder at the woman.

Walking away from Ava, leaving her in the hallway, is one of the greatest reliefs of Cohen's life.

eight

The Bloody Nose

Cohen doesn't remember with any precision the first time he held a baseball, the first time he stared, mesmerized, at the pattern of 108 red stitches holding together two strips of worn white horsehide. Because of those seams, the ball did not roll smoothly across the linoleum kitchen floor; rather, it lurched and leaned this way, that way, like someone trying to find their balance on a moving platform. He crawled after it, pushed it ahead, and watched it bobble along. He lifted it, tried to put it in his mouth, slobbered on it. For him, the baseball was part of being.

At three or four years of age, Cohen tried to catch the hardball as his father tossed it into his waiting arms. Calvin did not believe in starting with a Wiffle ball or a tennis ball—no, it was a real, standard-sized hardball from the very beginning. He tossed it to Cohen carefully, gingerly, the way you might throw an egg.

"Hold your arms out," Calvin said softly, stretching Cohen's arms taut, pushing them together, and tossing the ball so that it balanced between his milky elbows. It was less a matter of Cohen catching than it was of Calvin throwing

53

the ball accurately into his surprised limbs, but with each catch, Cohen grew to love the game more, this game of catch, this game that connected him with his father. When he caught the ball, his normally serious father smiled. That was all the reason he needed to love the game.

At the age of five, Cohen had his first glove, and he grew used to the rough inside edges against his fingers, the way it grew softer with time, the sound of the ball nestling into the webbed pocket, sometimes with a smack, sometimes with an oomph, sometimes like a punch in the gut. He threw the ball well by that age, and he felt like something special, hurling that orb through space.

"Good throw!" his father always said, sometimes pretending the force of the throw had stung his hand. "Yow!" he would cry.

"Nice catch!" Calvin shouted with each snag, or "Well, good try" with every drop. But the drops came few and far between by the time Cohen was six. The two of them would stand in the front yard of their home in the country, tossing the ball back and forth, back and forth, back and forth. It was like a conversation without words, except for his father's "Good throw!" and "Yow!" and "Nice catch!" and "Well, good try." It was how they connected, this ball circling, spinning through the air, a small world traveling back and forth at gentle speeds, the leather sound of a catch, the light grunt that came after a hard throw.

His father had taught him how to turn his glove: palm up to catch the ball if it arrived at stomach height or lower, and palm forward if the ball came in at chest height or higher. There was always the arc of the ball, the speed of its approach, the background of the large oak trees or a passing car or the great blue sky. Sometimes he peeked up at the house windows and saw his mother staring down at them, arms crossed, before looking quickly away.

He had his first baseball practice the spring after he turned nine. It took place on the ball diamond at the bottom of the hill behind the VFW. In those days, ballfields were not as immaculately kept—fathers mowed the outfield on their days off only after the grass was long enough to lose a ball in, and they dragged the dirt smooth around the infield with a section of chain-link fence weighed down with a handful of bricks pulled behind an old riding mower. In those days, a few weeds peeked through, and when he and his father walked quietly up to the third-base line, the infield was already filled with other eight- and nine-year-olds playing catch. Most of the throws were short or long or hit kids on the head or the leg or the chest. There were a few precious catches. For the most part, it was chaos.

Cohen stood there on that first day of practice in clean jeans and a white T-shirt and a red Philadelphia Phillies hat, staring into what seemed to be a cloud of electrons bouncing off each other—some kind of childlike attempt at creation, with random things colliding and erupting and amalgamating. He felt very much an outsider. There he stood, so still, so out of place, removed from that joyful, chaotic cloud of newness.

"Hey," the only girl on the field shouted. "Wanna throw?"

Cohen gawked at her for a moment, the one who had said those precious words. He looked up at his father anxiously, and his father nodded.

"Go on," he said. "Go ahead."

Cohen walked hesitantly onto the dirt field, his new baseball cleats rubbing on his heels, the static of those wild electrons alive all around him. The girl who had asked him to throw wore jeans torn at the knee and regular old tennis shoes, and her shirt was nearly washed through, but she walked around the field like she had been created for that diamond-shaped space.

The two of them threw the grass-stained baseball back and forth, back and forth, back and forth, finding a rhythm. At first Cohen had been uncertain about throwing with a girl, but he soon realized she was as good as him—no, she was better. The fields stretched out behind her on the other side of the tracks, and the sky was bigger than anything that had ever been. The air filled with the sound of baseballs hitting the chain-link fence or skidding across the hard dirt or making muffled trails into the grassy outfield. But with Cohen and his new friend, it was all *thwop, thwop, thwop* as the ball settled into each of their gloves. Back and forth without a drop, without a miss.

"I'm Ava," the girl called over to him as he threw the ball.

Cohen caught the information like a line drive and smiled. "I'm Cohen," he shouted. He threw the ball back, and for two nine-year-olds, the exchange of names was exhilarating, like finding a piece of fool's gold in the driveway.

His first baseball practice might have faded from his memory if it hadn't been for the sound of the train, the blast of its whistle, the deep rumble of its approach. But he looked at the tracks just as Ava threw the ball, and she realized what was happening and shouted, "Cohen!" He looked back in time to raise his glove, palm up, but the ball was too high so it skimmed like a skipping rock and collided with Cohen's nose.

Stars.

The beginning of the universe.

The inside of an atom, spinning.

Arcs of light and the rush of the train and he

was on his back, on the dirt, opening his eyes to the blue sky and oozing liquid drip drip dripping from his nose. He sat up, and kneeling beside him was his father and his new coach and his new friend, Ava. The blood dripped rhythmically down his upper lip, and he leaned forward and it dripped onto his white T-shirt in long streaks and onto his jeans, leaving small almost-black spots in the blue denim. He put his head back to keep from getting more on his clothes, imagining his mother's wrath, but it ran down the sides of his cheeks and trickled the smooth length of his neck. He could taste it in his throat, a slippery metallic kind of choking. He coughed.

"Spit it out. Go ahead," his father said, and Cohen heard embarrassment there in his flat voice, and a hint of shame that his son couldn't catch a ball thrown by a girl.

His coach led him through the arc of children staring, all baseballs suddenly motionless, horrified at this unforeseen outcome. He led Cohen through the dust rising in that early summer dusk, all the way to the bench, where he sat down and put his head back and held an old rag to his nose until the bleeding stopped. His father washed his face with water from the team thermos. It was cold, ice cold like melted snow, and he drank some too, to get the rest of the blood cleared from his mouth and the back of his throat.

Cohen locked eyes with Ava, and Ava squinted back and shrugged an apology. Cohen gave her a thumbs-up, which it turns out, in nine-year-old lingo, is the foundation of a friendship.

nine

The Trocar

"Oh, Dad," Kaye says, her head tilting to one side, tears welling up in her eyes. She reaches down and feels under the blanket for one of his hands. The machines beep on and on and on.

Cohen looks over at Beth.

"Are you okay?" he asks her.

She nods, biting her bottom lip. "I can't believe I found him," she says, her voice trailing off.

"I'm sorry," Cohen replies. "I'm really sorry, Beth."

She gives another quick nod, wipes her eyes. "I should get back to the funeral home. The police are still there."

"Call me if you need anything," Cohen says. "Anything. We'll sort it all out."

Beth leaves. Cohen watches as the numbers fluctuate on the machines, realizing he could easily sit there all day and become absorbed in the gradual rising and falling of his father's heart rate, anticipating the regular intervals. The blood pressure cuff suddenly vibrates and hums, filling with air, measuring, and spouting off new numbers to be examined and tracked.

A nurse moves wordlessly around the room,

adjusting this, making notes on that, propping Calvin up by sticking another pillow under his back. When she walks out, Cohen allows himself to look at his dad, really look at him, and what he sees is a human being he barely recognizes.

His father's skin is already graying, already fading. His mouth is slightly open, as if caught mid-sentence, and his eyes are closed. There is a large bandage under his jaw, above his voice box. His bald head reflects the light, and his ears seem larger now, as everything else about him shrinks away.

"Who was that outside the room?" Kaye asks Cohen, still rubbing their father's hand under the blanket. She seems to be seeking out distractions.

"What? Oh, that was strange. Do you remember my friend Ava from elementary school?"

"Vaguely," Kaye says. "Maybe not."

Cohen nods. "I think she's a police officer now. Or a detective. I don't know. She said she wants to ask me some questions."

Kaye looks back at their father. "What happened, Cohen?" She doesn't look up. She seems to go suddenly still, like a Catherine wheel when the wind dies away.

"I know as much as you do, Kaye," he says, glancing over at Johnny. "You okay, buddy?"

"Is Grandpa dead?" the boy asks matter-of-factly.

"No!" Kaye erupts, carefully releasing her

father's hand before gliding over to Johnny and kneeling down beside his chair. "No. Everything will be fine."

Cohen shakes his head but doesn't say anything. No, his father is not dead. He walks past Kaye and Johnny, over to the large window that looks out from his father's seventh-floor room. From that height, he can look over the city blocks, the streets, the alleys. He reaches up and puts his hand against the glass, and the coldness of it grounds him in that place. He is there, in the hospital. He is there, with his sister and nephew, and his father is dying.

Far below him, Cohen sees a woman standing on her front porch. Of all the houses that line that particular street, she is the only one outside. She's holding a baby, pacing back and forth. It's hard to tell from that far up, but it seems she is bopping up and down as she walks, perhaps trying to put the bundle to sleep. The sky is slate gray again, and behind that flat curtain the sun heads for the horizon. Flurries begin to fall, and the woman holds out her hand from under the porch roof, reaching for them.

Cohen watches her. She seems so far away.

He hears the door open behind him, but he doesn't turn. He's worried about where things will go from here. It was a mistake not to call the police immediately.

He's on the edge of a precipice, looking down

into unfathomable depths. He slides his hand down the cold glass and it makes a squeaking sound, so he puts both hands on the cold sill, still looking out over the city lit by gray light.

"Hi, I'm Dr. Stevens," a man says.

Cohen turns around and looks across the long room. The doctor is younger than he expects, looks half his age, and Cohen nearly cracks a joke about being at the hospital on a school day, then thinks better of it.

"I'm Cohen," he says quietly without moving from the window. "I'm his son."

"I'm Kaye," his sister says, the two words rushing from her mouth so fast that she repeats them more slowly. "I'm Kaye. Kaye. The daughter."

"Kaye," Dr. Stevens says, reaching out and shaking her hand. He walks over to Cohen and shakes his hand, nods his head solemnly. He glances down at Johnny sitting in the chair, appearing uncomfortable. He looks at Kaye and motions toward Cohen and the window. "Can we talk for a moment?"

Kaye nods, and the two of them walk over, standing on either side of Cohen.

"Have you heard anything about the . . . nature . . . of your father's injuries?" The doctor speaks in a hushed voice.

Both Kaye and Cohen shake their heads.

"Mm-hmm," the doctor says, staring out the

window for a moment. The silence lasts so long that Cohen considers asking a question, but as he takes a breath to begin speaking, Dr. Stevens resumes. "I'm not sure how much the police would like me to say, but he is your father, and I'd like you to know the severity of . . . what happened. I see no good reason to keep it from you, and there are decisions you will need to make."

Again, silence. Kaye glances at Cohen nervously. He stares down at the tiled floor, noticing the flecks, the seemingly random patterns. He feels the cold air radiating from the glass behind him and thinks of the woman on the porch, reaching out to catch the snow.

"Your father had a sharp instrument that pierced him here." The doctor reaches up and with his index finger points under his jaw where it meets his neck. "The instrument was pushed up into his brain. It was perhaps a bit larger than the diameter of a chopstick, long and pointy."

Cohen nods slowly. "The trocar? That's the only sharp instrument I can think of in the funeral home."

The doctor stares at Cohen for a moment, taking in the information.

"It wasn't some kind of knife? You're sure?" Kaye asks.

He does not remove his finger from that point on his jaw even as he continues. "There was also some embalming fluid injected at the site. Other toxic debris."

"Was it . . ." Kaye begins, but her voice fades.

Dr. Stevens slowly lowers his finger. Cohen nearly laughs, the way some people might laugh when thrust into a terrible but also absurd situation. He turns away and stares out the window. He looks down at the street. The woman is gone.

"Who would have done this to my dad?" Kaye whispers.

The doctor continues without acknowledging her question. "We are doing everything we can, but the damage done by the . . ."

"Trocar," Cohen repeats in a flat voice.

"The damage done by the trocar is severe. The fluid injected compounds the injury." He takes a deep breath and tries to sound sympathetic. "I don't expect your father to survive the night. We have made him as comfortable as possible."

Kaye makes a tiny sound like a hiccup or a chirp. She covers her mouth.

The doctor starts to say something else, stops, and puts up both hands as if in surrender. "I really shouldn't say anything else, not at this point. You can stay as long as you like. If you need anything, please let us know. There are blankets and pillows in the closet and the sofa folds out into a small, uncomfortable bed if you'd like to spend the night. But like I said, I don't expect this to drag on for a long time."

Kaye makes the tiny sound again.

Cohen nods. "Thank you, Doctor."

Dr. Stevens backs away, turns, and walks quickly out the door. The room smells of antiseptic and something else that Cohen can't quite identify. Toast? Soup? Kaye walks smoothly back to their father's side and searches for his hand under the covers while holding her other hand over her mouth.

Cohen turns to the window again. The sun is getting lower in the sky, dropping behind the taller buildings in the west. The streetlights came on while the doctor was speaking and now form neat, organized lines. The darker it becomes, the clearer Cohen's own reflection in the glass is. What does he look like to someone down on the street, glancing up at the seventh-floor window? He wonders if they can see him, the sad, tired man.

Kaye clears her throat and tries to speak. "Cohen, who could've . . ." But her voice is too heavy, and it folds in on itself and ends in silent weeping, the only evidence being the slight tremors in her shoulders.

Cohen looks over at Johnny. He is staring at his mother, biting his lip, one of his legs swinging under the chair.

"Hey, J," Cohen says, beckoning with a movement of his head.

Johnny stands and walks in moping fashion,

his head bent down and swaying back and forth. He doesn't lift his feet when he walks, sliding his cleats along the tile floor like ice skates.

"Take off your shoes if they're uncomfortable," Cohen suggests, putting his arm around the boy. They both face their reflections in the window.

"Nah. I'm okay."

"That snow was crazy, huh?"

The boy nods, giving a slight smile.

"When I was a kid, I never played baseball in the snow." Cohen peers through the window, trying to see the sky. "Pretty dark out there," he whispers. "But usually we can't see the stars. Not here in the city."

"Yeah."

"How's school?"

"It's alright, I guess." But the boy clearly perks up, either because he likes school or because he craves a distraction from what's going on around him.

"Learn anything interesting?"

He thinks for a moment, seeming to inquire silently of his reflection staring back at him in the window. It works, an idea is exchanged, and Johnny's face brightens.

"Do you know how fast light travels?" he asks Cohen.

"How fast?"

"One hundred eighty-six thousand miles. Per. Second."

Cohen looks down at the boy, whose fear and sadness have given way to amazement at this simple fact. Johnny's eyes are wide open, eyebrows lifted. There must be nothing in the whole world as astonishing to the boy as this one fact.

"Wow."

"Yeah. In one second. And did you know the light we see from the stars left those stars thousands of years ago? We're only seeing it now."

"That's kind of a strange thing to think about."

"Yeah," Johnny continues. "And some of those stars are dead but we still see their light. We won't know they're dead for another thousand years."

Cohen smiles down at Johnny. "You're a smart kid," he says. But a sadness transfers to him, perhaps at the word *dead,* perhaps at the idea of something being gone and no one knowing. Perhaps at the thought of that lonely light speeding through space, the last living part of a now-dead star.

"You're a smart kid," Cohen says again. "Probably too smart for your own good."

Johnny laughs, pleased at himself, and stares up through the glass, hungrily searching for stars.

ten

The Sock

The same spring Cohen met Ava, the same spring he took a baseball to the nose and leaked blood all over himself, he walked to his father's church one day after school, as he sometimes did. He passed their house and kept on for another mile or so, arriving at the church to find the front door unlocked. It was a warm day but the metal was cold. He had to pull with both hands to budge the heavy door, and it made a loud latching sound behind him that echoed in the dim, empty foyer.

There, the doors to the bathrooms. There, the place an usher always stood during the service. There, the double wooden doors that swung open into the sanctuary. The air smelled like pine mingled with the warm scent left behind by a recently used vacuum cleaner, one that had left angled lines in the bloodred carpet. The empty church filled him with a reverent, spooky kind of feeling, and he tried to breathe lightly.

Cohen pulled back the doors that led into the sanctuary and slipped in between them. They closed without a sound behind him. The air was still and warm. Light fell in stretched beams through the tall, narrow windows at the front of the sanctuary, and he walked forward, transfixed. The light seemed somehow solid, like gold bars. He moved silently down the center aisle, past each and every row, holding his breath in the stillness, all the way to the front where there was a rectangular wooden altar with words engraved on it.

Do This in Remembrance of Me.

There, the light fell all the way to the floor.

Small specks of dust floated through the bars of light, and at first Cohen didn't want to breathe for fear of blowing the holy light away. But then he leaned in close and blew gently, a breath of life, and the tiny dust planets swirled in and out of the light in circular patterns. Cohen smiled. The room was silent.

But wait.

There was one sound.

What was that? It seemed to be off in the distance, something out of place. The dust planets swirled back on themselves in the void of moving air, rushing back at Cohen. But he didn't notice them anymore. He didn't move. He listened like a rabbit disturbed by distant sounds. Of what? Wind in the grass? A shadow? His eyes held steady before looking one way, then the other. He took one step back, away from the beam of light.

He followed the sound to the left side of the church, about halfway back. He held out one hand at his side, grazing softly over each and every polished pew. They were made of oak, stained dark brown, and held swirls and patterns like fingerprints in the grain.

It was a small, persistent sound. Air moved through a forgotten window, pushing the white drapes against the paneled walls. But the farther into the shadowy side of the church he went, the clearer the sound became. It was the sound of people. Whispering. Moving. He stopped when he saw the two pairs of feet stretching out from between two pews. One pair of feet wore his father's shoes, the toes pointing down, and outside of them, toes pointed up, were the exquisitely painted, lime-green toenails of Miss Flynne.

Cohen wanted to dash off, run home, pretend he saw nothing. He was alarmed at the strangeness of how they were situated, how they took up physical space. He was torn between staying and going. Even though all he saw were tangled feet, all he heard were soft whispers, the air was electric with something new, something he had never encountered.

He took one step closer. He saw an object out of place, discarded on the carpet. Another step closer. It was one of Miss Flynne's white stockings, the very ones she often took off in Sunday school. It had a flower above the ankle—a rose? a tulip?—and at the top of it, a white ruffle, and below the ruffle, her initials:

HMF. He reached down without thinking and snatched the sock up silently, soundlessly. He stuffed it into his pocket as he walked backwards, faster as he went, returning to the center of the sanctuary.

There was an exit door on the far side of the large room. He could get out there. Would they hear the click of the door as it closed? Maybe, but he would be gone, and they wouldn't know he had been there. Each stride felt like a leap from here to there. He wasn't breathing. Faster now. Faster.

But he heard the sound of people moving, getting up. The sound of clothes pulled over bodies and a belt buckle clanging on itself. He fell to his hands and knees and crawled toward the door, but he heard louder whispers, whispers returning to the volume of normal voices. He rolled under the front pew and lay on his side, remembering Sunday nights, lying there in the heat of a summer evening. He remembered his mother never fanning herself, defying the heat, denying the sweat beading on her forehead, mouthing the words of his father's sermons. He imagined his father's words streaming out over everyone, exhorting, pleading.

He remained on his side under the pew. He thought he heard the main doors to the sanctuary swing shut, the ones he had entered through, but he waited an extra moment before looking out from under the bench.

Which was good, because his father hadn't left, so Cohen scurried back under the church bench.

He watched his father walk to the front, where he stood for a moment, looking up at the ceiling, his hands in his pants pockets, his collared shirt sloppily tucked in, his bald head dull in the dim light. His back was to Cohen, and it seemed a broad back, the strong back of an important man. His father's shoulders seemed powerful, and for a moment Cohen wondered if he had ever examined his father from that side, when he wasn't facing him. He could smell his father's cologne mingling with the scent of the pine polish someone had used to shine the wooden pews.

If Cohen hadn't seen what he had seen, he might have thought his father was a priest of old, the way he stood there, powerful, staring up at the ceiling as if he could see right through it, right through even the midday blue sky and deep into a distant universe. Or maybe Cohen would have mistaken him for some kind of angel without wings, a supernatural guardian over the altar. He would have been tempted to crawl out from his hiding place and grab the back of his father's foot to make sure he was flesh and blood, not principality or power.

But there was no getting around what he had—and hadn't—seen. What he hadn't seen fed his imagination, set up camp in a place that would never be forgotten. These images confused themselves in Cohen's mind, images of bodiless feet and the togetherness of his father and Miss Flynne in that all-too-tight space and the sound of words that weren't words and the lumpy presence of the sock he held in his hand.

He did not move from that spot.

His father moved, though—fell to his knees in a slow collapse onto the bloodred carpet, still looking up at the ceiling. He fell forward onto the altar.

Do This in Remembrance of Me.

Cohen's father was tall enough so that the front edge of the altar met his chest, and his head and shoulders fell forward, draping themselves on the wood. His head fell into one of the bars of golden light, and the light glared off it. His shoulders shook with sobs, and Cohen watched wide-eyed.

The sobs went silent after such a short time that Cohen couldn't be sure he had actually seen his father weeping. He could have easily counted the sobs if he had thought to do so. In the next instant, his father was still kneeling there, but now completely still.

Time passed. Cohen thought his father might have died, so he rolled slowly backward and rose like an apparition between the first and second pew. He walked up to the front of the sanctuary, stood behind his father, and realized he was asleep. His father had drifted off on the altar.

Cohen walked slowly backwards, backwards, backwards, then turned and pushed his way out of the sanctuary, out of that stuffy air, through the loud outer door and into the daylight.

He ran, and he didn't stop running, not until he made it to the green grass that led up to his own porch and the whining front door. He felt a strange sensation inside of him, something like anger, something like disdain, and at that age he couldn't correctly identify it as jealousy. But that's what it was.

He was jealous his father had been that close to Miss Flynne. He was jealous she had not chosen him. He was so filled with that aching jealousy and images of legs in between the pews and lime-green nail polish and his father sleeping at the front of the church that he had completely forgotten about the sock still balled up in his pocket.

eleven

The Question

Cohen sits quietly in the hospital cafeteria, staring into his black coffee. There are at least a hundred tables in the sprawling canteen, but there are only a handful of other people in the room, all sitting light-years apart. A woman wearing a navy-blue uniform and a hairnet walks from the kitchen to the food bar, her feet squeaking on the wet floor. A man and woman lean forward over their food trays, whispering to each other. The woman occasionally runs her fingers through her hair while her shoulders sob up and down. Three doctors sit around a table in the far corner, nodding, talking baseball, and grinning. Cohen can smell the pizza growing stale under the heat lamp and sees some kind of suede-colored gravy simmering. Outside the dark, tinted glass, headlights move through the city.

He becomes strangely aware of all the many floors above him, the weight of sickness, the muted sound of doctors and nurses coming and going through hundreds of rooms. They grab clipboards inside each one, analyze the treatment, proclaim the next phase, discharge the patient, or shake their head and sadly say nothing more can be done. Over and over again, on every floor, this is happening. Cohen feels buried.

An ambulance siren wails off in the distance, its sound steady and unchanging, as if it's not coming or going but simply waiting, screaming. Abruptly it stops.

He watches as Ava takes her coffee from the register over to the condiment station, adds sugar and cream, and stirs it all slowly with a black coffee straw. He wonders about this sudden reappearance of a long-ago friend. How will she go about it? Will she start by being friendly, or will she get straight to the point, interrogate him, ask him the *where were you on the night of, and can anyone verify your whereabouts?* Cohen thinks she looks worn. Perhaps that's the word. Or thin, but not physically thin—emotionally thin, like something stretched so tight you can almost see through it. This is the marked difference between the Ava he knew as a child and the Ava who has shown up in his life: a kind of thinness, a life that has been dimmed. But this vanishes or recedes when Ava approaches the orange plastic chair, pulls it out from the table, and sits down.

"Cohen," she says, shaking her head as if Cohen has magically appeared in front of her that very moment. She gives a smile filled with so many things that it cannot be anything but real.

Cohen sees the girl he once knew there in

the smile, the pretty nose, the wide eyes. He remembers all the baseball, all the bike rides. He returns the smile, and he, too, feels genuinely happy, if only for a moment.

"Ava," he says, and his voice is hoarse. He clears his throat and starts again. "Ava. How are you?"

She takes a sip of coffee. "Wow, that's hot. Watch yourself. I'm good. Good. It's been a long time."

"Was it graduation?" Cohen asks.

"Maybe. But even . . ." Her voice trails off.

Cohen knows what she was going to say, that even then it had been a while since they'd really seen each other, really spent any time together. Or something along those lines. They both know it, so it need not be said.

"Where do you live?" she asks.

"Still right here in the city," Cohen says. "I have an apartment a few blocks away from the funeral home."

Ava shakes her head and laughs quietly to herself, and her laugh takes him back thirty years. "It's a crazy place, this city, isn't it? I've nearly moved back a few times, but it never worked out."

"So, where are you?"

"Over in Middletown. Not far."

"But you work here?"

She nods.

"Did you ever . . . get married?" Cohen asks hesitantly.

Ava laughs again, that quiet, pleasant laugh, and she shakes her head, shrugs.

"Twice," she says, and there it is: a hint of sadness in her voice, probably something a complete stranger wouldn't have noticed. "And twice divorced. I guess I'm not much of a keeper."

Cohen tries to give her a look that is both understanding and full of consolation. "I doubt that's the case." He takes a sip of his coffee and doesn't want to put the paper cup down.

"You?" Ava asks. "Is there a beautiful Mrs. Cohen Marah at home bouncing babies? Herding the children? Bringing up the next in a long line of baseball-playing funeral directors?"

Cohen chuckles. "Nah, couldn't find the time."

"Really?" she asks, staring at him over her cup. She takes a sip. "Cohen the bachelor." She says the words like a newspaper headline.

"I'm too selfish," he says, shrugging. "Any kids?"

"One," Ava says, and the word slips out like a sigh. "A son. He's in high school. Spends most of the time with his father. My schedule is . . . inconsistent. He's a wonderful son, though. A wonderful boy."

"Does he play baseball?"

Ava's smile turns quizzical, melancholy. "Yes,"

she says slowly, quietly, in a new tone. "Yes. He does. Actually, first base."

Something like contentment drifts around them. Cohen is almost relieved that one of them had a son who's playing baseball.

"My nephew plays," Cohen offers, shrugging. "But he's young. Who knows if it will stick."

"It'll stick," Ava says. "It's in his blood."

Cohen hears the screeching sound of the couple at the other end of the cafeteria pushing their chairs back from their table, the clattering sound of a metal spoon falling to the floor. They walk the long length of the room, leave their trays on the counter, and slip back into the hospital's thoroughfares.

Cohen takes a long drink of his coffee. "Your parents okay?"

"My parents are fine."

Immediately Cohen realizes he shouldn't have asked, because the next logical question would be for Ava to return the question, to ask if Cohen's parents are okay, which they obviously are not. Or at least his father is not okay, and the fact that his mother isn't there either means they're estranged or she's dead. It is a conversational dead end.

For a while, the two of them stare into their coffee. Ava traces a crack in the table with her finger. She looks like she's been working for many, many consecutive hours. Maybe consecutive days.

"Cohen, we both know why I'm here."

Cohen frowns. "Do we?" he asks in a voice that's almost a whisper.

He has this sudden image of his father lying on the floor of the funeral home basement surrounded by that saintly ring of blood, his bald head shining. He can feel the blood on his fingertip from where he wiped the sole of his shoe. He rubs his fingers together beneath the table. He wonders if it's still there, that barely visible shade of pink, the red filling in his swirling fingerprints.

"I wish we'd be seeing each other under different circumstances," Ava says, now looking directly into his eyes.

Cohen clears his throat again and Ava waits for him to speak.

"Things could be better," he jokes, but his words fall flat.

"I'm going to talk to my boss about recusing myself from the investigation," Ava says. "I didn't realize it was you. I even saw your father's name on the report and it didn't hit me. I guess I always thought of him simply as Cohen's dad. I don't know if I could have even told you his first name."

Cohen nods again. Now he is far away, years away. He doesn't care. He doesn't hear. But he feels he should say something, feels he should make some kind of effort. It seems kind of her to step aside, kind of her to tell him that much.

He blurts the first question that comes to his mind. "How long have you been, you know, doing this?"

"You mean how long have I been a police detective?" she asks, smiling. "I started right after college. I was a state trooper for six years. Now, detective for, oh, I don't know. I lost count."

"What's your gut tell you?" Cohen asks, staring into Ava's eyes.

"What do you mean?" she asks.

"What's your gut tell you?" He shrugs, looking away nervously.

She shakes her head. "I don't . . ."

Cohen laughs quietly to himself. It sounds more like a series of gentle sniffs. "Do you think I did it?"

She crosses her arms, sighs, and sits back in her seat. Her face hardens slightly, and she returns Cohen's stare. Her eyes go flat, from glossy to matte in the time it takes him to put his coffee down. Her mouth has straightened out. She seems to be taking everything in—not only Cohen but the doctors who have finished their food and now lean back in their plastic chairs, arms crossed. The woman who has taken away the pizza. The three old women who enter. Everything is entering some sort of calculator, the equations are forming, the x's and y's transforming into values on either side.

This is a different Ava, Cohen thinks.

"When I sit here? Talking to you?" she says, and every sentence is a question now. "When I see my old friend? Drinking coffee?"

Cohen waits for her to continue.

"No. I don't think you did it. We don't suspect any foul play," Ava says. "Of course, everything must be taken into account. But it's looking like either an accident or a suicide." She says the last word quietly, reverently.

Cohen nods, shrugs. "All day, I've felt like it was my fault. Like I killed my father. Not physically. But still, it feels like my fault."

The two sit there without saying a word. Cohen can hear the kitchen staff in the back, cleaning up. The sound of spraying water. The sound of dishes rattling together.

"Can I ask you something, Cohen? Something I've been thinking about for a long time?"

He nods. He knows where the conversation is headed.

"Do you remember the winter of 1989?" Ava asks. "December? Just before Christmas? Because I do."

Cohen nods. Of course he remembers.

"I never would have believed it if I hadn't seen it for myself," Ava says, and now she is talking to herself as much as to him. "Sometimes I'm still not sure if I really saw it." She stands up. "Did I see it, Cohen? Was that real? Because if it was real, if I saw what I saw?" She shrugs.

It's like an old dream to him now, something he has pushed down and out of his mind for decades. But she's a detective now. She would be interested in tying up those sorts of loose ends.

Ava turns to walk away, but she stands there for another moment, perhaps waiting for Cohen to say something. Cohen isn't sure what he could say that would fill that silence in the right way.

Thank you?

Goodbye?

I can explain what you saw in December of 1989?

He doesn't look up again until he hears the swinging door squeak in its movement behind Ava at the other end of the empty cafeteria.

twelve

A Letter

July 17, 1984

Dear Co,

I'm sorry. That's all I can say. I'm sorry. I feel absolutely awful about what happened. I had no idea that's what Mom was planning to do, and I wouldn't have come along if I knew, or maybe if I knew I would have run ahead and warned you. At least we wouldn't have had to see it. But I didn't know. I thought we were just going to your baseball game.

I should have known, though. I should have known when I saw that look in her eyes all morning. She was in an absolute trance. She was so distracted, she burned all the breakfast food—the toast and the eggs. I cleaned it all up because after she burned it she walked into the living room and sat on the sofa, staring out the window. The house was full of smoke. The clothes I wore that day still stink.

Mom hasn't moved much since we got here. She mostly sits in this little green armchair we bought at Goodwill and stares out the window. The windows here don't have screens, and I'm always killing flies or bees that have come in. But she stares at the cars that go by outside. It's loud here. I miss our house. I miss the country.

Has Dad said anything to you since THE DAY? I often wonder what he thinks about all this. Does he tell you anything? I can't imagine him actually talking. He never has. But you know that. It must be quiet in the house, unless he's changed. I wonder if he's changed, now that it's just you and him. I hope he's changed.

Oh, I'm so sorry. What an embarrassment.

I sometimes wonder how we were born into this. I look around at my new friends here in the city, and so many of them—not all of them, of course, some have parents even worse than ours—have parents who are normal, who don't shout at each other in public, who are still married, and they eat meals together and both parents come to parent-teacher conferences. What happened to us? I mean, I know what happened. But why? Why us?

There's a nice boy here who says he goes to my school. His name is Jimmy.

I haven't made any close girlfriends yet, but maybe once school starts. Girls are weird, as you know (ha ha). Mom says I don't talk enough, I don't ask enough questions, I don't care enough. Maybe she's right about that, because I don't care much, I only wish we had our old life back. She's constantly pushing me to make friends with other girls, telling me to go talk to them, but I'm actually happy now. I don't need girlfriends. Not right now. I have Jimmy. And I have you, even though we're practically 100 miles away from each other. You have always been such a good friend to me.

I still miss you. I always miss you! And I'm sorry.

Yours,
K

thirteen

"Onward, Christian Soldiers"

Cohen kept Miss Flynne's sock all through the spring and into the summer of 1984, although if anyone had asked him why, he wouldn't have been able to explain it. In his room, there was an old dresser for his clothes, a piece of furniture his parents had picked up alongside the road. It had a few deep gouges on the top and most of the drawers were missing their handles. He tucked the sock under that dresser. Occasionally, when he lay in bed long after everyone else in the house was asleep, his mind spinning back through the sanctuary where he had seen and not seen his father and Miss Flynne, sleep wouldn't come. He would get out of bed in the middle of the night, walk blindly through the darkness, fish around under the dresser until his hand found the sock, and take it back to bed with him, lying on his back, holding it in both hands on his chest, jealousy an ember deep in the ash.

It seemed strange to do this, even to him, and he kept the secret hidden under a persistent shame he did not understand but could not shake. Perhaps it was the dawning of preadolescent confusion at the feelings he had for Miss Flynne, or perhaps it came from not knowing how to make peace with the searing jealousy he felt for his father. Or maybe it was a secondhand shame experienced on behalf of his father, who, based on the effusive tears and exhaustion he had laid on the altar at the front of the sanctuary, had much to be ashamed of.

As monumental a place as the sock seemed to take up in Cohen's mental and emotional space, it was remarkable how careless he could be with it. One morning, as he was about to catch the bus, he remembered he had left the sock under his pillow. Often his mother would make his bed— she was sure to find it.

"Cohen! Where are you going?" Kaye shouted. "The bus is here!"

He ran up the front steps, across the porch, through the banging door, his backpack thumping side to side, all the way up to his room. His mother was already there.

"Cohen!" she said.

He froze in place. "Yes?"

She turned and stared at him, shaking her head. She held his pajamas in her hand. "When will you remember to put your dirty clothes in the hamper?"

He nearly fainted with relief. "Yes, Mother." Not knowing any other way around it, he darted toward the bed, thrust his hand under the pillow, stuffed the sock in his jeans pocket, and raced back out of the room, his backpack colliding with the door frame and nearly twisting him off his feet.

"Cohen!" His mother's voice followed him down the stairs, but he didn't stop.

"The bus is here, Mom!"

It was this occasional forgetfulness in regards to the sock that led to him, on an early Sunday morning in July, sitting in Miss Flynne's Sunday school class and realizing that he had somehow, for some reason, brought her sock along with him. It bulged in his pocket like a secret that could not be kept any longer. He leaned forward in his chair and clutched his arms in front of him and to one side, trying to cover up the lump.

"Cohen," Miss Flynne said as she entered the small cinder-block room and passed him on her way to the chalkboard, "are you feeling okay?"

He nodded without saying anything. She looked at him with curiosity and seemed to decide to take his word for it.

He stared at her and an ache rose in him, an ache of sadness and anger. He wanted to take out the sock and throw it at her, shout, scream that he knew her secret, whatever it was, whatever she had been doing with his father. But Cohen never confronted anyone. He couldn't do it. So he sat there, leaning forward, his eyes filling with tears.

He wasn't prepared for the next surprise: Ava walked into the classroom carrying two baseball gloves. "Hi, Cohen!"

Ava had never come to his church before. He stared, his mouth open.

"Surprise!" Ava said, smiling. Her straight white teeth shone like a beacon. "My mom wants me to go to church. I don't know why. But I can walk here, at least when the weather's nice. I'm almost ten, you know. And I knew this was your church." Her smile merged into something bashful, and she glanced away, waiting for some kind of a response.

"Great," Cohen said. "Seriously. That's great."

More children came in, roughhousing, bumping against the chairs, throwing things at each other, but Cohen couldn't stop staring at Ava. It threw him off balance, seeing her anywhere but the ballfield or in passing at school. "What's with the mitts?"

"Oh, these? My dad says I should always take a glove with me, you know, to practice."

"Why two?"

She shrugged. "Who am I going to practice with? I thought you might want to throw after church."

The baseball she had lodged into one of the gloves fell to the floor and rolled the short distance to the front wall. Miss Flynne was writing a Bible verse on the chalkboard, the tapping sound of chalk sliding along. She glanced down at the ball over her shoulder, placed the chalk in its tray, and reached down gracefully, picking up the ball and eyeing the group.

"Whose is this?" she asked, trying to look stern but only managing to barely lessen the smile she always wore. She held the ball up. It seemed to weigh down her fragile wrist.

Ava raised her hand. When Miss Flynne saw that it was a new child who bore responsibility for the rolling ball, kindness surged to the surface again. "And who might you be?" she asked, tilting her head.

Cohen sighed. Her perfectly round head. Her long and wistful neck. He glanced down at her feet, but she had not taken off her shoes. She wore stockings without a monogram. Maybe he should simply return the sock secretly, leaving it in her Bible or in her purse or even under his chair.

"I'm Ava. This is my first Sunday. I'm friends with Cohen Marah."

Some of the boys in the back laughed.

"Welcome, Ava, friend of Cohen," Miss Flynne said, as if Ava was a princess from some faraway land. "Welcome. Keep this safe while you're in class, okay?"

She handed Ava the ball, turned back to the blackboard, and finished writing the verse.

In the beginning, God created the heaven and the earth. And the earth was without form, and void; and darkness was upon the face of the deep. And the Spirit of God moved upon the face of the waters. And God said, Let there be light: and there was light. And God saw the light, that it was good: and God divided the light from the darkness. And God called the light Day, and the darkness he called Night. And the evening and the morning were the first day.

"Today," Miss Flynne said, her voice hidden under the roar of still-talking children, "we're talking about the first day of creation."

After Sunday school ended, Cohen and Ava walked up to the sanctuary and sat with Cohen's mother and sister, stood when it was time to stand, and sang hymns about war.

"Onward, Christian soldiers!
Marching as to war,
With the cross of Jesus
Going on before.

"Christ, the royal Master,
Leads against the foe;
Forward into battle,
See his banners go!

"Onward, Christian soldiers!
Marching as to war,
With the cross of Jesus
Going on before."

They listened to Cohen's father regurgitate the sermon Cohen's mother had written about the light and the dark and how the separation between the two is in the very first verses of the Bible, which shows that God is a God of drawn battle lines and conflict always brewing. From the very first day. Cohen lost track of his father's voice and became distracted with Ava's presence, so close beside him that he could see individual wisps of hair floating out of her braid. He glanced over at his sister on the other side of his mother, and he wondered what stories she was making up in her head and which forest she was journeying through, and to what end.

And there was Miss Flynne in the pew directly in front of his mother. Her breathing was slight, like a doe hiding in the undergrowth.

After the final hymn, they filtered outside through the crowd and put on the baseball gloves Ava had brought with her. The boys who had laughed at the friendship between this boy and girl were suddenly envious, scuffing their shoes absentmindedly on the sidewalk, hungrily watching the ball sail. Ava and Cohen threw it to each other there in the soft grass in front of the church, and the baseball flew through the speckled light that fell between the leaves. Cohen always felt incredible comfort while throwing a ball, the gentle back and forth, the soft popping sound of a good catch.

"Are you ready for the big game next Saturday?" Ava asked.

"Sure," Cohen said. "We haven't lost yet."

Ava threw the ball, this time harder than usual, and Cohen made an imperfect catch, the ball smacking against his palm instead of settling into the pocket.

"Yow!" he shouted, throwing his glove to the ground. The ball fell out and rolled a few feet away.

Ava laughed. "Am I throwing it too hard for you?" she asked sarcastically.

Cohen grimaced, shook his head, picked up the ball, and threw it back. He had an idea. He needed to put something in his glove where the palm of his hand sometimes caught the ball. Padding would soften the sting. He fished Miss Flynne's sock from his pocket, laid it flat on the palm of his hand, and stuffed his hand into his glove.

There. That was better.

"What was that?"

"Nothing. Only a little padding."

"I can throw the ball hard. I tell you all the time, and you never listen!"

"C'mon, give me everything you got!"

As the ball made its orbit through the air, as the seams spun and the dirty white leather rotated in space, and as Cohen raised his mitt to welcome it, a commanding voice spread out from the church.

"Cohen Marah, you take that glove off this instant! We do not play baseball on Sundays!"

Cohen's glove absorbed the ball, and he looked over at the front of the church. His mother stood there, fire in her eyes.

fourteen

The Confession

"Hello, Father James?" Cohen says into his phone, still sitting in the hospital cafeteria, staring at the doors Ava left through. An employee turns off a row of lights, throwing the back section of the large cafeteria into darkness.

The man on the other end of the telephone line clears his throat and replies with only one word, but even that one word emerges slow and thick with sleep, like gravel ground together. "Yes?"

"Father James, I'm sorry to bother you so late."

Another empty moment. Another clearing of the throat. The words emerge in reluctant scratches. "Is this Cohen Marah?"

"Yes, Father. Yes. It's Cohen."

For a moment neither one of them says anything.

When Father James still doesn't speak, Cohen stumbles on. "I know it's late. I know. I'm sorry. I need to talk. To you."

Another pause. A sigh. Words spoken barely above a whisper, words that wish they didn't have to be said. "Cohen, you do remember that I retired in January? That I am no longer the rector at Saint Thomas Episcopal Church?"

"Yes, Father," Cohen says reluctantly, as if the priest has mentioned something completely irrelevant to their conversation. The score of a minor league baseball game. The current temperature. The price of cotton in Australia. "I know. I know. I . . . I need to talk, that's all. My father is dying."

He tacks that last sentence on in hopes that it will turn the tide in his favor. He had wanted to keep that information back for a bit longer like a trump card, but it slips out before he knows what he's saying.

Father James clears his throat again. "I am very sorry to hear about your father," he says, moving ahead tenderly. "Father Richard or Reverend Laura would be more than happy to visit your family in the hospital. Even now, in the middle of the night. I can call them for you if you would like. Priests are used to this kind of thing."

Cohen sighs. "It's not only my father. I need . . ." Here he pauses for such a long time that Father James finally speaks.

"Cohen?"

"Yes, well, I need to confess, Father James. I need to confess. And I miss you, and I'm not comfortable confessing to Father Richard or Reverend Laura. They are both very kind. But they're also both very young. I'm not sure they have much life experience, as far as that goes."

"Cohen," the priest says in a kind voice. He

seems to have regained his composure. "I am honored that you still see me in that role. I am thankful to have served as your rector for so many years. Truly, I am. But Father Richard and Reverend Laura are your spiritual leaders now. Either one of them is quite capable of receiving your confession. Of that I am sure. Quite sure. In fact, I regularly confess to Father Richard, and I find him both gracious and understanding."

"But Father, you *know* me."

"Cohen . . ."

"I never practiced confession until I came to Saint Thomas. Did I ever tell you that? I'm sure I have. You're the only person I have ever confessed to. Not often, I know. But still. You are the only one."

Cohen looks away from the cafeteria doors and stares out through the glass at the quiet city, the occasional late-night car drifting past, its headlights glaring against the tinted windows. In the halo of the streetlights, he can see the snow drifting down, lazy, out of place. *It's March,* Cohen thinks. *None of this should be happening.*

"Please, Father," he says, and in those two words is everything in the world he cannot say.

Father James sighs for what feels like the tenth time. Their conversation is like a war fought in small skirmishes, battles made up of sighs and long pauses and heavy silence. Cohen can picture the priest scratching the white hair on top of his head, the way he always did when Cohen would ask him a difficult question or come back around to the same old subjects, the same old doubts and confusions and hesitations.

"Okay, Cohen. Yes. I can meet you in the chapel in thirty minutes. But you need to consider conferring this practice from me to the new leadership at the parish. Perhaps we should sit down together with them and talk through your . . . what shall we say? Hesitations?"

"Yes, Father, I will. I think that's a very good idea. Thank you, Father. I will see you in thirty minutes. Thank you."

Cohen hangs up quickly, before Father James can change his mind. He stands and pushes his chair under the table. The employee turns off another row of lights, and the approaching darkness follows him across the room. His footsteps make a lonely sound on the hard tile. The church is five blocks away. He'll walk.

When he leaves, pushing his way through the doors, the employee turns off the last row of lights behind him.

fifteen

Eli, Eli, lema sabachthani?

Cohen drifts slowly to the church, giving the retired priest extra time to make his way there. He marvels, as he always does when out in the middle of the night, how quiet the city is, how dark, how full of shadows and passages and steaming alleys. The snow stops falling for a moment.

Cohen can see the Saint Thomas steeple rising, a tall black tower against the night sky. He remembers the stars from his childhood, when his family lived outside the light-polluted city. It was a marvel to him when he learned how far away they were, how long it took the light to reach him. He thinks of Johnny and remembers when he was the one in awe that the light he was seeing was thousands upon thousands of years old.

But there are no stars tonight, at least none that he can see. Small, upward-facing lights illuminate the red-brown brick of Saint Thomas, and interior evening lights push the stained-glass colors onto the street. He turns before he gets to the main entrance of the church and walks up the long, covered walkway to the chapel. Off to his right, the fountain sends its endless supply of water up to where it gathers before running over the edge of one pool, then another, and finally back into the ground from where it came. Time does not stop. He arrives at the large glass doors that go into the side of the old church. He tugs on the handle, and the door reluctantly budges.

Inside the door, he cleans his shoes off on the mat before turning directly into the small chapel. It's warm inside. A large red oriental rug stretches the length of the room. Chairs skirt the outside. There are small bookshelves holding rows of Bibles and copies of *The Book of Common Prayer*. A low altar runs along the front, and behind that a podium, and behind the podium, hanging on the blue wall, is a painting of the crucified Christ. Cohen stares at it for some time, taking in the mournful face, the crown of thorns drawing ruby-red beads of blood, the golden flecks in the background. The face has been painted with the expression of forlorn abandonment, eyes turned down.

Cohen remembers the verse from his childhood Sunday school days. These things rise unexpectedly, like debris shaken loose from the floor of a lake during a storm. He never knows what will surface.

Eli, Eli, lema sabachthani?

My God, my God, why have you forsaken me?

He is brought up out of his reverie by the sound

of Father James clearing his throat from behind the temporary confession screen standing at the front right of the small chapel. The priest has already situated a chair for the confessor. Cohen stares for a moment at the shadowy outline of the priest, the only thing he can see of him through the screen.

More old memories surface. Cohen sees the Beast crawling out from under the car, nearly shapeless, its shadowy limbs somehow present but also formless. He feels again the terror when he realizes it is coming across the street. The fear rises in his throat. He coughs.

The voice of the priest pushes back those nightmares, his voice gentle and kind. "Come," he says, clearing his throat. "Have a seat, Cohen."

Cohen, without thinking about it, removes his shoes and walks to the front, sits quietly in the chair, and feels an unexpected surge of emotion. Tears, or the beginnings of tears, form in his throat and his eyes. He swallows hard, and he can only say two words. "Father James."

"First," the priest begins, "allow me to read this from *The Book of Common Prayer.*"

He pauses and Cohen can hear the rustling of thin pages. There is something there in the air, something quiet and holy. Something he has forgotten or left behind. Again he remembers the stars.

"Reconciliation of a Penitent," the priest reads,

"or Penance, is the rite in which those who repent of their sins may confess them to God in the presence of a priest, and receive the assurance of pardon and the grace of absolution."

"Thank you, Father."

Through the screen, Cohen can see Father James nod his head. "Confession is a holy sacrament, a physical sign of the unseen sacred. You may begin when you are ready, Cohen."

Cohen nods. He feels the presence of so many things—the gentle patience of the priest, the knowledge that only a few blocks away his father is dying, the memory of things from his past. The lingering doubt in God that has followed him his whole life. Night pressing in around the church.

"Bless me, Father, for I have sinned."

When Father James speaks, Cohen still can't see his face clearly through the screen, even though they are close together, but he can picture the priest speaking with his eyes closed as he often does. Every word he speaks is genuine, as if he's making up the confession script for the very first time, as if no one has ever spoken these words before.

"The Lord be in your heart and mind, Cohen, and upon your lips, that you may truly and humbly confess your sins: In the Name of the Father, and of the Son, and of the Holy Spirit. Amen."

Cohen crosses himself clumsily and licks his

lips, wondering what that would be like, the Lord upon his lips. He remembers Isaiah's burning coal, Miss Flynne telling them the story with flannel Isaiah on the board alongside a golden-haired angel reaching down, touching his lips with a live ember. He closes his eyes and repeats the words he has come to memorize since joining Father James's parish a decade ago.

"I confess to the Almighty God, to his Church, and to you, that I have sinned by my own fault in thought, word, and deed, in things done and left undone, but especially . . ."

Cohen pauses, unsure of how to continue.

"But especially," he says, and again he stops. He opens his eyes, staring at the warm rug beneath his feet and then up at the painting of the Christ. The downturned face. The disappointed eyes. The ruby red. The gold flecks. The wall behind the painting is a soft, baby blue, like the sky on a spring day.

"Go ahead, Cohen," Father James whispers.

"But especially," Cohen says in a voice so quiet it gets lost in the room, "especially in regards to the death of my father."

sixteen

The Final Inning

Cohen grabbed his mitt, jumped out of the car, and ran across the parking lot to the ballfield. He stopped where the parking lot ended and the wilted grass began and looked back for a moment at his father, who slammed the heavy car door and trudged through the heat waving up off the ground. He walked in a way that was weighed down by early July, with its humidity and long days and the sense it gave them that summer would never end. The world would never cool. Fall and winter and spring were forever banished.

Calvin wiped the sweat from his head with the white handkerchief he always carried. He started at his forehead and continued down to his face where he dabbed his eyes and cheeks and finally his neck, rough as it was from not shaving. It was Saturday, noon, and he didn't shave on Saturdays. Cohen didn't like the way his father looked on those weekend days, unfinished, transient, like a hobo. By the age of nine he had already become more comfortable with the clean-shaven man with the shining head, preaching in a suit, than he was with his Saturday father, the one who walked the house in slippers, stubble rough and clothes sloppy.

Cohen felt the pull of the ballfield but couldn't look away from his father. Something about him on that day seemed weary, but not at the beginning of weariness, when it is new and surprising, and not in the middle of weariness, when it seems you have a long way to go and have nearly grown used to it. No, his father seemed end-of-the-line weary, when it appears the hard days of life will never end. He looked like he might collapse at the next step. Or the next one. Or the next. Cohen stood there watching his father cross the parking lot, and he felt weary for him.

These thoughts slowed him down as he turned and walked into the grass. A line of parents had already formed, some in lawn chairs, some standing with arms crossed, all of them ready for this season to be over. The mothers read magazines or did crossword puzzles, and the fathers spoke to each other about the heat and how high the corn had grown, and it being only the middle of July.

Cohen put on his glove.

He stopped, frozen in place, barely inside the chain-link infield fence.

"Hey, Cohen!" Ava shouted, but he didn't look up.

It wasn't in his glove. He had left it in his glove, but it wasn't there. He bit his lip. He searched around in his mind, trying to remember where he had left Miss Flynne's sock.

He ran back past the line of lawn chair parents, back past his lumbering, Saturday morning father, into the parking lot toward the car. Calvin stopped, watched Cohen go past, and didn't say a word.

Cohen got to the car, yanked open the door, and looked on the floor of the passenger side and under the seat and, for good measure but no good reason, in the back seat and all through the driver's side, but it wasn't there. The sock was nowhere. But it wasn't nowhere—it was somewhere, and that's what concerned him, the somewhere it might have ended up.

Cohen held his baseball glove on the crown of his head, pulled it down with worry, and thought back through the morning. Had he tucked it under his pillow? Left it under the dresser? That would be the best possibility, but he thought he remembered fishing it out from there. Had it fallen out of his glove when he was eating breakfast or walking to the car? Was it lying in their yard, a white flag, a shouting witness? He could imagine it there, limp, patient, the letters looking up at the hazy summer sky.

HMF.

He ran back to where his father stood. "Dad," he said, breathless, "we have to go home." It was a prayer, a plea.

The team had already assembled on the bench, the coach shouting out positions and batting order. The game was about to begin.

"What?"

"We have to go home. I'm not feeling well. We have to go."

"Cohen, this is your last game. You look fine. What's wrong?"

"I just . . . Dad, we have to go."

His father stared at him, squinting in the sun. He stood there like a statue, a pillar. He reached into his deep pocket and drew out the hanky again, wiping his head, his eyes, his cheeks, his neck. He was shaking his head slowly before he even finished cleaning away the sweat.

"Cohen, it's your last game. I don't know what you're up to, but we're not leaving, not now."

A voice from the bench. "Cohen Marah, second base, batting sixth!"

"Did you hear that, Son? Now get out there. Stop this nonsense. We'll be home soon enough, and then you can do whatever it is you so badly need to do."

"But . . ."

His father didn't say anything, but his stare deepened. Cohen turned, shoulders sagging, and drifted in the direction of second base.

"Hurry up!" his father shouted behind him. "Get out there!"

"Hustle, Cohen!" his coach echoed.

But Cohen couldn't hustle. He couldn't hurry. The weight of every bad thing that could happen in his life pulled down on him. What if his mother found the sock?

The July humidity rose from the grass, and the air smelled of the deepest greens, the kind that settled in among forest shadows. The sky was a molten white with small patches of blue.

The game started and Cohen scanned the hill by the VFW, waiting for his mother's car to come down from the main road. The longer it took her, the heavier the sense of dread in his gut. It was a churning, poisonous thing. She was rarely early, but she was at every game by the end of the first inning. He kept looking over at the lane, so often, in fact, that he missed a first-inning grounder hit his way. He never missed grounders. They were his specialty.

"Stay in the game, Cohen! Keep your glove down! Bend your knees!" his coach shouted.

"Pay attention!" his father yelled.

"Hang in there, Cohen. You got this," Ava said from first, questions on her face, a quiet curiosity in her voice.

Cohen passed the time by sinking down inside himself—it was the only place he could go. The second inning ended and the third inning started and still there was no sign of his mother and Kaye. His at-bats were distracted strikeouts, and seconds after he returned to the bench he couldn't have recalled a thing about them. Cohen returned to the field, sure something had gone terribly wrong. He thought he might throw up on the infield, and he considered it, wondering if it might be his only ticket home, his only chance to get back and make things right before everything veered off the tracks.

The heat bore down on everyone. The home plate umpire became overheated and kept walking over to the visiting team's bench every other batter, breathing heavy and dumping water on his head and red face. Under his arms, his shirt was dark and soaked. Before Cohen's team got their second out that inning, the umpire fainted, sort of folded in on himself and drifted forward, nearly crushing their undersized catcher. Both coaches ran onto the field and knelt over the man, and for a few glorious minutes the chatter among Cohen's teammates was that the game would be called. They couldn't continue without an umpire. They could all go home, and Cohen could find that stupid sock and burn it or chuck it in the creek or tuck it in something and throw it away, because nothing in the world was worth this amount of dread. He imagined the relief he would feel at church the next day, the sock discarded, the anxiety gone.

The umpire walked gingerly back to his car, refusing help, drifting in and out of parking spaces until he found his own vehicle. The teams' coaches seemed resigned to the game's ending, everyone saying what a shame it was the season had to end this way, but to Cohen's horror, his father walked over to where they were talking.

Cohen's feet were glued to the ground, and he was very aware of each drop of sweat as it trickled down his temples, his cheeks, his nose, his chin. What strange twist was this?

His father volunteered to take the umpire's place. His father, while being a dedicated baseball man, had never umpired a game before in his life. But there he was, pulling on the huge padded chest protector like a reverse turtle shell, slipping the black umpire mask onto his face, cleaning off home plate with a tiny brush so that a small cloud of tan dust rose around him, before he squatted down behind the catcher and started calling balls and strikes.

Where was Cohen's mother?

What was his father doing?

What strange apocalypse was unfolding in front of him?

Inning after inning passed, and his mother's continued absence was the confirmation of his greatest and most horrible nightmares. She had never completely missed any of his games before. She had found the sock. She was on her way to kill his father. She had committed suicide, her body in the basement. Kaye was on the run. He should be too. He eyed the cornfield, wondering if he could get lost in it.

His father, meanwhile, seemed to be enjoying himself, and he was doing a capable job, his strike zone acceptable to both batters and pitchers alike. His authority as a pastor found a strange companion in the world of being an umpire, and when he shouted "Strike!" or "He's out!" his voice was remarkably reminiscent of those Sunday night services when he tried to preach the lost home. Every pitch was a prayer, and he answered in an even voice. In between innings, he removed his mask and wiped his face and head and neck with his handkerchief. At first Cohen thought his father was simply squinting, but when he looked closer, he was taken aback.

His father was grinning. As if he was enjoying himself. Cohen had never seen his father grin before, not like that. His father smiled, yes, especially when speaking with parishioners and sometimes even while he preached or told a story. He laughed occasionally, usually at Kaye when she said something clever—often his father's laughs were mirrored by his mother's flatline look of disapproval. But Cohen had never seen him grin, not like that, and he certainly didn't expect it in the midst of the heat and the sun and the dust. Grinning. Like a boy.

"Cohen!" the coach called out as they took the field for the last inning. "Take the mound."

Cohen's heart stopped. His coach wanted him to pitch? When his father was the home plate umpire?

Cohen weighed his options. He could run away, and immediately this seemed the most viable choice. Running meant he wouldn't have to explain himself to anyone. He could pretend to pass out, the second victim of heat stroke on that hot July day. But he wasn't sure of his ability to fake unconsciousness. He could refuse his coach.

But Ava was there, smiling her encouragement, handing him the ball. She was running back to first base, already shouting for him. And so he found himself stepping onto the mound.

He was mindful of each breath. He tried to rub the sweat off his forehead and cheeks with the back of his gloved hand but only succeeded in spreading it around, stinging the corners of his eyes. He swallowed hard. The baseball felt heavy, unwieldy, as if it were growing in his hands. He took another deep breath, went into his windup, and pitched the ball.

The batter didn't swing, although it was a lovely pitch on the inside half of the plate, about belt high.

"Ball one," his father said.

Cohen, catching the ball thrown back to him, did a double take. That was a perfect strike— the way it had left his hand, flown through the air, and nestled into the catcher's mitt, with the catcher barely having to move his hand to catch it. What was his father doing?

Now anger nestled in with the nerves and the doubt and the desire not to be on the pitcher's mound on that hot July day. What was wrong with his father, that he would call a perfect strike a ball?

Cohen reached back, threw the next pitch, grunted as it left his hand. He watched it spin toward the catcher, again belt high, this time on the outside half of the plate. The batter didn't swing.

"Ball two," his father said, and Cohen stood there for a long moment staring at the umpire, the decision maker, his own father. Another perfectly thrown pitch. Another strike. Yet he had called it a ball. Again.

Cohen reached up and caught the ball the catcher returned to him, but he didn't turn to go back to the mound, not at first. He stood there staring at his father, shouts and protests and complaints lodging behind his tongue, waiting to erupt from his throat.

"Play ball," his father said tersely.

Cohen said nothing. He turned. He got ready to throw another pitch.

"You got this, Cohen!" Ava said.

"Right down the middle, Cohen!" his coach shouted.

A group of birds darted overhead, making for

the fields and the waist-high corn. A sudden breeze blew, rustling the stalks, heaving the flat clouds across the metallic sky, kicking up dust. The sun glared from behind those clouds, a bright presence that took up half the sky. Cohen reached back and threw another pitch.

This last pitch—and it would end up being Cohen's last pitch of the game, the last pitch of the season, the last pitch of his entirely too brief baseball career—was perfect, a fastball right down the middle of the plate. He had managed to harness the anger, the frustration, and all those pent-up words in the back of his throat and direct it into that final pitch. He expected the batter to swing at such a perfect pitch, but he didn't. He stood there and stared as the ball sailed into the catcher's mitt and made a satisfying pop.

Cohen waited for the strike call.

"Ball three," his father said in an almost disinterested voice.

"What?" Cohen shouted, and everyone on the field stared at him, the nine-year-old pitcher arguing with the umpire. Kids his age never argued with umpires.

The fathers stopped talking about the corn, and the mothers looked up over the edges of their magazines. His father didn't say anything in response, but his back stiffened, and he flipped up his mask so that it rested on top of his head. The two of them stood there staring at each other through the dust and the wind and the heat.

The catcher didn't seem to know what to do so he threw the ball back, but Cohen didn't even try to catch it. He was still staring at his father. The ball drifted over his shoulder, thudded behind him, and rolled into the grass. Cohen kept staring at his father. He reached up and pushed the brim of his ball cap back, but he didn't look away.

Cohen could have gone on indefinitely, staring his father down. He knew he had been wronged; he knew the universe was on his side, and that sense of righteousness filled him with resolve. The birds left the sky a clean slate, and still he didn't move. The clouds drifted from west to east and the corn grew, and still he stared at his father.

"Play! Ball!" his father said again, taking off the mask and squeezing it in white-knuckled intensity.

But it was too late. All of it was too late. Cohen had thrown his last pitch. Something else was coming, a different kind of fury altogether, and its first movement caught Cohen's eye. He looked up the lane that led from the VFW down to the ballfield, and there came his mother's car over the hill, an old Volkswagen Rabbit, silver, the sunlight glaring from the windshield.

He could have convinced himself everything was okay and everything would be okay, except for the way the car didn't slow to take the slight curve at the bottom of the hill, veering into the grass and stirring up more dust, or the way his mother didn't take a parking spot but drove right up to the ballfield.

"Play ball!" Cohen's father shouted again, fury gathering at the edge of his words. He had not yet seen the car. He had not yet seen his wife opening the door, careening out, leaving the door open behind her. But Cohen had, and when his father realized the stare-down with his son had broken off, he turned to see what his son was looking at.

Cohen's mother didn't stop at the line of parents who did not now know what to pay attention to—the argument between the pitcher and the umpire or the woman storming the field. And she didn't stop at the gap in the chain-link fence where the coaches stood speechless at the disagreement between father and son. She pushed between them. And she didn't stop inside the fence where the grass ended and the dirt infield began. And she didn't stop at the infield but walked right up to home plate, right up to where Cohen's father clutched the umpire's mask. She poked her index finger into his incredibly puffy chest protector, her finger sinking in, not even touching his real chest.

"How could you do this?" she said in a voice that was simultaneously tears and rage and a refusal to be disappointed by someone so clearly less than her.

Calvin didn't seem to know what to say. Cohen's glove fell from his hand and landed palm up in the dust. The wind died down. The corn stopped rustling. The clouds stopped moving.

"You are nothing without me! Nothing!" she screamed, poking his chest protector with each and every word. Kaye came wandering from the car, taking each step as if it might be the step where she fell through the crust of the earth.

"You are disgusting and immoral! Immoral! And a sinner! And you will go straight to hell for this!" Cohen's mother screamed.

By now Calvin had recovered enough from the initial onslaught to speak, and even though he asked a question, Cohen could see his guilt creeping out from the edges of his face, the wrinkles around his eyes, the slouching of his shoulders. He no longer squeezed the mask—it hung at his side, hooked tenuously by his index finger, ready to drop.

"What are you talking about, Rachel?" he asked quietly, seeming to forget he was the home plate umpire at his son's Little League ball game. He didn't shush her and lead her away. He didn't ask her if they could talk about this some other time. No, his guilt drowned him, and he could do nothing but offer halfhearted denials.

But Cohen's mother was out of words. She was spent. Her sobs, the ones she tried desperately to hold down, came out like coughs. She wiped her eyes fiercely with the back of her hand as if she wanted to rip them out, angry at the tears they produced. She reached into her pocket and pulled out something small and white and balled up, and she threw it down into the dirt where it rolled to rest directly on home plate.

The sock.

HMF.

She turned and walked away, and when she reached Kaye she grabbed her by the arm in fury, as if Kaye had been the unfaithful one. She dragged her to the car, Kaye's numb half-steps stumbling to keep up. And then they were in the car, careening again up the hill and out of sight.

Cohen's father took out his handkerchief in the midst of that profound silence. He wiped his head, his eyes, and his neck and put the hanky in his pocket. He bent down and picked up the sock and put it in his other pocket. He looked once at Cohen, and the expression on his face was one Cohen had never seen before—he looked lost, unsure of where to go or how to get there.

Calvin dropped the umpire's mask, took off the chest protector, and laid it carefully on the ground. He stopped to say something to the coach but didn't seem to know what. He walked through the stunned and embarrassed crowd to the car, where he waited for Cohen without saying a word.

seventeen

A Letter

October 12, 1984

Dear Co,

How are things back home? Here in the big city—and let me tell you that Philly is the real deal, no small city like the dinky one you're living in but big and scary and full of monsters. Ha ha. Me and Mom are okay. The new school is better than I thought it would be and I'm meeting some nice girls. I like walking to school, and the sound of the city at night is cool. It makes me feel very small.

I miss Dad's breakfasts, though. Mom has been on this health-food kick so all we have in the house is something called muesli? I had to look at the box just now to be able to spell it. It tastes like sawdust with little chunks of wood in it. I keep wanting to threaten Mom that if she doesn't buy some bacon I'm running away and coming back to live with you guys, but I don't think she's at the joking stage yet. Ha ha. Sometimes she buys this super healthy bread, and then I can have toast, but even the butter we have is weird. Oh well.

How's Dad handling everything? I feel so sad for him. His whole life is falling apart. I'm kind of glad I'm not there to watch it happen. You and I both know Mom isn't the nicest person to live with, so I'm sure there are some things he doesn't miss, and he probably enjoys his quiet nights. You know how he was always begging us for quiet. But it must be lonely around there, especially on Sunday mornings.

Do you guys go to church anywhere? Mom and I visited a few different places, but everything here in the city is stuffy stuffy stuffy. I should have written those words in all caps. I don't know how much longer we can keep up this search. Sunday mornings are so awkward. But you know Mom. She probably thinks that if we missed a week of church we'd be signing a one-way ticket to h-e-l-l.

(I wrote it like that in case Mom reads this letter before she sends it. Are you reading this, Mom? That's not nice, if you are. Ha ha.)

Do you like the new apartment? Do you have a nice room? Are you scared with all the bodies in the basement??? I would be terrified. Mom said I can visit in the summer, but that was after she said "maybe" so many times that I kind of wonder if she isn't putting me off until the summer when she'll say no again. She seems desperate to keep me away from Dad. I think she's scared I might decide to move back in with you. It makes me so sad sometimes when I think about it. I try not to. Maybe when I visit, you can show me around and we can have a sleepover in the basement with all the bodies and tell ghost stories! Wouldn't that be terrifying?

How's your friend Ava? Do you have a girlfriend yet that you're not telling me about? There are no boys here worth getting to know. Including Jimmy. They are all big-city know-it-alls.

Please write again. I miss you. I love you.

K

eighteen

And All My Other Sins

"But especially, especially in regards to the death of my father."

Cohen pauses, and the words are absorbed into the carpet, into the sky-blue wall, into the downturned face of the crucified Christ. Father James says nothing. He waits for Cohen to finish his confession. That has always been something Father James has been good at, something Cohen marvels at: his ability to remain quiet for such a long time, to wait when words are expected. His patience is uncanny.

Cohen looks up again at the painting. It feels precisely as if the disappointment on the downturned face of Christ was painted there for this very moment. Cohen thinks the painting might as well have been titled *The Eternal Disappointment of the Christ in Regards to the Life of Cohen Marah*. He races through the final words of confession, and even as he's saying the words he knows at least part of what Father James's response will be.

"For these and all other sins which I cannot now remember, I am truly sorry. I pray God to have mercy on me. I firmly intend amendment of life, and I humbly beg forgiveness of God and his Church, and ask you for counsel, direction, and absolution."

"Cohen . . . Cohen," the priest says in a gentle voice. "Slow down. This is a prayer you are saying from your heart. Your soul! It is an offering to the eternal force that created the universe, the force that created you. Slow down, my son, there is no rush. Think of the words you're saying."

Silence.

"Should I say it again?" Cohen asks sheepishly.

Father James lets out a low grunt that is somewhere between a chuckle and a snort.

"For these and all other sins which I cannot now remember," Cohen says again, slowly, "I am truly sorry."

Cohen pauses between each phrase, trying to catch the words in his mind before they evaporate.

"I pray God to have mercy on me."

He takes a breath.

"I firmly intend amendment of life."

He becomes acutely aware of how late it is.

"I humbly beg forgiveness of God and his Church, and ask you for counsel, direction, and absolution."

They sit there without saying anything. Cohen glances one more time at the eyes of the crucified Christ, hoping the sense of disappointment has lessened. The heat kicks on, and warm air rushes into the room from the low vents, rustling the pages of a prayer book someone left open on one of the chairs. Exhaustion overcomes all of his defenses. His eyes are heavy. If the priest doesn't speak soon, he might fall asleep there in the chair.

"Before I absolve you, Cohen, I must encourage you to take anything—anything—the authorities need to know . . . should know . . ." He stops. "Cohen, are you saying you took your father's life?"

Cohen glances at the screen, looking for the eyes of his confessor, but when all he can see is a shifting shadow, he stares back at the floor. "No, Father. Not physically. But I am concerned that I may have caused his death. Indirectly."

"I see."

"Do you?"

Father James pauses. "No, not completely."

Cohen tries to find the priest's eyes behind the screen. Time passes strangely there in the chapel. He can't remember what time it was when he left the hospital. When he walks outside, will the sun be rising? Or are there still hours and hours of night remaining?

"We had a . . . conversation. An argument? I told him some things he didn't want to hear. When I left his house the night before, we were both very angry. I worry he may have . . ."

Again, he's overwhelmed by this sudden desire

for sleep. He considers asking the priest if he can spend the rest of the night right there in the chapel, asleep on the warm rug, curled up beside one of the heating vents.

"I worry he may have taken his own life. Tried to."

"I see." Father James peers out at Cohen from behind the confession screen and sighs. "Our Lord Jesus Christ," he says quietly, and again Cohen can picture him speaking with his eyes closed, "who has left power to his Church to absolve all sinners who truly repent and believe in him, of his great mercy forgive you all your offenses; and by his authority committed to me, I absolve you from all your sins: In the Name of the Father, and of the Son, and of the Holy Spirit. Amen."

"Amen," Cohen whispers.

"The Lord has put away all your sins."

"Thanks be to God."

"Go in peace," the priest replies, "and pray for me, a sinner."

PART TWO

Tuesday,
March 17, 2015

*In the midst
of the waters . . .*

Genesis 1:6

nineteen

The Beast

After everything came tumbling down—after the tornado of shouts and awkward silences, after the furiously packed bags and his mother dragging Kaye from the house, after they drove away, leaving him in the middle of the country road— came a long, slow stretch of days and months and years when Cohen felt mostly numb. In their passing, they were lonely and quiet. But when Cohen looked back on those years from age nine to fourteen, they were blank. He knew he lived them. He knew he existed then, during the latter half of the 1980s, but there was very little to remember.

During the fog of the first few months after his mother left them, his father made an awkward but rather quick transition into a new occupation, from pastor to funeral director. The church would not have him, not after what he had done. There were rumors about Miss Flynne of the decorative socks, Miss Flynne of the neon-green nail polish, that she had fled west. Cohen never saw her again.

Kaye and Cohen's mother found a place to live in Philadelphia, closer to her own family, and

Cohen and his father moved into an old apartment above the funeral parlor, right there in the small city only a few miles from their old place. The country road gave way to a grid of cement and concrete and macadam. The forest of tangled oaks and maples and pines transformed into straight lines of sycamores lining streets named after the monarchy: King and Queen and Prince and Duke. A sky once filled with the light from distant stars was overwhelmed by streetlights and headlights and the glow of the monolithic hospital a few blocks south.

The previous owner of the funeral home hadn't lived in the apartment. It had been empty for years, unused, and smelled like shadows, so they left the windows open for the rest of the summer and into the fall. Cohen lay stretched out flat in his bed and tried to sleep but couldn't for the sound of the city and the heat and the presence of all the bodies coming and going in the basement.

"That is no place for a boy," he had heard his mother hiss to his father during one of their rare in-person encounters, soon after the separation, just before the divorce. His father had only stared at the floor before looking back up at her with empty eyes. It was as if, now that the woman who had written his sermons was gone, he could not find the words.

Cohen had wondered if his mother might be

right, if a funeral home was no place for a boy to live. He took to wandering the apartment at night, not because he was especially brave but because it was only slightly less terrifying than lying in his bed, waiting for a resurrected corpse to come for him. If he remained in bed, he stared through the dark at his bedroom door, the very same door that always seemed to be creaking open ever so slowly. He couldn't take his eyes from it or the door handle, which always seemed to be rotating as someone or something tried to slide in and join him.

At some point during those lost years, he began getting out of bed and wandering. He carried a flashlight and an aluminum Louisville Slugger baseball bat, hidden during the day between his mattress and box spring. He soon located, and knew how to avoid, the loose floorboards so as not to alert his father to this new nighttime restlessness.

Not that his father would have heard him. When they first moved into the funeral home apartment on the second floor, his father had begun taking a nightly glass of port. Which soon became two glasses. Which soon became four tumblers each night before bed. His father's snoring reverberated in an outward ripple the way his preaching always had, and it could be heard from anywhere in the second-floor apartment. Cohen could even hear his father's snoring in most areas of the first floor, where the coffin displays and chapel were located.

But then came 1989, when a blurry half decade ended and the memories began again.

It was winter, and everything stood sharp and dry. He was awake, standing in the dark kitchen, when the sound of a car traveling at a ridiculously high speed eased its way into the silence, the high whine of an engine at its max, the squeal of tires going too fast around a sharp turn. He opened the window, stuck his head out into the freezing-cold air, and saw headlights bobbing and weaving, going back and forth from one lane to the other, coming fast.

The car came up the street and onto his block without stopping at the traffic lights, and the driver lost control, slid sideways, rediscovered the car's traction, and shot off the road, slamming into the blue post office box and lurching to a stop near the house across the street from Cohen's living room window. He sat staring, eyes wide. The car remained eerily still on top of the post office box, tilted to the point that it might fall over on its top, steam or smoke rising from the engine.

Various lights winked on as people who had heard the crash pulled themselves from their beds and came to their windows. But Cohen wasn't paying attention to the house lights. He was completely absorbed by what crawled out from under the wreck.

At first he thought a shadow was stretching from the side of the car, perhaps because one of the neighbors had turned on their outside light. It was like a slowly spreading pool of darkness, but it had a form, which made him wonder if the driver of the car had been wearing some kind of a costume. But it was no costume, and he was not coming out of the door.

"What?" Cohen whispered, reaching down for the previously forgotten Louisville Slugger without taking his eyes from the spreading blackness. At that moment, at that same exact moment, all the streetlights in the town winked out. Maybe the car had hit something that brought on the darkness. Maybe some other car had also crashed and taken out a utility pole. Whatever had happened, the city fell into a deeper layer of inky blackness, and the only remaining light came from the windows of houses where people had woken up, and these were few.

The thing that climbed out from under the car still had no clear shape, but Cohen saw enough of it to know that it had a head, and it had things like arms and legs, but not in a million years could he have described it. There was something of death about it, and the strong, metallic smell of fresh blood swept up through the open window where Cohen stood.

The thing, the Beast, the whatever-it-was, had something like eyes and something like a face, and it looked up at the window and saw him. He knew it. He could feel that it had seen him, and its seeing of him was an ache that filled his mind.

The thing began moving to cross the empty, dark street toward the sycamore tree and the glass doors of the funeral parlor.

Cohen froze. He squeezed the baseball bat, held it in two white-knuckled hands. Should he shout for his father? Should he run and make sure the doors were locked? Should he go hide?

Sirens pierced the night, and flashing lights approached from a long way off. The thing turned and looked at the lights, and it moved in the opposite direction, vanishing down unlit Duke Street. For a moment Cohen thought he could see the darkened trail it had left, like a slug's. A trail of cold and fear.

He realized he had barely been breathing, and his hands trembled as he moved to put the flashlight away, laid down the bat. He sat with his back against the wall, and the cold night air rushed in over the windowsill behind him and poured down his back. He heard the loud sound of a siren outside the funeral home, and the shouts of neighbors. His father, now moving noisily through the house, stumbled out the door, going to see what was happening.

twenty

The Boy

"What are you thinking, Cohen?" Kaye's voice comes to him from another sky, some far-off horizon, drifting through the morning light that filters into the room. "Did you hear me?"

"I'm sorry," he says, pulling his gaze away from his father's bald head. He notices his father's hair is coming in around the edges, a white-gray stubble returning now that he hasn't shaved in a day or two. "I was somewhere else."

"What are you thinking about? You haven't been saying anything. Where did you go last night?"

"Out," Cohen says, shrugging. "I needed some fresh air." He looks into his sister's imploring eyes. Her being has always oozed with kindness ever since he was young. She was the doting older sister, rarely antagonizing, almost always encouraging.

He looks at her round stomach and smiles, trying to change the subject. "How are those two holding up?"

She grimaces. "Heavy. Uncomfortable. I'm so ready to have them out here, where I can hand them off to you or Brent or . . ." He can tell she almost finished her sentence with "or Dad." She lifts her hand to cover her mouth, composes herself.

"What is your doctor saying?"

"About the date? They want to take them three or four weeks early. That's only two weeks from now."

"I didn't realize it was so soon," Cohen says.

She shrugs. "Or the week after that. They're recommending a C-section, and they don't want to wait until I go into labor, so at my next appointment we're going to pick a date."

"Will Brent be back in time?" Cohen realizes that in the chaos he hasn't even asked about Kaye's husband, how his travels are going, or if he can come back earlier.

"He'll be back. As long as these two can hang on for another ten days. These overseas trips have me tied up in knots."

"I'm here too, you know. If you need me."

"I know you are." She sits back in the chair, her legs spread as if she might give birth at any moment. She rubs her round stomach with both hands, partially closes her eyes, and groans with the heaviness of it all. He stares at her and the ripeness of her body. The impending birth feels weighty and overwhelming. He would panic if he were her. If he had two humans growing inside of him, nearly ready to fight their way out, he would wilt in the face of what had to be done.

With her eyes still half closed, she asks Cohen, "Where were you? Last night."

He pauses. "I went over to see Father James."

"Really?" She seems happy to hear it.

"Yeah, I needed to talk."

"I'm glad you're still going to church. I'm glad you're talking to someone." She opens her eyes, raising her eyebrows, a playful accusation.

"I talk to you!" he protests.

"No, you don't, Cohen. You don't talk to me."

They both turn and look at their father again. Their gazes return to him over and over again, like children running to a window to watch an approaching storm.

"Do you remember when he used to play monster with us?" Kaye smiles. "When he hid under that brown blanket and stayed completely still until we climbed on top of him?"

Cohen does remember. It's a memory from too far away. It resides in a catalog of memories of his father he has not perused in a long time, from before the blank half decade.

"He terrified me when he did that," he says. "He'd hold me down until I screamed. It was awful, actually. I felt trapped, like I couldn't breathe."

"Do you remember how hard he would laugh?" Kaye asks, shaking her head as if it's hard to believe. "He would come out from under that blanket, face all red, breathing heavy, sweating, laughing until he cried."

Cohen nods. It's true. He has completely forgotten so many things.

"You bring up something like that," he says quietly, "and I don't know what to think of Dad."

Kaye nods but doesn't speak.

"I really don't." He looks at her as if she has the answer. "I don't feel like he and I have had a conversation, a real conversation, since before Mom left."

"You say 'since before Mom left' like it was her fault."

Cohen shrugs. "And even before that, if we did talk, it was about how to catch a ball or how to run faster or how to turn first base. How to check the runner. How to hit the cutoff man. How to properly put a worm on a hook. It was always about something that had nothing to do with us."

He stares at Kaye again. He wonders if she knows what he's talking about, if she can help him make sense of it all. He feels like he might cry, and the emotion frustrates him.

"He always loved you," Kaye says. "I could see it. I was jealous of it."

"Jealous?"

"Sure," she says, but there's no bitterness in her admission. Only a blooming regret. "The way you two threw that ball back and forth for hours? The way you'd watch baseball games and endlessly debate things I knew nothing about?"

She pauses as if trying to decide if she has gone too far, said too much.

"He loved both of us. Loves both of us. I know that. But his love for you was so deep." She raises her hand to her mouth again, and when she speaks again, it's in a whisper. "Why do you think I went to live with Mother? Why do you think I signed Johnny up for baseball as soon as I could?"

Cohen sighs and runs his hand through his graying hair. "I'm sorry, Kaye."

"Why do you think I'm having these babies?" She cries quietly.

Cohen stands, puts his hand on her shoulder, leans down and wraps his arm around her, and lets her drain her tears on him. But for some reason, for some inexplicable reason, he moves on quickly to the hospital room window and stares out into the morning.

He shakes his head. "I'm sorry, Kaye," he says again, quietly.

The two of them are there together for what seems like a long time, the equipment beeping, flurries falling outside again, drifting through the air, lost, finding their way. There is a heaviness in the room that comes with confession. There's a crack in the relationship they once had, and light shines into new places.

Kaye clears her throat. "Have you talked to anyone at the funeral home?" she asks him.

"I talked to Beth. She's got it under control. We had to transfer a lot of our work to the church while the police look around the basement. What they let us move, anyway."

"Will we be okay?"

"To be honest, it's kind of a relief. You need a break from the place—you've been putting in way too many hours. Beth and Marcus are doing what they can. I've got the pastor taking over the funerals on our schedule—only one this week, thank God. We're limping along, but we have some reserves. We'll be okay for a few weeks, until . . ." He's not sure how to finish. *Until we get through this? Until Dad dies?*

Their conversation is cut short by a commotion in the hall, the sound of an IV rack falling over. Shouts. Expletives.

Cohen leaves Kaye and his father and goes to the door. He sticks his head into the hallway and sees a boy flopping out of the neighboring hospital room, arms and legs flailing as if he was pushed out. The boy looks like he's in high school. He wears a green John Deere baseball cap, a green T-shirt with the sleeves cut off, jeans held up by a large-buckled belt, and work boots that add weight to his movement. His face is pimply, and there's a haze of fuzzy brown hair on his top lip with matching patches of it on his cheeks. He carries a look that is equal parts surprise, anger, and disgust, and a sadness he can't quite hide.

Coming out after him is a man who could be Cohen's age, maybe a little older, dressed like the boy but wearing a heavy coat. He has a mustache that starts above his upper lip then eases all the way down along the sides of his mouth, ending sharply at his jawline. His teeth are a pearl gray, his eyes bloodshot from exhaustion. He grabs one of the boy's tight biceps in his huge paw, but just when Cohen expects him to erupt in angry shouts, the man says nothing. His grip squeezes tighter, a boa constrictor. His anger continues to grow. But he says nothing.

The two stand there, a statue that could easily be titled *Father and Son*. The young one's face begins to turn to ash, his mouth goes into an even harder line, and though the boy hides most of it, Cohen can see it, can recognize it gathering: pain. The father's grip tightens even more, his fingers going white. The boy begins to wilt under the clamp on his arm, turning from defiant teenager to compliant little boy. Cohen expects the boy to collapse to his knees or cry out, but the man releases him, takes two short steps backwards, still staring at the boy. He spins back into the room.

The boy reaches up quickly and rubs the spot on his arm, the spot that is now alive with the disturbed red branding of his father's hand. He closes his eyes and turns his neck. It cracks loudly. He continues rubbing his arm until he sees Cohen staring at him. His hand stops. His mouth, which had begun to soften, finds its plumb line again.

The boy stares at him. "What are you looking at?" he asks, and Cohen thinks he sounds relieved to have discovered someone who might be lower on the food chain.

Cohen shrugs. He doesn't know what to say. But the kid keeps staring at him.

"That your old man?" Cohen asks. He doesn't know why those are the words that come to him. He doesn't know what he's trying to do—avoid getting beat up in the hospital? Help a kid deal with an abusive father? Pass the time?

The boy glares at him for a moment. He takes a deep breath and shrugs, an almost violent movement, like a lion shaking its mane. "Yeah. So?"

"Who are you visiting?"

"Why do you care?" the boy blurts, but one thing he still seems to have is a conscience, and Cohen can tell he feels a little guilty for his sharp response. The boy moves nervously.

"Just curious," Cohen says calmly.

"My grandpa," the boy says, his voice shifting a few degrees into a normal, conversational tone. He starts rubbing his arm again, slowly, automatically. Cohen glances at the fiery red lines the father's fingers left. "He had a heart attack a few days ago. The doctors screwed up. Someone gave him the wrong medication. Now he's probably gonna die."

Cohen's eyes widen. "Seriously?"

"Yeah," the boy says. He starts to say something else but decides against it, saying only the same word again. "Yeah."

"I'm sorry," Cohen says quietly.

"Not your fault," the boy says, staring first at the floor, then down the hall, then at the door to his grandfather's room as it opens.

People emerge from the room, walking in single file. First, the boy's father, still at the edge of erupting, his face red, his hat pulled down low. He is like a bull worked up to the point of charging: one more provocation, no matter how small, will be enough to send him on a violent spree. After him, a woman. Cohen guesses she's the boy's mother—he gets his fine facial features from her. She has a delicate nose, downcast eyes with thin eyebrows, wispy brown hair. Her mouth is sad and the only truly beautiful thing about her face. To Cohen, something about her resembles a walking apology, the kind of woman who believes everything is her fault, that she deserves every chastisement she has ever received—and there have been many. She glances at Cohen, but when their eyes meet, she looks away.

145

Behind them, a white-cloaked doctor. He looks worried, frustrated. Cohen wonders if what the boy said was true, if it's this doctor's fault that the grandfather is dying. The door swings closed behind them. The clicking sound of the latch is that one last thing, that one final provocation, and the boy's father turns in a red rage.

Cohen thinks he'll have to be the one to pull this man off the doctor. But he's not a physical person—he has never been in a fistfight with anyone.

The man raises a finger and points at the doctor, but words can't find their way through the maze of his anger. His breath heaves in and out of his mouth so that small beads of white spit gather at the corners. He rips his baseball hat off and throws it on the ground at the doctor's feet, and he takes three quick steps in the doctor's direction. Cohen has to give the doctor credit—he somehow keeps from backing away. The man's finger is still raised, now an inch from the doctor's sculpted nose, two inches from his designer glasses. The man's eyes are wild, two tornadoes, and now that his hat is on the ground, his oily gray hair stands on edge.

The doctor trembles. Cohen takes a step closer.

But the man says nothing. He turns away. He grabs the boy by a clump of his shirt under his chin and wrenches him to the ground. "Get my hat," he mutters.

The man's wife falls in line behind him like a shadow.

twenty-one

The Current

"What was that all about?" Kaye asks as Cohen comes back through the door.

"We need to keep an eye on Dad's medication," he says, looking closely at the various IV bags, reading words he doesn't understand. He walks back around the bed to the chair that has become his and sits down. He's tired. The long night is catching up to him.

"While we're being honest," Kaye begins.

Cohen looks at her, eyebrows raised. "You mean, while you're being honest."

"Okay, while I'm being honest. Cohen . . ." She pauses, looks at him. "I feel like you know something about Dad you're not telling me."

He feels a rigidity spread up his spine, immobilizing him. He grips the armrests of the chair like a man afraid of flying. His eyes lock on to his father's face. His strong features. The lines in the wrinkles around his neck. The small hairs that populate the ridges of his ears. The faded scar at the corner of his eyebrow. Cohen can barely breathe.

"Did the doctors tell you something you're not sharing with me?" Kaye asks, almost pleading.

"Did you see something at the funeral home you're not telling me about?"

"Kaye," he whispers, shaking his head. "I don't . . ."

Before he gets any further, the door to the room opens. A nurse comes in, checking things, looking at clipboards, glancing at the IV bags, and monitoring the equipment. Behind the nurse, Ava.

"Hi, Kaye," she says. "Hi, Cohen."

"Ava," he says, surprise in his voice, and a question mark.

"I'm sorry about your father," Ava says to Kaye, shaking her hand. "I don't know if you remember me. I went to school with Cohen. I'm Ava."

"I'm sorry," Kaye says. "Vaguely. I wasn't around much after seventh grade."

Ava nods, looking over at Cohen. "I was wondering if you have a minute?"

"Have you found out anything about what happened to our dad?" Kaye asks.

"Nothing for sure," Ava says. "And my boss has taken me off the case, officially. Unofficially, I'm still snooping around." She smiles after the last sentence and looks knowingly at them, as if she is doing the snooping as a personal favor to them.

"Where do you want to talk?" Cohen asks.

"Actually, my boss is wondering if you could

come over to the funeral home, walk through the basement with him, answer a few more questions? He doesn't know much about how the operation works. He's hoping your insights might help us out."

"Sure," he says, standing slowly, stretching, a yawn slowing him. "Do you mind if I go, Kaye?"

"No," she says. "Go ahead. But can you take the overnight shift tonight? I'm exhausted. And Johnny didn't do well without me at home."

"Of course," he says. He walks over to Kaye and kisses the top of her head. "I'll be back soon. After that, you can go get a shower," he jokes.

Kaye swings playfully at him, smacking him on the hip, but her hand grasps his jacket for an extra moment before letting go, and her eyes lock with his as if she's trying to find the answer to her earlier questions, the ones he avoided. *Did the doctors tell you something you're not sharing with me? Did you see something at the funeral home you're not telling me about?*

He meets her gaze for a moment, and there it is, the face of the girl from his childhood. He remembers seeing her in the back window of the car as she left with their mother. Her chin was on the top of the back seat, her hair pulled back in a ponytail, her eyes afraid and wondering. Her hands gripped the back of the seat on either side of her chin, and she raised the fingers of one hand, only her fingers, in a sort of wave. They drifted in a sad rhythm like seaweed in a current. Then they were gone. She was gone.

He doesn't know if he wants to tell her their father might have committed suicide. He doesn't know if he can tell her it might have been his fault.

He nods to Kaye, trying to be reassuring, before turning back to Ava. One of the machines beeps a long, steady pulse. He gives his father one last glance before walking out the door.

twenty-two

The Trailer

Cohen came home after school the day after seeing the Beast, not thinking of where he was or where he was going. He wandered into the basement, not aware of his father working at one of the examination tables, wiping tears away with the back of his wrist. And what Cohen saw right there in front of him, what his father's job demanded of him that day, was too much for him, too much for any fourteen-year-old.

He stared for a moment, and at first he didn't know what he was looking at, the two blackened pillars side by side on the table. He wondered why his father would take such care in examining burnt wood, two pieces about Cohen's size. A realization came up to him out of the depths of his mind. They were children, and he saw the vague chalky outlines of faces, of chins. They were burned children. That realization made it into his consciousness before the other urgent message his brain was sending.

Cohen! Look away!

But it was too late. He had seen it. He had seen them.

He drifted backwards, bumping a table. He

turned and ran, his father choking out words after him, his voice a wreck of emotion. But Cohen fled, pushed open the door at the top of the basement stairs, and burst through the back door, nearly screaming, holding one of his hands over his mouth to keep the sound in. He ran to his bike and rode it all the way north on Duke, east on Liberty, under the bridge, through some neighborhoods, under the highway, until he was slipping along on the same small roads that led out to their old house.

But he didn't get to the old house. He dropped his bike in the ditch along the country road, still not thinking, still panicking, and fled into the woods, propelled by something, something his mind was already trying to block out. That thing he ran from, that thing he had seen, it was already like a dream slipping beyond his ability to recall, a sad or terrifying dream that left its residue scattered throughout his brain in pieces he could not put back together. That memory, that thing that came before he had fled the funeral home and run into the woods, would always be smoke to him, smoke and the bitter taste of ash.

He stumbled farther into the woods, through an old cemetery, and up a hill. It was December— cold, cold December—and the leaves on the ground were brown and the branches all ended in reaching, frostbitten fingers.

There was a halfhearted path up the hill, a

path he remembered from when they had lived in the country. He followed it farther than he ever had, even beyond the train tracks where he had never been allowed to go, and the sadness in his stomach was like a peach pit: tough and ugly and somehow coming up hard against any other thought that cut through. He wondered if he would feel better if he threw up. He stopped and leaned against a tree, but he didn't have the nerve or the know-how to make himself vomit. He wondered maybe if he thought about throwing up enough it would happen, and he tried to think about the time a substitute teacher had thrown up in his classroom when he was younger. But that only made him smile, because he recalled how Ava, also in the class, had pretended to throw up the rest of the day, sending people scattering.

Ava. He missed her. When he and his father moved into the city it had meant a new school, new friends, new acquaintances. He had not wanted to play baseball anymore. He had only seen her twice since then, two chance crossings that stood out in those dull years. She had looked at him, both of them too bashful to cross the empty space of years, and he had wondered if she ever thought of him, what she thought of him, and whether or not she remembered what they had together when they were innocent children, before his world fractured.

Cohen walked farther, crested the hill, and

looked down into a large hollow. The bank that led down was covered with leaning blackberry brambles, stripped bare by a season of birds and a season of winter. Their thick, thorny stems were a dull red in the winter light, each a single strand, but thousands of them, so that the hollow was nearly impenetrable. They cluttered the ground around the trees and swayed when the wind picked up.

Beyond the blackberry thorns, down farther in the hollow at the bottom of the bowl-shaped valley, sat the lonely husk of a mobile home. The door swung open and closed, open and closed, as if someone unseen walked in and out over and over again. Part of the trailer was blackened from a fire, and there were slashes in the roof. The trees around it were black too. Cohen wondered how the trailer had burned without setting the entire forest alight.

If he had come in the summer, when the blackberry brambles grew their lush green and the oak and maple and sycamore leaves crowded together in the upper gaps, he never would have seen the small mobile home. He wondered if there was a way down to it, and if anyone lived there or if it was abandoned. He thought it could make an interesting fort, a place for him to get away when he needed to.

He made his way around the hollow, probing the blackberry bushes for a way through, constantly turned aside by their thorns scratching his hands and snagging his coat. When he pulled away they made a loud tearing sound on the fabric. The air smelled crisp like ice, and the smell of smoke was coming up from the trailer, as if the fire had taken place not too long ago. His skin felt tingly, his nose numb with cold. He kept going, though, circling at the top edge of the hollow, looking for a way down.

He had nearly about made it all the way around to where he had started when he heard voices. He hid behind an especially wide oak tree, his feet propped on the beginnings of the roots where they reached into the ground.

"Will not!" a boy's voice said in earnest tones.

"Will too," a girl's voice said, and when she spoke, her words weren't argumentative at all. They were simply correct, and she knew it.

Cohen held his breath. He peered around the tree, then ducked back behind it. He had never seen those children before. He peeked around the tree once more. The boy wore a long-sleeved T-shirt but no jacket in the cold, and the holes in the knees of his jeans gaped like large, sagging mouths. His light brown hair stuck up in strange places, as if he had recently woken up. The girl had the same forlorn appearance, but her hair was much darker, and there was something very pretty about her. He couldn't decide what it was. He was sure they were brother and sister, and they looked to be about his age.

The two of them walked side by side, each carrying a walking stick. As they were about to pass the tree where Cohen was hiding, they stopped. The boy stared at something on the ground. The girl looked up and scanned the slate sky.

"I don't know why you think it's going to come back here," the boy muttered, tracing the frozen ground with one of his bony fingers. "There's nothing left."

"It always comes back," she said in a hoarse whisper, and Cohen felt a chill race through his body, so strong it made him tremble.

It always comes back.

He leaned closer to the tree. The rough bark sanded his face, but the sense of feeling something, anything, on that cold, numb day was a good thing. It reminded him he was alive.

It always comes back.

"So, are we going to sit here and wait?" the boy asked, as if that was the stupidest possible thing they could do. He didn't sound scared at all, only impatient and annoyed.

The girl raised her hand and shielded her eyes, still staring at the treetops. "Maybe we're here for another reason," she said in a mystical voice.

"Okay, your royal weirdness," he said. "Now what are you talking about?"

"You know how I've been saying we need one more person to help us?"

He nodded, poking at the ground viciously with his walking stick.

"Maybe that person is here," she said.

Cohen's mouth went dry and his heart raced. He leaned in tighter against the tree and held his breath, closed his eyes. Had she seen him?

"I don't see nobody," the boy said. "Besides, the two of us can handle it now. We're different. We don't need nobody else."

"Maybe he's hiding because you're being rude," she said. Her voice was louder, and there was something fierce in her, something emerging.

"Who?"

"The other person we need to help us find it."

"I . . . don't . . . see . . . nobody," the boy said again.

"Maybe he's hiding because . . . you're . . . being . . . rude," she shouted, her voice echoing through the woods. The sound of it was like the crashing sound ice makes when a frozen river breaks apart in the spring. The voice terrified Cohen, and he simply had to look, had to see the source of this furious sound, so he peeked around the tree again.

The girl seemed larger now, though that could have been because she stood up straight and tall when she shouted. Her skin was whiter than it had been before, or it seemed that way—whiter than white, as if she was dead. She dropped her walking stick and held her hands out in front of her.

Cohen's gaze darted to the boy, expecting to see signs of someone humiliated, someone giving in. Who wouldn't give in to the incredible power the girl seemed to have? Who could resist that shout, that look?

The boy, that's who.

He stood his ground and raised his walking stick with both hands. They seemed ready to strike each other. Something seemed to push Cohen out from his hiding place, something in him that knew what it was doing, or thought it did.

"It's me," Cohen said, stepping out from behind the tree. "It's me. I'm the one who's here. I'm Cohen. And I'm not hiding, not anymore."

He had no idea why he did it, why he revealed himself to them. Maybe he was scared of what they were about to do to each other. Maybe he thought he had seen enough horrible things to last him the rest of the week, or the rest of his life. Maybe he wanted a closer look at the girl.

The boy looked over at him first and let his stick swing down to his side. The girl seemed to deflate back to her quiet self. Her hands came down slowly, and there was color in her cheeks again, but only small round spots of it.

She sighed, and when she spoke she sounded

exhausted. "Yes, it's you. Finally. I'm glad you're here."

Cohen looked back and forth between the two, trying to decide who to speak with. The girl seemed friendly, but she was also exhausted and he had seen her fury. She intimidated him. The boy, on the other hand, was a little more . . . well, normal, but also seemed like he might be mean, possibly even cruel.

Cohen looked back at the girl. "Who are you?" he asked, rubbing his hands together in the cold.

But the girl sat down on the hard ground, once again clutching her walking stick, and said nothing. She seemed even smaller than before, the whole wide forest growing up around her, the sky drowning her. Cohen looked over at the boy.

He hesitated. "I'm Than," he said reluctantly.

"What's her name?" Cohen asked, amazed at his own bravery.

"That's my sister, Hippie."

She smiled a tired, wry grin.

"Is that really your name?" Cohen asked.

She shrugged, clearly unwilling to fight about it. "It's fine."

Cohen smiled. Than did too, but his grin was caustic and cynical. Cohen didn't know what to think of him, whether or not he could trust him, whether or not he could like him. But Hippie . . . Cohen fell for her immediately.

"Did you hear us talking?" Than asked.

"Not much," Cohen explained, not wanting to sound like a snoop. "Not very much."

They stared at him.

"Well, you know, I mean, I heard you're looking for something."

Than looked nervously over at his sister, but Hippie's eyes didn't leave Cohen.

"Do you know what we're looking for?" she asked in a calm voice.

He started to shake his head, but an image stopped him. It was the image of the car crash—when he'd stood beside the open window, hearing the approach of a speeding car, the crash. The darkness that had come out. That's what he couldn't stop thinking about. The darkness that had crawled out from under the car. The Beast he had seen coming for him. And in that moment he knew.

"Maybe," he whispered. "I might know."

"Ha!" Than laughed skeptically and turned away, swinging his stick at a large oak. A piece of bark broke away. A breeze rustled the bare bones of the trees, carrying the scent of the burned-out trailer up the hill to where they stood.

"What?" Cohen asked.

Than shook his head, still laughing to himself. "You haven't seen nothing. No way. Not possible."

"What did you see?" Hippie asked.

The wind in the trees died down. The woods

were nearly silent, as they are in the winter when the birds are mostly gone and the squirrels are not flitting through the undergrowth. In the winter it's only the wind that brings life to the trees, but in that moment the wind had stopped and Cohen could feel his own heart beating.

"I saw a car crash," he said. "I saw a car crash."

"And?" Than demanded.

"And . . . and I saw a shadow. A darkness. A Beast?"

The change that came over Than's face was comical. It was as if someone had turned him into a wax figure, his mouth posed in an open position, his eyebrows raised.

Hippie smiled. "Yes. I knew it. I knew it was you."

Cohen looked at her but didn't ask the question.

She answered it anyway. "You can help us. Yes. You."

"With what?" Cohen asked.

Than started walking away, making his way around the path that circled the bowl in the hills.

Hippie nodded toward her retreating brother. "Follow him," she said, still smiling.

"Where are we going?" Cohen asked, suddenly very aware of how far he was from home and how much trouble he would be in if his father found out he had left the city on his own, gone clear beyond the railroad tracks.

"Down there." Hippie pointed with a slightly

bent finger down the hill to the charred mobile home with its burned roof, its blackened walls, and its door that kept swinging open and closed, open and closed, even when there was no wind.

twenty-three

The Accident

"Mr. Marah?" the detective says in a thin voice.

Cohen looks around the funeral home basement as if he can't remember how he arrived there, and it feels surprisingly foreign to him, this place where he has worked nearly every day of his adult life. It's empty now, and he hasn't seen it that way before. He glances up at the ceiling, wishing he could see the sky. But he can only see a water-stained drop ceiling, a grid of yellowing, once-white squares. Whoever turned on the lights turned on only one switch, so half the room is dark.

"Mr. Marah?" the detective says again. "I know this is probably difficult for you. We only have a few questions. After that, you can head back to the hospital to be with your father."

Cohen looks at him calmly. The man doesn't look like a detective—he's short and thin and wears large glasses. His hair is wispy and parted, and he has large hands for his size. He looks more like an accountant or the manager of a factory that makes buttons.

"Call me Cohen."

"Of course. Cohen."

Cohen looks over at Ava. She gives him a soft, encouraging smile.

"Cohen," the detective says, "when was the last time you saw your father?"

"I guess the night before all this. Was that Sunday night? The days are all running together."

"Okay, Sunday night." Every word the detective speaks is weighed down with suspicion, as if he does not expect Cohen to answer truthfully, as if the next question might be the one to undo him. "Can you tell me about that?"

"Sure." Cohen looks around the room. This is what he doesn't want to talk about. He wonders if he starts down this road whether he'll be able to stop. "To be honest, it wasn't a pleasant conversation."

He pauses, deciding that, all things considered, he should be as honest as possible. He feels on the verge of losing track of what's true and what's not. The stories inside of him are becoming tangled cords. Why he thought his father was dead. When he first arrived at the scene. When he last saw his father.

"I went up to the apartment to let Dad know I was heading home for the night."

"This was on Sunday night?"

Cohen nods.

"What time?"

"I don't know exactly. It was late. Maybe around eleven."

"Eleven p.m.? That's late. And your elderly father was awake? Okay. Go ahead."

"He's always awake at eleven p.m.," Cohen says defensively. "This is a funeral home. People don't schedule their deaths between the hours of eight and five."

The detective does not respond to his sarcasm.

Cohen shakes it off. "I went upstairs." He motions toward the back of the basement and the stairs that go all the way up to the apartment. "I was working down here, getting some things together, nothing big. So, upstairs, I knocked. He didn't answer, so I went in. He had obviously been drinking. He drinks." Cohen rubs his eyes. "He drank." He shakes his head. "Whatever. Anyway, he was on the sofa, as usual. He had a drink in his hand."

"He didn't lock the door?"

"The door?"

"The door you entered the apartment through? You said you knocked and walked in. The door wasn't locked?"

"Good question," Cohen says, thinking. "I don't remember if it was locked. I do have a key."

"So, you can come and go as you please, here in the funeral home and also upstairs in the apartment?"

Cohen feels a rise of exasperation, tamps it down, and nods. "Yes. I come and go as I please. I lived here for many years. This is where I work, and that is my father's apartment. Don't you have a key to your parents' house?"

He stops. He takes a deep breath, begins talking, stops again, and the breath eases out in a long sigh. He shakes his head, trying to clear a path through all the memories that have been bombarding him since the morning he stepped over his father's body.

Ava speaks quietly. "You were saying that he drinks?"

"Yes. Right. He drinks all the time. Anyway, I told him I had decided I was leaving."

"Leaving?" Ava asks.

"Yeah, leaving. I told him I wasn't going to work here anymore." He looks over at Ava. "I can't do it anymore. I'm vanishing into all this. All this death. I've been trying to quit for years, a decade maybe? I've been dropping hints every so often. But he ignored them. He couldn't imagine a future for this place that didn't involve me. Even though my sister works here and is way more capable than me. It was always about me." He looks around at the strangely empty basement.

"So you felt trapped?" the detective asked, peering over his glasses.

"I'm done. Anyway, that's what I told him. I was done. I'd give him some time to find someone else."

"How did he take it?" Ava asks. She glances

at the other detective, and he gives her a barely discernible nod.

"Not well." Cohen gives a short gasp of a laugh, air out through his nose. "Not well. This place is everything to him. Everything. I was supposed to take it over from him, and my son after that, on through the generations." He stares at the floor. "I don't actually have a son, in case you wondered."

The three of them stand there in silence. Two other police officers orbit around them, taking notes and pictures and whispering to each other. The heat turns on, making the police tape flutter.

"How long are you guys going to be here?" Cohen asks.

"We're almost finished," the detective answers. "I brought these two back to take a last look at a few things, but we should be out of your hair in the next day or two."

"What did your father say when you told him you were quitting?" Ava asks. There is a quiet kindness in her voice.

"He erupted. He had just finished his drink, and he pulled back his arm like he was going to throw his glass against the wall. But he didn't throw it. He slammed it down on the coffee table. He didn't let go of it, and he stared at it while he asked me why I had 'such disregard for everyone but myself.' Those were his words." He pauses and shrugs. "He was right. I am a very selfish person."

"Cohen," the detective says, "was that the last time you saw him before what happened here?"

Cohen swallows. He looks not at the detective but at Ava. "Yes."

"You didn't see him the morning of?"

"No."

"Where were you that morning?"

"I was supposed to be here. But I didn't come to work, not after what we said to each other. I figured he needed some time to cool off, take in the news that I was quitting. I thought he might need some space. You can ask Beth. I think she was here all morning. I didn't come in."

"Yes, but she wasn't here when it happened," the detective says in a deliberate voice. "Were you?"

"I told you, I didn't come in for work."

"Where were you?"

"At home." Cohen sighs. "By myself. With no one to corroborate my whereabouts."

"Where do you live?"

"A few blocks over, on Lemon Street." He looks at Ava. "I went to Johnny's baseball game."

"Your nephew, correct?"

"Yeah."

"Which would have been after . . . this?" the detective asks.

"I don't know," Cohen says, raising his voice. "What time do you think 'this' happened?"

"Cohen," Ava says, "you don't have to get

upset with the detective. We're only trying to figure out what happened to your father."

Cohen stares at her for one loaded moment.

"Would you like to know how we found him?" the detective asks in a monotone voice.

Cohen thinks the man has already arrived at his conclusion. From here on out, everything is part of a drama already written. "Yes."

The detective takes a few steps around one of the examination tables. "Your father was lying here, on the floor. He had fallen down. The instrument used for embalming had been thrust up through the bottom of his jaw, up through the back of his throat, and into his skull."

Cohen winced. "The trocar."

"The trocar?" the detective repeats.

"Yes. Trocar. It's the instrument we use to remove everything from the body cavity during the embalming process." He walks over to the counter that lines the wall, pointing to one of the cabinets. "May I?"

The detective nods. Cohen opens the door and pulls out a long piece of metal that looks like an oversized eighteen-inch screwdriver, except it has a three-sided blade.

"This is inserted into the body two inches above the navel and three inches over. Once it's in and connected to the machine, it sucks out all the body fluids. You have to work it around to get everything, like a vacuum. After that's over, we reverse the action and use this same tool to inject the body with embalming fluid."

The three of them stare at it.

"Could it have been an accident, Detective?" Cohen asks, breaking the silence.

The detective raises his eyebrows. "You tell me. Seems unlikely, don't you think? It would take quite a lot of force and a considerable amount of bad luck."

Cohen shrugs, handling the trocar lightly. "The other option is foul play, right? This thing isn't a weapon. Usually it's attached to the tube. It's very rare someone would be handling it on its own. Although . . ."

"What?" Ava asks.

"It does occasionally get clogged. Bits of bone or other matter get stuck inside. If that happens, you have to take it off the hose and clean it out. Dad would have disconnected it, then walked from here over to the sink on the other side of the room." He stops where his father had been lying, frowns. "Bodily fluids could leak onto the floor. You could slip while carrying it. My father is an old man. He could have come down on the table, the blade up."

He bends over at the table where he had once, a million years ago, stepped over his father's body. He wedges the trocar between one of the countertops and the bottom of his jaw. He looks over at Ava and the detective, frozen in place, an accident in motion. The point of the trocar presses under his jaw, under his tongue.

He stands and walks back to the cabinet and puts the trocar back in its place. "Will that be all, Detective?" he asks, looking at Ava.

"For now, Mr. Marah. We will need to speak with your sister as well." He pauses. "Mr. Marah?"

Cohen glances over at him.

"I wouldn't leave the area if I were you. Not for a few days, at least, until we get some things straightened out."

"Why would I leave the area, Detective? My father is on his deathbed."

The detective stares at him. "Very well. Thanks for your time."

twenty-four
The Gun

Than led the way around the small valley, his stick beating a slow rhythm on the cold ground. Hippie walked behind Cohen, and he felt a bit like a prisoner in a war movie, the one forced to walk in between his captors. But Hippie was kind—she was no captor—and she asked him questions about where he lived and what his family was like, her voice coming up to him from behind like a pleasant memory.

Than stopped and turned, waiting for them. He looked at Cohen and rolled his eyes, shook his head. "This way," he muttered, plunging stick first into the briars that lined the bowl-shaped depression in the woods.

At first Cohen wondered how they were supposed to make their way through. He held back so Hippie passed him, and as she did she looked up into his face, and he saw something different there in those green eyes, something foreign. He gave a weak smile and followed her.

That's when he realized there was a path. The narrow trail struck into the briars at an angle that made it easy to miss based on the direction he had been circling. Sometimes he had to raise his arms straight up above his head to avoid the reaching thorns, and sometimes he had to turn sideways. Than plunged ahead, disregarding the reaching stems, some of them clinging to him as he passed, then springing back. Hippie's movement was more like a glide than a walk, and the blackberry briars seemed to brush off of her as if they were feathers.

As they descended through the thickets, as the path circled around the hill, lower and lower, the smell of smoke got stronger. The odor of charred and blackened life. The wind came back, sweeping through the branches and clinking them all together, and some old branch that had long ago broken off but had still somehow been entangled finally fell to the earth, crashing into the undergrowth.

Than whipped around, facing the crash. Hippie's face went straight to the sky, her hand shielding her eyes from the glaring winter white-gray, and she ducked. Cohen felt his heart thudding in his chest and froze. What were Than and Hippie so afraid of?

Cohen couldn't move. He wanted to turn and run, but he couldn't even do that. He glanced back and forth, from one side of the depression to the other, waiting for who knows what. The wind that had first started high in the branches now dropped in among the tree trunks and flowed through the vast expanse of thickets like water.

The long, red-black stems of the blackberry bushes rose and bowed, swayed from side to side, as if the presence of the children disturbed them.

"C'mon," Than hissed, moving ahead at a trot. Hippie glanced back at Cohen, and he saw she was nervous. She nodded, a small kind of encouragement, and it loosened his body from that fearful paralysis. He nodded back, a smaller, less determined gesture, took a deep breath, and followed the two of them down the hill.

The blackberry thickets went on for a long time, but they thinned out in the small yard around the mobile home. The only real reason you could call it a yard was that there were no trees, the thorns were few and far between, and there was some semblance of grass, but—and this was true especially in the winter—it was sparse and tan and brittle.

Littering the space outside of the trailer, like supports strategically placed to help weeds grow, were various plastic things for children. A small blue plastic swimming pool, cracked and upside down. A miniature plastic slide, orange with teal-green steps. A red tricycle with flat black tires. But what made these things seem even stranger was the fact that they were all in various stages of melting. Those closer to the blackened section of the trailer were almost unrecognizable; those farther away were less obviously melted, but the subtle nature of their deformities felt odd, somehow scary. The slide, for example, was farthest away and at first glance seemed unharmed, but the steps sagged ever so slightly.

It was as if the entire world was melting there in that hollow, as if something so powerful had passed through so as to affect even the basic molecular structure of things. Cohen wouldn't have been surprised to look over and see Than's face half melted, or Hippie's feet slowly dissolving into the ground.

What he did see when he finally pulled his gaze from the warped playthings was Than approaching the door, the very same one that was still banging open and closed, open and closed. It hung on by only one hinge. There were no real stairs, only cement blocks that had been stacked in a haphazard half pyramid like some kind of Mayan structure. They were blackened from the fire.

Hippie stood with her back to the trailer, looking up and away, slowly turning as she watched the crest of the hill closely. Cohen was transfixed by her.

"What's your name?" Than hissed, startling Cohen.

Embarrassed that he had been caught staring at Hippie, he tried to sound nonchalant. "I told you. Cohen."

"C'mon, Cohen," Than said, coughing up his name as if he thought it was a pseudonym.

Cohen made his way through and around the melted plastic remnants. "What are you guys doing here, anyway?" he asked.

Than shushed him.

"Sorry," Cohen whispered. "What are you doing here, anyway?"

Than glared at him. Hippie walked to the door, and soon the three of them were standing there in a small huddle, Than up on the seared cinderblock stairs, Cohen with his back to the mobile home, Hippie with her back to the forest but still looking up into the sky. She was always looking up.

Than grabbed the door and held it motionless. The absence of the slapping sound it had made while swinging back and forth caused a deep silence to descend. Cohen hadn't even realized how much of a comfort that repetitive sound had been, but standing there with nothing now to separate him from the sounds of the forest or the smell of the burned house, he felt exposed.

"Remember that thing you saw?" Hippie asked.

"In the dark?" Cohen asked. "On the street corner? Yeah. I remember."

Hippie's eyes left Cohen and traveled around the trailer as if taking everything in for the first time. "It did this," she said quietly.

"That shadow thing did this? I thought this was a house fire."

Than sneered, laughed to himself, and shook

his head. "No, man, the shadow thing, as you call it, did this. No ordinary house fire."

"What, can it breathe fire?" Cohen joked, but the other two didn't seem to find it funny. "C'mon," he said. "Seriously. What is it, some kind of a dragon?"

"No." Than turned and walked into the house. "It's a Beast." When he opened the door the whole way, it swung out and away from the house on its one lonely hinge before falling off entirely and crashing to the ground. Hippie didn't give it a second look—she scaled the pyramid of blackened cinder blocks and disappeared into the house behind Than.

Cohen stood there, staring. He wanted to leave. Or at least most of him wanted to leave. He turned and saw the place where the narrow path scaled the small hill and wound its way between the thorny blackberry shoots. It was a winding way, and it was tempting. There were too many things here he didn't understand, too many things he couldn't put his finger on, but that was what kept him from leaving. He wanted to know more about what he had seen.

He walked up the cement block steps and they wobbled under him. The last step up, the one from the highest block and into the trailer, was a monumental step, and he had to reach up with both hands, grab the inside of the door frame, and pull himself in. No matter how much he told himself that he had chosen to go in, no matter how he reminded himself that he had climbed in willingly, he still couldn't shake the feeling that he was being swallowed.

The darkness inside the burned-out mobile home could be felt, like humidity. It was like its own environment—heavy, sticky—and even though it was a cold winter day, the darkness made him feel like he was sweating. He reached up and pulled the collar of his coat away from his neck to let in some fresh air. He cleared his throat and waited for his eyes to adjust, at least a little bit. Under his feet, with each step, was the grinding of broken glass. He had once stepped on the skeleton of an opossum in the woods, and the floor of the trailer felt like that, like a bed of old bones. He took another crumbling step.

A flash of light. He jumped back, raised his hands. Than laughed.

"Easy, Than," Hippie said.

"We're here to find something," Than said to Cohen. "Hippie's going to watch the door. Me and you, we're going to look. Got it?"

"Okay. What are we looking for? I thought we were looking for the Beast."

Than rolled his eyes and shined his flashlight into Cohen's face again.

"Than," Hippie said.

"Fine," he muttered, lowering the beam.

Cohen's eyes were dazzled, and it took them some time to readjust to the darkness.

"We're not looking for that thing, not yet," Than said. "We're on the lookout. There's a big difference."

"So . . ."

"So," Than continued, turning and walking toward the back of the trailer, "we're looking for something someone left here. Something that will help us destroy it."

Cohen looked over at Hippie in frustration. "You can't tell me what we're looking for?" he asked.

"We don't know. Not for sure," Hippie said quietly, never looking away from the hillside. "Than seems to think there might be something we missed, something useful."

"You were here before?"

Hippie sent a glance at Than, and in the half-light coming through the door, it looked like a warning.

"I can't tell you what we're looking for because I don't know what we're looking for," Than said, leading Cohen slowly back into the hallway.

"So how will we know . . ." Cohen began, but Than turned and shined the light in his eyes again.

"Just. Look."

"Fine, fine," Cohen muttered, shielding his face with his hands.

"You start in this room," Than said, turning into the first room on the left. He walked brashly through the small space and flung up the blind that covered the window. Daylight eased its gray way in. He stomped out and went back to the hallway, his flashlight bobbing from side to side as he walked.

Cohen looked around. The back half of the mobile home hadn't been as affected by the fire. The rooms still smelled of smoke, and a few of the walls had turned brown due to the heat that had climbed up the other side of them, but they were intact. There was a small single bed with a pink blanket, a side table with a lamp that had a white shade, and a pale green rug spread on the floor over the top of the nasty tan carpet that stretched wall to wall through the trailer. He lifted the mattress and peered between it and the box spring. He opened the closet door warily, but it was empty. He stared hard at the ceiling, the light fixture, and even pulled up the heat register in the floor. Nothing.

What was he looking for, and where would he find this unknown thing?

Cohen approached the window. There was a thin, stained white sheer tacked into the wall with pushpins above the window frame. He pulled it to the side so that he could look out into the front yard again. He saw the melted toys. The bramble-covered hillside. The naked trees, tall at the top of the hill, dark against the gray sky. He scanned the blackberry thorns for any movement, any sign of the Beast.

A jolt of panic surged through him. Was he alone? Had the other two left him? It was the same feeling he had walking up the stairs at night, when he was certain a hand was preparing to seize his foot.

He turned and trod over the throw rug, the worn tan carpet, and peeked into the hallway. He glanced into the living room, but Hippie wasn't there.

"Hippie?" he said, his voice swallowed quickly by his fear. Or had he even spoken out loud? Had he only called for her in his imagination? He was finding it difficult anymore, identifying the line between what was hard, concrete, real, and what was not.

"Than?"

He heard a rustling sound farther back in the trailer, deeper into the shadows. He took a few steps into the hall, passing a pitch-black bathroom. It smelled like bleach and bug spray and feces. The next room was almost as small as the bathroom, but it had a window.

"Hippie?" he called back over his shoulder.

He thought he should leave. But there in the small room, under the window without a curtain, was a leaning desk. One of the back legs was missing, and it had been propped up against the wall. Gray winter light glared off the light wood. Besides the desk, the room was empty, not that there would have been room for any other furniture. The floor was some kind of fake laminate made to look like hardwood. It creaked and moaned under his feet.

Dirt smudged the window in round dots, the dusty remains of some other day's raindrops. Cohen ran his hand over the desk's smooth top. An urge came over him, and he opened the top right drawer. It made a scraping sound as if the runners were broken. There were some old receipts there, disorganized, torn. Balled-up gum wrappers. An empty cigarette pack.

He pushed the drawer closed, looked over his shoulder, and opened the bottom drawer. Empty.

"Than?" he shouted over his shoulder. He could still hear Than in the back bedroom. It sounded like he was sliding metal hangers along a clothes rack. "Hippie?"

Cohen opened the top left drawer, the smallest of all. There was another empty cigarette pack. He picked it up and looked inside, the plastic crinkling in his hands. He set it down on top of the smooth wood, pushed the drawer closed, and opened the bottom left drawer. He stared down into its depths.

This drawer was full of envelopes stuffed with old yellowed things like coupons, more receipts, and paper clips. It held a pair of scissors, a stapler, a yellow fly swatter, and blue glass cleaner, now leaning and leaking onto all the other things. And under it all, buried in the mess, was a shoebox.

He gently removed everything and stacked it in a line on the desktop. He handled each and every object as if it was part of a bomb that would explode with any jarring, any shaking. The plastic bottle of glass cleaner was sticky on the outside. He hated that. He hated having a mess on his fingertips. The fly swatter still had insect guts on it. The stapler was jammed—he knew because he tried to shoot a staple out into midair.

He pulled the shoebox out with two hands, placed it on the desk among everything else, and stared at it for a moment. He was convinced, for no particular reason, that something living resided on the inside, and he waited for this unknown thing to move the lid. The box was navy blue with an American flag on the front and back. The lid had a single white stripe down the middle, and the corners were worn and broken so that it didn't sit quite right on the box. He pushed the lid aside.

Inside the box were random, unmatched socks. Children's socks and adult tube socks. Dress socks and even a few long women's stockings. He pushed them here and there, hesitantly stirring them in the box with his index finger to better see what else might be inside. He was worried that a mouse might have made its home there.

But as he moved them to the side and his hand went deeper into the shoebox, he felt something cold, something hard, something that was most definitely not a sock. He grabbed it and lifted it out. It was heavy and dangled from his hand, and he held it like a live thing.

It was a revolver.

He had never held a gun before, unless you count the BB gun he almost never used, the one propped in the back of his closet. He stared quietly at it, wondering if it was loaded. He took it in the palm of his hand, the black metal curving. He pointed it at the window and closed one eye, lining up the sight with the other eye. He imagined seeing the Beast and following it in his sight as it crept down the path among the briars. He found its head there somewhere in its shadowy mass.

Bang.

"That's it," Than said, startling Cohen, who jumped and nearly dropped the gun.

"Hey!" He took a deep breath, shaking his head. "Why are you sneaking around like that?"

"That's it," Than said again. "You found it."

"This?"

Than nodded. He held out his hand.

Cohen gave him the gun without thinking twice. Than flicked out the cylinder and spun it. Each chamber was empty, like a vacant eye socket.

"In there?" Than asked, motioning to the shoebox full of socks.

Cohen nodded.

Than shook his head and laughed to himself, and he seemed less a boy than a wizened old man. "I looked in that desk last time," he said, laughing again. "But I didn't look in the shoebox."

He reached into the shoebox and felt around beneath the socks. Cohen heard the sound of metal things clinking together like a wind chime. Than pulled out a handful of bullets. He stuffed one in each empty chamber, and they clicked into place.

"Well," Than said, and that was it. Cohen kept waiting to see what was to come of this find, what it meant, where it would take them. But Than said nothing more.

"Where's Hippie?" Cohen asked.

Than looked up at him, and most of the questions in his eyes about Cohen had left. But there were still a few in there, and they made him squint. "Outside."

The two boys stared at each other, Cohen with his back to the window, Than with the gun in his right hand and a fistful of bullets in the other. They seemed to reach some kind of understanding, a mutual agreement that while they did not like each other, they had clearly been brought together for some reason.

Than seemed to soften. He looked over his

shoulder before speaking. "Look, this needs to stay in here." He paused. "In case we find the Beast. In case we need it." He gave Cohen a knowing look. "Just in case. But the thing is, we can't carry it around, and we can't tell Hippie about it."

"Why not?"

"She hates this kind of stuff. It will only upset her. Promise me."

Cohen sighed. "So where do we keep it?"

Than looked around the room. The sun had dropped lower outside, and the whole trailer was beginning to feel more like a cave than a house. Long shadows of old trees leaned down the hill.

"Hey, where are you guys at?" Hippie shouted in through the front door. "We should get going. It'll be dark soon."

Than stared at Cohen as if waiting for him to suddenly shout out that they had found the gun. When Cohen didn't say anything—in fact, he stood there holding his breath—Than shouted back, "Be right out."

Than walked over to a small heat register in the floor, the kind that lifts up out of the hole. There were no screws holding it down and it came up easily out of its metal sleeve. He put the revolver down inside the vent, and Cohen heard it ping against the metal air duct. Than looked over his shoulder one more time. He put the remaining bullets inside one of the socks and lowered it down beside the gun, then slipped the register back into place.

"Got it?" he asked Cohen, and Cohen couldn't tell exactly what he meant by the question. He could have been asking, "You understand not to tell Hippie, right?" or "You see where I put it, right?" or "You do know if you do anything I don't like, I'll shoot you, right?" But Cohen nodded, because sometimes the only answer is yes.

The two walked back out through the front door frame—the door was still on the ground—into the light of that gray day, and after the darkness of the trailer, even the slate sky seemed to glow. A cold wind swept through the forest, rustling the winter branches, moving the brambles to rasp against one another.

Hippie looked up at them.

"Nothing," Than said quietly, brushing past her and starting back up the winding trail that split the thorns.

She looked at Cohen. He shrugged.

The three of them moved through the blackberry brambles like shadows. Once at the top, as they walked back through the woods toward town, Than moved ahead. Hippie slowed and Cohen drew up beside her.

"Was that your house?" Cohen asked Hippie in a timid voice.

Hippie nodded, staring off into the distance.

She turned and looked at Cohen, and her eyes were like steel. "We have to find that thing. We have to stop it before it does anything like this again."

Hippie's glaring eyes startled Cohen, and he nodded without saying a word, his mouth hanging partially open. He licked his lips— they were suddenly dry, brittle in the cold. He swallowed. Hippie turned away from him, and the look on her face was both regal and childlike. Her pronouncement made her seem older than she was.

"We have to find that thing," she muttered again, and Than looked back at them. He reached up and tried to hold down the unruly patch of hair at the back of his head, but as soon as he moved his hand, the hair stood back up.

By the time they got back to the train tracks and walked over them, back into territory Cohen was familiar with, he had drifted into the lead. Than had paused to stare up into the sky. The tops of the trees started waving again, this time in long, bowing motions as if they were sweeping the sky clean. Cohen hadn't thought it possible when he had run up into the woods only a few hours earlier, but he was ready to go home.

The gun was part of the reason for this. He was glad for every step between him and it. He felt as though he had been given a head start, and now the gun would come after him, that shiny blackness, that cold, hard steel, those handfuls of bullets. They would come slowly out of the trailer after the sun had set, sneaking through the dark like a mean dog that had slipped its leash. Yes, he was glad Than had left it in the trailer. He only wished he would have found a screw to fasten the air vent in place. A screw, he thought, could have kept it there, could have kept the gun from following him.

But there was happiness inside him too, happiness that he had found friends. When his father had been found out, when they had left the church, Cohen lost most of the friends he had. And now Sundays were quiet and slow, or spent at a stranger's burial while his father presided as funeral director.

He missed Ava. He still thought about her. It was good to have friends again. Even if one of them was like Than.

The wind flared up again, swirling the winter smells of cold, dead leaves and things waiting for spring. They parted without saying goodbye, the three young people, and Cohen found his bike and pedaled furiously for home.

twenty-five

The Missing Mother

Cohen emerges out of the funeral home basement and into the bright day, shedding his meeting with Ava and the detective like a thin skin. He takes deep breaths of the early spring air, and his body aches with weariness. He reassures himself he can sleep that day in the hospital room, once Kaye goes home and it's only him and his father. He has not yet spent time alone in the room with him. He wonders what it might feel like.

"Cohen!" a voice calls out, and he turns to find Ava walking fast to catch up.

"Hey," he says.

"Mind if I walk with you?" Ava asks, settling in beside him.

"No."

"I'm . . ." she starts, and then she stops.

He tries not to look at her, tries not to give her the satisfaction of him wanting to know what she was going to say. He can feel her looking at him, and she begins again.

"I'm sorry about the things I said last night in the cafeteria. I didn't mean to imply that I thought you're capable of killing your father." The words come out like a prepared speech. Cohen wonders if she's been thinking her way through them only this morning, or if she was up in the night rehearsing, rewording.

"We're all capable of terrible things," he replies.

"I know. I see it almost every day."

"I could be responsible for my father's death, even if I didn't push that trocar into him. Which I didn't do, by the way."

She looks at him again, and this time he glances over, meets her gaze.

"We can kill people without ever touching them. Those things I said to my father on Sunday night? I think they killed him."

"You think he committed suicide?"

Cohen sighs and shakes his head back and forth slowly. "I don't know. But he was alive on Sunday night, before I said what I said. I saw how my words ate him up. The next time I saw him, he was . . . well, you've seen him. My words did that. I don't have any doubt."

"That's not killing someone," Ava says. Her words are quiet and earnest. "That's not your fault, Cohen. We can't control how people respond to the way we live our lives. Besides, it looks like an accident to me."

"How do you mean?"

"Well, I've never seen someone kill themselves with one of those things. There are much easier ways." Her voice trails off, and Cohen can tell she doesn't want to talk about it.

The two of them stop at the corner of Duke and Frederick, staring up at the hospital building, waiting to cross Frederick Street.

Finally Ava speaks. "I'm going to go, Cohen," she says, sounding like she doesn't think she should be there.

"You're welcome to come up if you'd like."

"No, but I will come and visit again." She reaches up and holds Cohen by the arm, above his elbow. It is an unexpected, intimate touch. "I'm sorry. I shouldn't have said those things last night."

He watches her turn and go back the way they came and then walks the rest of the way to the hospital. He passes three or four rooms that have their doors open—inside each one is an elderly man or woman, most of them asleep with their mouths open. They do not have visitors. A nurse makes eye contact with Cohen and smiles, walks past him into one of the rooms.

As he approaches his father's closed door, he sees the boy wearing the same John Deere ball cap, sitting on the tile floor, his back against the small space of wall between his grandfather's door and Calvin's.

"Hey," Cohen says to him.

"Hey."

Cohen stops and looks down at the boy. He seems softer on that day, worn down, perhaps by a lack of sleep or another confrontation with his father. Who knows.

"How's your grandfather?" Cohen asks.

"He's gonna die," the boy says, staring straight ahead.

"I'm sorry."

"Nothing for you to be sorry about. He's old." In a strange moment of wisdom, the boy looks up at Cohen. "We're all gonna die. You know that, right?"

Cohen gives a sad smile. "I'm a funeral director. I'm well aware of the fact."

The boy looks away. "How's your dad?"

"He's probably going to die too."

"Probably?" the boy asks, allowing himself the luxury of a slight, wry grin.

"Well, you know. Soon. Anytime."

The boy scrunches up his mouth and nods, as if he's seen every weary thing in the world and this is the truth of it.

"Is your dad here?" Cohen asks.

"Nope."

"Your mom?"

The boy laughs quietly to himself. "She took off. No one knows where."

"What do you mean?"

"I mean she's gone. Last night she went to bed, this morning she wasn't in the house."

"Really?" Cohen asks. "Does she do that often?"

The boy looks up at Cohen and there is worry in his eyes, behind the haughty carelessness he tries to wear on his face. "Nope. Never."

"Any idea where she went?"

The boy shakes his head. "No one knows. Looked everywhere. Dad's really losing it, first with the doctor basically killing Grandpa, and now Mom taking off." Concern fills his voice. "You see him, you walk in the other direction, you hear, mister?"

"I'm Cohen, by the way," Cohen says, reaching his hand down to the boy. "You don't have to call me mister."

The boy hesitates, then reaches his own hand up. It's small and callused.

"Thatcher," the boy says, nodding.

"Why are you sitting out here, Thatcher?"

The boy purses his lips and moves his head back and forth in a nonnegotiable no. "I'm not sitting in there, not while Grandpa's dying. I don't want to be there when it happens. Not by myself."

"It's nothing to be afraid of," Cohen says. "I've seen a lot of people die."

"I haven't seen it, not once, and I don't want to see it."

"Why not?"

"Something's going to leave him, his soul or whatever, when he dies, and I don't want to be there when that happens."

"Fair enough."

The two of them pause, Cohen with his hand on the door, Thatcher with his back against the wall, eyes staring straight ahead as they were when Cohen first walked up.

"What's your mother do, Thatcher?" Cohen asks, not sure where the question came from.

"My mom? She's a nurse."

"And what's your dad think about her being gone?"

"Dad? He's mad at her, real mad, even though she didn't do anything. After what this doctor did, he's mad at every doctor and nurse in the world. I guess he took it out on her pretty good last night."

"Did he take it out on you too?"

"Maybe," Thatcher says, shrugging off Cohen's concern. "I hope he doesn't find Mom. I hope she runs and runs all the way out of here, as far as she can."

Cohen takes a deep breath. "I have to go in here, Thatcher. My sister needs a break. But if you need anything, let me know. I'll be sitting in here most of the day, and through the night too."

Thatcher nods. He looks like he might say something but he doesn't, so Cohen goes into his father's room.

twenty-six

The Doorbell

Cohen parked his bike in the alley that ran along the funeral home and stopped for a minute, holding his breath to see if he could hear his father moving around inside. Nothing. The sun had sifted its way down through the buildings, down through the trees, and the streetlights came on randomly in the near dark, some of them emitting a low buzz before flickering to life.

During his ride home, thoughts had circled around in Cohen's mind, but one more than the others: whether he would ever see Hippie and Than again. He wondered where they lived, who they were. He left his bike and walked around to the back door, crept inside, let the door latch quietly behind him, and listened again.

All was silent. He went up to the second-floor apartment. The kitchen light was on, but no one was there. He found his father on the living room sofa, staring at the floor, a finger's width of amber-colored liquid at the bottom of a tall drinking glass.

"Son," he said in a dim voice.

"Hey, Dad," Cohen said hesitantly, waiting.

"Where've you been?" When his father spoke,

197

he didn't look up from the floor. His words all came out together, without spaces.

"Out with friends."

His father nodded knowingly, as if Cohen had said something so true it hurt. He raised the glass, had second thoughts, lowered it, and held it with two hands between his legs. "I'm sorry," he said.

"For what?"

His father chuckled suddenly, and then the humor vanished and he was staring vacantly again. "For what. For what? For everything."

Cohen went over and sat on the floor, leaning his back against the wall directly across from his father. Something about the situation opened fourteen-year-old Cohen's eyes, and he saw his father in a way he never had before. He saw him not as some far-removed god but as a person, a real live flesh-and-blood person. This glimpse of his father intrigued him and frightened him all at once. He wanted to run to his room and lock his door, but he was paralyzed by curiosity.

"I'm sorry you had to see those children today in the basement," his father whispered.

"No," Cohen said. His father's words were like a splash of icy water on his head, running down his neck, down his back. "No."

"No, no, it's okay," his father said, his voice going on in a droning hush. "It's okay. It's okay. They're better off now. They're in a better place."

Cohen felt frozen in place. Now he definitely

wanted to run. He needed to leave. He felt the threatening thickening of his throat and knew he might be sick. But he couldn't move his legs. He kept shaking his head.

"It's bad, isn't it?" his father said. "This world. It's a bad situation. There's not much in it that doesn't lead to some kind of disappointment, some kind of sadness. But those kids, they're okay now."

There was a rushing sound in Cohen's ears. "No," he mumbled. "No."

"Cohen," his father said. He sounded so far away. He sounded like a lost boy whispering into the woods. "It's okay. Son. It's okay. They're in a better place."

Cohen kept shaking his head, but his father wasn't looking at him. He was only gaining steam, and he picked up his glass, threw the drink down his throat, and pounded the glass back on the coffee table. "But I will tell you this right now. The father who did this is not getting away with it."

Cohen looked up, startled at the change in his father. There was a simmering rage there, poorly caged beneath the alcohol. It could slip out if it wanted to—something had opened the lock, knocked the door ajar.

His father squeezed his eyes closed and shook his head. "They're looking for him now. He killed them in that fire—it looks intentional—and they're hunting him down. But my eyes are open too. And if I see him first . . . If I find him . . ." His voice trailed off but found itself again. "I might get him too. I might get him first," he whispered. "I might. He came around here the other night, looking for his kids, I guess, looking for the bodies. It's an awful thing. They say he's mad at me for something, mad that I couldn't make 'em look better. Couldn't do an open casket for the family."

Cohen's father choked on something, maybe his drink, maybe his own saliva, maybe regret, and he coughed hard for a long time. When he spoke again, it was in a hoarse mutter. "There was nothing I could do. That was his fault." Tears came up into his eyes. He looked at Cohen, his eyes pleading for his son to believe him. "Nothing. There was nothing I could do. But if he comes around again, he'll know."

The doorbell to the funeral home rang. Cohen's father looked up, confused, as if it was the first time he had ever heard such a sound, as if he wasn't sure what he should do.

But Cohen didn't hesitate. "I'll get it," he said. His father grunted his assent.

Cohen jumped up, walked quickly through the apartment door, took the stairs down to the display room, and walked through the loosely arranged coffins without turning on a light. The streetlights cast a yellow glow through the double

200

glass doors at the front, the ones that led directly out onto Duke Street, and in the glow Cohen had a hopeful thought—maybe it was Than and Hippie. Maybe they had found him.

Through the glass, Cohen saw a single shadow. He paused, took a few more steps, and opened the door.

"Ava?" he said.

"Hi, Cohen," she said, vapor escaping from her mouth with each word.

twenty-seven

The Contractions

Cohen peeks into the room. His father is in the same exact position he was when Cohen left: head slightly tilted forward, arms at his side, feet pointing up at the bottom of the hospital bed. There are new pillows under his arms. His face is somehow older. His sleep seems even deeper, although it might only look that way because the light has changed. The sky is blue through the far window, an icy blue that hints at the edges of spring, and a silvery light trails from it, threading into the room.

Kaye sleeps in her chair, stirs, and rubs her stomach with both hands without opening her eyes. She lets out an almost silent sigh that turns into a moan. She turns from one side to the other, now facing away from the door. Cohen moves into the room, holding the door handle so it won't latch loudly. When the door bumps up against the frame, he walks over to his father's side, pulls up a chair, and sits down.

The room is outside of time. There is the piercing blue sky, the bright natural light in that half of the room, the unlit shadows falling over him and Kaye and their father. There is the shallow breathing of his father, the labored breathing of Kaye sleeping. There is the barely audible beeping of the machines, the silent drip of the IV, the humming of the blood pressure cuff, inflating again on his father's bicep, deflating, measuring, silent, letting out a single beep. There is the growth of the twins inside Kaye, their silent adjustments, their preparation for birth.

Kaye sighs again, and Cohen hears her sit up.

He looks at her, away from his father. "You okay?"

"I'm okay."

He nods at her stomach with a question on his face.

"Yeah, I think they're doing okay too. Nothing serious."

"Contractions?" he asks.

"Nothing serious."

"You need to get some rest."

"What do you think this is?" she asks.

"No, I mean rest in a bed. Someplace comfortable. Not all bent up in a chair."

Kaye shrugs. "I'm okay. I'll go home now that you're here."

"Good."

The light outside seems so fickle, and the flat, slate-gray clouds return, sliding into place, erasing the blue. Flurries fall again for a minute, and the snow begins in earnest, mixed with a sleet that taps the glass.

"Ugh," Kaye groans. "I hate driving in that."

"I'll call you a taxi," Cohen says, looking back at their father.

"No, I'll be fine," Kaye says, leaning forward in her chair as if about to rise. She stops. "What did the police say?"

"Nothing, really. Just more of the same. You know."

"No, I don't know. That's why I asked."

He shrugs and speaks without turning away from their father. The matte of his bald head looks grayer, reflecting the clouds. Cohen realizes he can't remember what his father's eyes look like when they're open.

"They told me a lot of the same stuff the doctor told us yesterday."

"Did they say how it happened?"

"Same thing the doctor said. The trocar. Probably an accident."

"An accident?"

"They don't know. It's hard to tell. No one else was there, Kaye. We might never know."

"What do you think happened?"

"I think they're probably right. Could've been an accident. Dad's older, not as careful. Drinks most of the day. He could have been carrying it with him across the room, slipped, came down on it. You know how sharp it is." He looks at Kaye. She winces. He shrugs again. "Could've been."

"Or?"

Cohen swallows hard. "He could've killed himself, Kaye."

She grimaces. "Like that?"

"It's not likely," he admits. "But possible."

"Did someone else do it?"

"I don't think there were any signs of a struggle. It wouldn't be easy to push the trocar in that precisely if you were fighting."

Kaye pauses, closes her eyes, and rubs them with her fingers. "It seems a cruel accident if that's what it was."

"But we've seen our fair share of those," he replies.

He hears her rise from her chair, and the filtered gray light grows darker in the room as the sleet stops and the snow falls, heavier now. Cohen glances at the window, and the movement of the snow reminds him of the way it hits a windshield when you're driving through it. He feels a sense of movement, a sense of falling, as if the hospital room is plummeting through the snow, as if the entire building is falling. It gives him a sense of vertigo, and he looks back at his father's form under the sheet.

Kaye walks up behind him and puts her hand on his shoulder. "What aren't you telling me, Cohen?" she whispers.

His back stiffens under her touch. But a moment later her hand dashes from his shoulder to her stomach.

"Oh," she says, grimacing and bending over slightly.

"Kaye . . ." he begins.

"It's nothing," she says. "Pre-labor pains."

"Pre? How 'pre'?"

"What happened, Cohen?" she asks him with a knowing glance.

He braces himself against the window frame. "Dad and I had an argument Sunday night. I told him some things he didn't want to hear. He was very, very upset." Cohen looks at Kaye, feeling drained and weary. "I don't know. I can't help but think that it's connected to this."

"What did you argue about?"

"Me quitting." He looks at Kaye hesitantly. She sighs. He has talked with her about this before.

A nurse comes in, the same nurse he saw in the hallway. She gives him the same smile. Cohen looks at Kaye, her deep eyes. This is his sister. When his father dies, she will be all he has left. She and Johnny and the twins on their way. And he'll be responsible for them somehow; their fates will be tied up with his. Does he have it in him, this kind of responsibility?

"Get some rest, Kaye," Cohen says. "Go home. Drive carefully." He looks up at the clock above the door, his voice catching. He clears his throat. "We can talk about it later. Promise. Now get some rest. I'll stay with Dad."

twenty-eight

A Choice

Cohen sits beside his father's bed, and for a long time there is nothing. No nurses come into the room to check the numbers and write on the clipboards and stare at the IV. No doctors dance around the inevitability of what is to come. The hospital goes on all around him, but he is there inside the cocoon with his father, waiting to emerge, waiting for something to happen.

The ridge of his father's arm is right in front of him, and he leans forward, unlatching the guard on the side of the bed and lowering it before hunching even farther forward and resting his forehead on his father's forearm. It feels soft under the sheet, not sinewy as he remembers it. It seems unbelievably small, this once powerful forearm, and uncharacteristically fragile. He hasn't noticed this in recent years, the decreasing of his father in old age, but now it seems so obvious. How could he have missed it? How could he not have seen his own father getting old?

Cohen turns his head so that he's facing his father's feet. He closes his eyes.

There is an image in his mind of how deliberate

his father always was when embalming bodies. The methodical care he took to restore them to lifelikeness. The way he turned from a body, taking off his long rubber gloves, sighing with satisfaction. There was something familiar there, something that perhaps reminded his father of preaching a good sermon.

For the first time since all of this started, since Cohen stepped over the body of his father yesterday, he wishes he could ask one last thing. The disappointment that had haunted Calvin, that had hung like the strands of a spiderweb about his eyes, was it a disappointment he felt in Cohen? Or was he disappointed in himself, that he had somehow let it all happen, had somehow let everything fall apart?

Cohen feels a hand on his shoulder, and goose bumps slide up his neck. His father is touching him. His eyes pop open, but he doesn't dare move his head. There, his father's feet, motionless. There, under his head, his father's left forearm. There, on his shoulder, his father's right hand.

He jumps.

"Mr. Marah! I'm sorry! I didn't mean to startle you."

It's his father's doctor.

Cohen shakes his head, trying to regain his sense of being. He clears his throat. "No, I'm sorry. I must have drifted off."

"You and your sister have spent a lot of hours here. I can tell your father meant a lot to you."

Cohen nods vacantly.

"I think it's time we have a frank conversation about your father's health."

Cohen nods again, feeling like a bobblehead doll.

"Mr. Marah . . ."

"Please, call me Cohen. My father is Mr. Marah."

"Of course. Cohen." Dr. Stevens pauses, and when he speaks Cohen can tell the words are familiar to him, the way a prayer becomes rote. "Your father is not going to recover."

Cohen stares out the window. "Yes," he says in a whisper. "Yes, I know. I didn't expect him to last this long." He says the last sentence almost as if he's trying to reassure the doctor that he has done a fine job, that none of this is his fault.

"You and your sister need to have a conversation about when the right time might be to remove life support."

"Yes," Cohen says. He walks to the window and looks out over the city, the city that for so many years brought their dead to his father. The city that handed over its bodies for his father to remake one last time, to present as if they were sleeping. He feels tears rising along with another layer of weariness, and he tries to push it all back in with the heels of his hands, pressing them up against the bones around his eyes. He realizes he's crying not at the death of his father but at the passing of a man who had shrunk from his life and lived it out mostly drunk in a second-floor apartment, burying his neighbors. And they never even knew him.

"She'll be back in the morning, I believe," Cohen says, his voice halting like a drunken man finding his footing. "My sister, that is. We'll talk about it then and let you know."

"Thank you for understanding," the doctor says. "I'll come by in the morning."

Cohen watches a new round of snow fall on the city. A west wind kicks in and for a moment the snow moves sideways along the glass. When he turns to ask a question, he realizes the doctor is gone.

It's only him and his father.

twenty-nine

Appeared and Disappeared

"Ava, what are you doing here?"

Cohen moved through the glass doors of the funeral home and sat down on the sidewalk. Ava leaned her bike against the funeral home brick and sat down beside him. It was so dark. The streetlights hummed. Cohen pulled his arms across his chest—he hadn't grabbed a coat, and the air was freezing.

"My family moved into the city," Ava said. "About six blocks away. It didn't take me long to ride my bike here. I didn't even know if you'd be here, but it was the only place I thought to look."

A siren sounded in the distance, and the sound always made Cohen suddenly aware of the world around him, the fact that others were living, breathing, experiencing a very different reality from his.

"How are you?" she asked.

"I like your bike."

"Thanks," she said, brightening. "My dad got it for me to make up for moving here. He said I could get to know the city."

"You shouldn't be out at night, not by yourself," Cohen admonished.

"I guess it got late fast," Ava said, unconcerned. "It gets dark quick."

Cohen couldn't figure out why he suddenly felt like he wanted to be mean. He knew she reminded him of the day his mother left, and that was something he didn't want to think about. And he didn't want to talk about his parents—not his mom, who he had only seen a few times since those days, or his dad, who was apparently too far gone to get off the sofa and come downstairs to see who rang the bell.

"Still play ball?" he asked.

"Softball," she said. "They don't let girls play baseball in middle school."

"Why, 'cause you're better than everyone else?" It made him mad thinking she wasn't allowed to play, and the meanness he had felt evaporated.

She grinned. "Yeah, probably."

They sat there quietly for what felt like a long time, cars occasionally passing, the streetlights flickering, humming. A couple walked past them holding hands. A kid their age rode his skateboard in the middle of the street, skipping up onto the sidewalk to avoid oncoming cars, the wheels making rhythmic clacks as they passed over the sidewalk seams.

"Do you like it here?" she asked.

He shrugged. "It's okay."

"Do you . . . have any friends?"

212

He thought of Than and Hippie, the closest thing he had to friends in the half decade he'd lived in the city. He didn't want to tell her about them, although he didn't know why.

He shrugged again. "Not really."

She stood up and dusted off her jeans, pulled her bike away from the wall, swung one leg over it effortlessly. He watched her closely out of the corner of his eye. She moved even more gracefully than he remembered. She was prettier than he recalled.

"I guess I'll see you around," she said.

"Come over again sometime," he blurted out, not sure where the words came from, and she grinned.

"See ya, Co," she said over her shoulder. She rode south, and he watched her carefully as she appeared and disappeared, in and out of the streetlights.

He stared south on Duke for a long time after she was gone, and even though he was freezing cold, he waited as long as he could before going back inside.

thirty

A Letter

December 5, 1989

Dear Co,

Well, little brother, who knows what 1990 will bring around for us! We're only a few weeks away from a new decade. I guess we have a lot to look forward to. I miss you.

So what was this, our fifth or sixth Thanksgiving apart? I stopped counting after the second one because it was too depressing. Ha ha. Mom did the now-normal rotisserie chicken for the two of us, candied sweet potatoes (which is one of the few really good things she makes), green beans, and donuts for dessert.

She's really fallen apart. I mean, not in presentation—she still dresses real sharp and I can't remember the last time I saw her without makeup on—but more in general life skills. She never cooks anymore. The microwave is king in this house! Ha ha. And I think she might be smoking! Crazy, huh? I can't be sure. I haven't seen her do it. But some evenings she "goes for a walk" and comes back smelling of more than just the city.

Mom, smoking. I know it's hard to believe. I might as well have told you she was doing hard drugs or stopped reading the King James Version. Ha ha.

She doesn't go to church anymore, so I don't go either. Sometimes I wonder if she still believes in God. That's a strange thing to wonder, I guess. I still believe in God even though we don't go to church. At least I think I do. I still pray anyway, and I guess I wouldn't bother if I didn't still believe at least a little bit.

Okay, so I have to ask you something. Mom said that Dad told her you have a girlfriend? Come on, little brother! This is the kind of stuff I don't want to hear from Mom through Dad! You've got to keep me in the loop! I demand you tell me in your next letter! Ha ha. Of course, we both know Dad's not doing so well, so maybe there's nothing to it. Anyway, let me know.

Gotta go. Love you.

Yours,
K

thirty-one

The Beast Comes to Visit

December of 1989 would always remain in his mind as a month of eternal gray, a month of things hidden in shadows. He was fourteen and finding things out, fourteen and seeing his father for the first time, or a kind of father he had never known before: a human father, a failing father, a rock-bottom father. It was a month of cold rain, and sleet when it was colder, and sometimes wet snow that melted on the sidewalks and sent ashy water down the gutters, half freezing where it sat in puddles. There may have been a few days of blue skies in that long-ago month, but Cohen would never remember them.

Yet there were things like blue skies: the letters from Kaye that he read over and over, kept in his pocket until the paper started to wear thin and the penned words blurred, fuzzy and memorized. And bike rides with Ava, laughing all the way down Duke to the empty ice cream shop, or sitting out on the sidewalk talking until the streetlights flickered on and she would jump on her bike, proclaiming her parents were going to kill her for being late yet again. No one died from being late more times that December than Ava.

But the days of that month continued, deeper and darker, and still there was no sign of Than or Hippie. Or the Beast. Every day as Cohen walked to his middle school in the city, he looked for them. Down every alley. Through every window. In the back seat of every passing car. Even with Ava he sometimes felt distracted, looking over her shoulder.

At night he drifted through the house, lonely and awake, peering through the windows, into the city, aware of the bodies in the basement waiting to be embalmed or buried or, somehow worse, cremated. On some nights he felt independent and strong in his solitude, a boy making his own way in the world, and on those nights he slipped quietly from one level to another, from one room to the next. But on other nights, on most nights, he felt lonely, like the last person on earth, and every noise was a body resurrecting. His parents' separation nagged at him like a small lump under the skin, the kind that grows so slowly you don't even notice until one day you bump it and realize it is tender and has taken on a life of its own.

The knowledge of the gun in the air vent of the mobile home also made him uneasy. He stared into the middle-of-the-night shadows and wondered again where Than and Hippie had gone. He hoped the Beast hadn't gotten them.

One day in mid-December as he walked home, he saw them.

They stood across the street, nonchalant. Than kicked at a crack in the sidewalk, scuffing his shoes. Hippie gazed up at the pale sky, scanning for something. Always looking, always watching out.

Cohen jogged over to them. "Hey!" he shouted, waiting for the light to turn. Than looked up and when he saw who it was, he rolled his eyes, shaking his head in exaggerated fashion, but Hippie gave Cohen a smile. He wanted to preserve it. He wanted to see her smile all the time.

"Hi." She waved shyly, her hands in fingerless, navy-blue mittens.

Cohen looked up and down the street and ran across, his backpack heavy on his shoulders. "I live right over there," he said, pointing at the funeral home.

"The funeral home?" Than asked. He might as well have said, "In the dumpster?"

Cohen shrugged. "Yeah."

"Wow," Hippie said. "That's cool."

"You want to see inside?" Cohen asked, wondering immediately why he had asked.

Than tried to feign indifference, but Cohen could tell he was intrigued.

"Sure," Hippie said.

"What are you guys doing, anyway?" Cohen asked as they walked slowly through the afternoon.

"Same old thing," Than said.

"The Beast?" Cohen asked, lowering his voice.

Than wrenched his mouth and rolled his eyes again, as if Cohen couldn't possibly understand the weight of what he was talking about. Cohen glanced at Hippie to see if she found him as annoying as Than apparently did, but she was staring at the sky while they walked. His eyes caught the narrow line of her neck, the softness of her jaw. Her skin was pale, almost translucent, and narrow lines of blue crept along like streaks of minerals in rock. She looked at him, and he quickly looked away, turning red, trying to think of something else to say. But nothing came.

Cohen stopped in front of the funeral home. He cupped his hands against the dark glass and peered in.

"No one's there," he said, relieved. He looked over at the other two, wondering if they'd lost interest, but they both seemed eager to go in. He pulled open the door only part of the way so that the chain of bells hanging inside wouldn't do their loud dance. Than went in first, then Hippie. Cohen looked over his shoulder and followed them inside.

The air in the display room, the main area of the funeral home, felt fragile. To the right was a closed set of double doors that led into a small chapel. It mostly went unused, since nearly everyone in town attended church and had their funerals at First Methodist or First Baptist or Saint Thomas, but every so often someone came in who didn't have a church, and they needed a small space for a funeral. So Cohen's father would hand him a list of things to do: dust the wood in the room, wipe off the small pulpit, vacuum the carpet, brush off and arrange the chairs. The smell of wood polish always took him back to The Day He Saw His Father Cry on the Altar or The Beginning of the End or The Day He Shouldn't Have Picked Up That Sock.

When he turned to say something to Than and Hippie, they were gone.

"Guys?" he hissed, not wanting to shout, not wanting to attract his father's attention if he was upstairs in the apartment. "Where are you?"

He walked away from the chapel into a disordered group of coffins, some open like the mouths of clams, some closed, some standing up against the wall, some stretched out. He looked under them and around them and behind them.

"Than, this isn't funny," he whispered as loud as a whisper can go. "Hippie? Where are you? I hope you're not hiding in a coffin—I don't think you can breathe in there."

He was crawling under a few coffins along the wall, pulling back the heavy drapes to see if the two were hiding there, when he heard a sound that made him freeze in place. The discordant clanging of the string of bells over the front door. Someone had come into the funeral home.

He quietly shifted behind the curtain, drawing the heavy fabric around him as slowly as possible. He tried to hold his breath, but that didn't last long, so he measured his breathing. Long, slow, still inhale. Long, quiet, controlled exhale.

Something grabbed his hand and he nearly screamed. It was Hippie. She was already there, hiding behind the curtain. He looked down at where their hands were joined. It was exhilarating—her white skin was cool to the touch, smooth, and soft. He looked up at her face to see if she was as enraptured as he was, but she was peeking out from behind the curtain, her eyes wide open. She looked at him, and he could only see half of her face. The other half was hidden in the folds of the curtain. But he knew what she was mouthing to him.

"The Beast," she said silently, exaggerating the movement of her lips, her tongue. She said it again. "The Beast."

They both looked out from behind the curtain. At first Cohen didn't see anything different about the room. There were the coffins and their corresponding shadows drifting through the legs of the narrow tables that held them up. A long line of slanting light came in through the front door. All the way across the room, the doors that led into the chapel were closed, the lights off.

In the far corner he saw something moving, something gathering, shifting into shape, the way spilled metal shavings will congregate in the presence of a magnet. Whatever it was in the corner, the shadows in the room leaked toward it across the floor, sliding along, in no hurry whatsoever. The shadows themselves were moving. Cohen felt a strange ache in his chest, a deep breathlessness, and a scream formed in his throat, a scream he wouldn't let out, so it sat there and ached. The drawn shadows left behind a dull, shadowless room, but somehow this didn't make the space brighter—it simply meant there was nothing to contrast the light. Everything had turned a thousand shades of gray, and it felt like an old black-and-white movie.

The shadows gathered in the corner and took shape, and the Beast rose, the top of it brushing the ceiling, swaying back and forth as if looking for something. Or someone.

Cohen glanced over at Hippie, his eyes wide. She returned his gaze, the whites of her eyes shining. She squeezed his hand harder, now with both of hers, but he realized she wasn't afraid. She was tense and alert and every muscle in her neck and shoulders and face was on edge, but she wasn't afraid.

"Where's Than?" he asked soundlessly.

She shook her head, a series of back-and-forth twitches. She didn't know.

But in that moment they both saw him.

Than was halfway across the room, crawling under one of the coffins on his knees and forearms. He looked like a mountain lion dipping under a fallen tree as it approached an unsuspecting deer. His knit cap was pulled on tight, and some of his hair leaked out the sides in a wild fringe. He moved without making a sound.

Cohen and Hippie didn't dare move. The Beast shifted toward the chapel door, and even though it didn't have an identifiable face or eyes they could see, it seemed to pause by the crack in the door as if it was examining the chapel.

Than looked over his shoulder at Cohen and Hippie, raised a single finger to his lips. *Shh.* He crawled farther forward, came out from under the coffin, and rose silently to his feet. He crept toward the Beast. It turned. Than shouted and ran into the darkness.

Before Cohen knew what he was doing, he had clawed his way out of the tangled curtain and followed Than. Hippie was right behind him. The Beast turned on all three of them, growing, pulling in more darkness, roaring. It was the sound of a forest fire rushing through the undergrowth, a hissing, spitting, rumbling sound.

The Beast tossed Than aside, and he floated through the air before slamming into the wall. He slumped into a huddled, motionless mass. Hippie pulled her way past Cohen, stopped, planted her feet firmly, and raised both hands. At first Cohen thought he saw it stagger, diminish, but if it did, it only lasted a flash of time.

The Beast seemed to laugh, and it was a laugh that shifted into anger as it rushed at Hippie. Her head spun as if she had been slapped, she flew to the side, and her head cracked against a coffin. The Beast turned.

Cohen felt the blood drain out of his face. He thought he might pass out, but in the overwhelming intensity of the moment, he felt a rage rising. It was a rage born from every other intolerable aspect of his life: his parents' separation, the parts of his new life in the city that he did not like, his father's increasing distractedness. Everything he hated stood there in front of him in the form of that darkness, and he sprinted toward it.

The Beast consolidated into a denser substance, lower, even more sinister. It threw itself at Cohen on his first approach, and he felt his head snap back, felt his body soaring, felt the carpet on the floor as he burned his way along it on his back. He lay there for a moment, certain his neck must have been broken, but as he felt the fibers under his fingertips, stared up at the bottom of a coffin he had slid under, he realized he was alive. He could move. He wasn't afraid.

Cohen lurched to his feet again, raced at the Beast, and paused outside its grasp. It swung and missed. Cohen drew back his hand and aimed, but as he threw his fist forward, the Beast struck him again. His jaw made a loud cracking sound, and one of his back teeth dislodged with a sickening creak. Again he was on the floor. Again he stared up, this time with the warm taste of blood in the back of his throat.

From his spot on the floor, moving only his eyes, he looked over at Than, who still hadn't moved from where he lay against the wall in a heap. Hippie was on her back, unconscious. The Beast moved toward her slowly, savoring the stillness of its enemies. It leaned over her and roared again, and this time dark strands of shadow leaked from its unformed mouth, dripped down onto the floor beside Hippie's face like veins of mercury. Hippie still didn't move. The Beast drew closer to her face.

Cohen looked around for something he could use as a weapon, but there was nothing. He sighed. Hopeless. Determined. He stood on shaking legs and ran at the Beast. It never saw him coming.

He gathered himself and jumped onto what seemed to be its back, put his arms around the amorphous head, and squeezed. It roared and thrashed, and Cohen squeezed tighter. The Beast rushed backwards, smashing him over and over against the wall, but still Cohen held on. It jumped and his head hit the ceiling. It fell and rolled over on top of him—his ribs creaked under the strain and his breath was wrung out of him, but still he held on.

The Beast slowed. Rolled onto its side. Cohen squeezed hard one last time, and it stopped. That was all. It stopped. The shadowy essence of it that seemed to be constantly swirling turned motionless. Cohen closed his eyes, gasping for breath, and each breath shot a searing pain from the bottom of his rib cage up under his arm. His face felt inflamed, burnt. He raised one hand up, his fingers brushing swollen cheeks. He swallowed a thick wad of phlegm and blood.

The Beast stirred. Cohen sighed. He had nothing left, nothing remaining to fight with. He wondered if this was the end, and deep inside, under the ash of his disappointment at life, a small ember flared up. An ember of relief. The end did not frighten him.

But it was not the end. The Beast, instead of turning on him, moved in crawling fashion, oozed along the carpet, and dissolved in the afternoon light that came through the glass door. One moment it was there, the next it was gone.

Cohen had never felt this way before—joy and pain, relief and terror. He rolled over to reach for Hippie, to bring her back, to help her.

But she was gone. He looked over at the wall. Than was gone too.

He rolled onto his back and wept, not at their

absence but with relief that it was over. He lay there for a long time, until the gray winter sky faded and dusk coated the glass door, and the streetlights slowly turned on, one after the other.

thirty-two

The Sleeping Father

When Cohen crept upstairs after dark, bruised and aching from the Beast, he found his father asleep on the sofa. There were cans on the window ledge above the couch and a lone glass tumbler on the coffee table with a thin golden skin coating the inside. Cohen limped over and picked it up, hobbled to the kitchen sink, and turned it upside down. Only a few drops fell out, but it gave him a certain satisfaction, emptying the glass before his father could. He moved to put it down, but he was distracted, still trembling, and his hand hit the faucet, knocking the glass into the sink where it shattered with a sound that split the air.

His father moaned from the sofa. Cleaning up the glass was the last thing Cohen felt like doing, but he thought if his father came into the kitchen in the state he was in, he might very well slice himself open. So he carefully pushed the shards into the corner of the sink with a towel, bunched everything together, and threw it in the trash, towel and all.

The air in the apartment was cold and thin, like the atmosphere at the top of a mountain. Light shone through the windows, pale and anemic. He wondered if his father had turned the thermostat down again. He was always complaining that he was hot while Cohen walked the house in layers, trying to stay warm.

Cohen went to the bathroom and cleaned himself up, washing his face with icy water, putting a bandage on his hand, and swishing the blood out of his mouth. He reached gingerly inside and felt the tooth, one of his molars. It wiggled. He groaned. It would have to come out. He took a deep breath, closed his eyes, and leaned against the wall. He reached in and pulled on the tooth. Once. Twice. Again. Finally it made a grinding scrape and he felt a snap as it gave way. The pain made his vision cloud over.

The hole in his gum where the tooth used to be oozed blood, and he kept spitting it into the sink, gargling water, spitting, gargling. Trying not to choke. He remembered the baseball he'd taken to the nose when he was young, that old familiar taste of blood. When the bleeding slowed, he crammed some paper towels into the back corner of his mouth and cleaned the sink and the mirror and turned out the light. He was so tired.

He walked over to the sofa where his father still slept and nudged his shoulder with one hand. "Dad," he said, his voice muffled by the paper towel still in his mouth.

Nothing.

"Dad," he said louder, shaking harder, but his father didn't respond. He was far away at the end of a dark tunnel, at the bottom of a well, out of reach. Cohen clenched his jaw and rubbed his cheek, feeling where the tooth used to be. He walked over to the wall opposite the sofa, sat down, and waited.

He realized he wanted more than anything in the world for his father to be concerned by his injuries, even to be angry. Cohen would take anything—derision, fury, sadness, empathy. Especially empathy. Someone else's hand on his bruises, someone else giving him a glass of water, someone else folding a cold cloth and draping it over his forehead or gently packing the hole in his gums with cotton gauze. But his father slept and the room grew dark and Cohen sat with his back to the wall.

Then, movement.

His father moaned, came up from that faraway place. He moved his mouth and licked his lips like a man waking in a desert, and his hand blindly swept the table, reaching for the glass. When it encountered nothing but flat space, he stopped, and for a moment Cohen thought he had fallen asleep again. There was another distant moan, another drawing together of his mouth, now trying to find saliva. Calvin put his elbows on the sofa and sat up halfway, squinting in the dim light that came through the window. He tapped each and every can, a gentle snapping motion with his index finger, hoping that one of them was not empty, but each one leaned lightly, a few falling over and rolling aimlessly on the window ledge.

"Dad," Cohen said, this time in a quiet voice, nearly a whisper, but his father heard him and turned in his direction. He stared into the shadows, squinted his eyes as if the darkness was light. When he saw Cohen, a kind of remembering flooded his face. *Yes, of course,* the look seemed to say. *I have a son.*

"Cohen," his father said, or at least tried to say, but the word stuck in his dry throat. He rubbed his neck.

Cohen retrieved a glass of water from the kitchen, and his father drank it all down without stopping. When he finished, he took a quick gasp of air, sat up slowly, and placed the glass on the coffee table.

"Cohen," he said again, nearly finding his normal voice.

"Hi, Dad." Cohen hoped his father would see his wounds, his bruises, his pain, but it was dark in the room, and they could barely see each other through the half-light.

His father nodded, pondering some faraway thought. "Oh," he said quietly, as if to himself. He looked at Cohen sideways, out of the corner of his eye, and Cohen sat down on the sofa beside him.

"The police came," Calvin said.

Cohen felt like he was under a spotlight. Did someone find out about the Beast? The gun? Did someone tell his father they saw him riding his bike out of town? He was fourteen. He didn't have an accurate sense of the kind of things police got involved with.

"Really?" he managed to squeak out.

His father nodded, turned to him in the dark room, and stared directly at him. "You need to be careful. They're still looking. They think the father . . . he might still be . . . coming by here again."

Cohen nodded, a wave of confusion moving through him. He remembered what his father had told him when he'd returned that night.

It's okay. Son. It's okay. They're in a better place.

A better place.

He realized he was still nodding, mindlessly moving his head up and down. He stopped.

"Are you okay?" his father asked, suddenly aware that something was wrong. But it was a concern that came too late.

"I'm fine," Cohen said in a monotone voice. "I wrecked my bike, but I'm okay."

They sat there in the dark together for a long time, both of them awake and not saying anything. Cohen realized he felt like he understood his father better in those moments of quiet, when he had no expectations, than he did when he wanted his father to say something in particular or ask about him or show some tangible sign of caring. In the silence, he could hear his father's thick breathing; he could hear the movement of his father's fingernails on his shirt as he scratched his shoulder; he could hear the rumbling of hunger in his father's stomach.

But in the silence, he also felt like they were moving further and further apart.

Calvin stood slowly, Poseidon rising up out of the water, pillows falling to the side and the blanket slipping to the floor. His shadow lumbered along the wall as he walked into the kitchen, barely lifting his feet, his soles making sliding sounds on the floor.

Cohen didn't move, except when his fingertips touched his tender jaw or his tongue hesitantly explored the soft hole hiding under the wad of paper towels in his mouth. He leaned his head back on the sofa and could almost see the night sky through the window. Living in the city meant there were rarely visible stars, but there was always a glow, the culmination of streetlights and office lights and passing cars. There were always sounds too: the wheezing of a truck as it labored to a stop at the next traffic light, the squeaking of old brakes, the throbbing beat of rap music thudding its way from a car with a custom exhaust.

He heard his father rumble through the cupboards, doors slamming, glasses colliding. The silverware drawer opened, and his father came out and sat at the couch, a plate of food in front of him on the coffee table.

"Why's it always so dark in here?" he muttered.

Suddenly Cohen didn't want his father to see his bruises. He didn't want his father to have the satisfaction of worry, because now it would mean nothing to Cohen. It was too late. It was always too late. He went to the door, trying to hide his limp.

"Where are you going?" his father asked, taking a large bite.

"I'll be back," Cohen said over his shoulder, and again he wanted his father to stop him, to care about where he was going enough to press for information.

But the only thing he heard was the fork hitting the plate, loud chewing, liquid gathering at the bottom of a new glass.

thirty-three
A Shadow You Can Hold

On that night, still feeling the sting of his father's inability to see him, Cohen walked into the display room of the funeral home and realized he felt no fear. None. He looked around, and all he felt was peace in the darkness. He wandered among the coffins, his fingers gliding over their smooth surfaces. He meandered to the chapel and peeked in through the door. He walked over to the curtain where he and Hippie had waited, hidden, earlier that day. He crawled under the coffin in front of the window, and he pulled himself behind the drapes. He remembered the sensation of holding Hippie's hand, feeling every movement of her fingers. Had he really felt even her fingerprints, even the lines on her hand?

The room was silent except for when the heat kicked on, stirring the air, moving the dust around, gathering up the essence of the newly dead from the basement and scattering it through the house. Cohen thought again about the Beast. He found himself listening intently for any of the doors to open, for footsteps on the sidewalk outside, for the parking of a car on the street. He watched the headlights pass the glass door and willed the shadows to keep moving.

Exhaustion set in, and the heat from the vent below the curtain moved the fabric in a fluttering pattern, the same way a spring breeze coming through the window would have moved it. The hot air gathered around him, and he drifted into a kind of light sleep, infiltrated by shadows and warm walks on soft grass and the wispy movement of weeping willows. He dreamed of the old days, playing catch with his dad under a blue sky, smiling over at Ava during a baseball game, running out to catch the bus with Kaye, his family sitting down to eat dinner on a night when no one fought. Deeper into sleep he went, down into darker dreams of wandering through empty churches and tripping in a field of high corn, only to stand and realize he couldn't see his way out. He ran in one direction, pushing the corn out of his way, the thin leaves stinging his hands and the skin around his eyes.

He woke up with a start, certain he had heard the gentle sound of bells followed by the glass door easing its way shut.

Wide awake, he slid behind the curtain as far as he could, trying to disappear. He wondered if maybe he had only jumped awake at the sound of the heat turning off—it usually made a kind of thunking finale—and it could have been the ensuing stillness that pulled him out of that dream. He could still feel the corn like thin razors on his skin.

He sensed movement on the other side of the room. He tensed, looking out from behind the curtain with one eye, but the room was too dark. He could see nothing. A car passed outside, and a shaft of light scanned the room from left to right like a flashlight sweeping the shadows. He held his breath. Another car passed, and this time he was sure of it—he saw something moving across the back of the room, away from the chapel. Past all the coffins.

In his direction.

He swallowed hard, amazed at how loud a swallow can sound in complete silence. He tasted the blood in his mouth, and again his tongue touched the hole left by the missing tooth. His jaw throbbed. He leaned from one side to the other and realized something was behind the curtain with him. His heart nearly stopped. The thing, whatever it was, gradually touched his hand. Cold and moving.

He screamed.

Hippie screamed back at him.

"What is wrong with you two?" Than hissed from across the room.

Cohen was so scared he couldn't talk.

"Seriously," Than said, disgust in his voice. "Why don't you babies go to bed and I'll catch up with you in the morning?"

Cohen's flash of fear was being replaced with an indignant embarrassment. "What are you two doing here?" He first looked for Than, but when he couldn't locate him he turned to Hippie. Her smile was water on a fire.

"Did I scare you?" she asked, trying unsuccessfully to stifle a giggle. He had never heard her like that, truly and unreservedly happy.

He couldn't stop a small smile from pulling at the corners of his mouth. He took a deep breath and let it out in a relieved rush. "What are you guys doing here?" he asked again, shaking his head, still trying to communicate how annoyed he was.

"We're tracking it," Than muttered. He crawled along the floor with a flashlight, trying to hide the beam, staring into the carpet.

"The Beast?"

"When did you come down here?" Than asked.

Cohen shrugged. "Maybe an hour ago. I don't know. I fell asleep."

"Have you seen anything?" Hippie asked in a kind, sincere voice.

"No. Nothing."

"Heard anything? Nothing outside?" Than asked.

"No." Cohen paused. "Are you guys okay? From this afternoon, I mean. Where did you go?"

Than grunted. "We took off. Needed to regroup, figure out what's next."

Hippie reached over and tugged on Cohen's shirtsleeve. "You were amazing."

Cohen felt a rushing in his ears at her touch. If the Beast had walked through the funeral home door in that moment, he would have stood to his feet and walked calmly toward it, fearing nothing. But there was no target for him to aim this surge of bravery and emotion at. He froze in place, not wanting her to move her hand.

"What are you looking for?" he managed to ask Than. His own voice sounded far away, as if it were someone else's.

Than waved them over. "What do you think, Hippie?" he asked, and there was awe in his voice, and something that sounded strangely like fear.

Hippie and Cohen bent down beside him, getting lower, lower, until they were both on their hands and knees. Hippie grabbed a pen from one of the tables, reached out, and slid it along the stiff carpet. Something black and sticky like tar clung to the pen and dragged along the carpet fibers. Cohen's insides churned. At first he thought it was blood, but it was darker, the color of ink. He glanced nervously at Than.

"That's it," Than whispered.

"What?" Cohen asked.

Than turned on the flashlight and shone it at the black substance clinging to the pen—it shone like a liquid but didn't move. It stuck there.

"What is it?" Cohen asked.

Hippie pursed her lips. "The Beast is injured. This is the trail it leaves behind, pieces of itself."

"That's a shadow?" Cohen asked. "Like, a shadow you can hold?"

Hippie paused. "Now we can track it."

thirty-four
The Last Thing to Go

Time moves on, and for many hours Cohen cannot look at his father lying in the hospital bed. One of the nurses mentioned that the last thing to go is hearing, and the thought that his father might still be able to hear him, might be aware of his presence, unsettles him. It sends him up out of his chair and over to the window, where he watches as the sky gradually dims from platinum to silver to slate to ash. It is inside him too, the grayness.

He glances at his father, gives a sort of wince, and turns back, feeling the cold glass. He moves his fingers along it slowly, as if trying to placate winter, convince it to lumber off, make way for spring. The sky and the snow and the fading light divide, separate, become their own elements. They are no longer connected. Cohen also feels disconnected, fragmented, as if all the times of his life are straining one from the other—his childhood, his adolescence, his adulthood. Who is he? Which of these Cohens is standing here in the room with his dying father, looking out over a silent city?

Confession. Again the concept flashes through

241

his mind, and now it's dark and he doesn't know how long he's been staring out at the streetlights that seem more yellow than white, the brake lights and the long streaks they leave behind on the wet streets. He sits down and falls asleep.

When he wakes up, a nighttime nurse has crept into the room, moving like a shadow. "Hi," he says quietly, rubbing his eyes.

"Hello," she says. "Anything new in here?"

"No. I don't think so."

"Okay," she says, adjusting Calvin's pillow, moving his arms so they're across his chest. "We'll move him around a bit more in the morning to try to keep away the bed sores and maintain circulation."

Cohen doesn't reply. He bites his lip. Does she know the situation? Does she know he's dying, that the doctors have given him up for dead? Why move him now? But he doesn't say anything.

Midnight.

He is suddenly wide awake in a way he has not been for days, and he wonders if he can get into Saint Thomas Episcopal Church. He seems to remember someone saying they usually leave at least the chapel unlocked. There is something about sitting in there at night in the dim lights, staring at the mesh of the confession screen, that seems like it would help. He considers calling Father James to see if he might meet him for confession again, but he also feels bad asking him to come out into a cold night.

Cohen glances at his father. Should he leave him like this? What if his father dies while he's gone? Kaye would be mortified if she found out Cohen left him; she would be devastated if their father died alone in the room.

Cohen looks up at the clock again. He decides to go to Saint Thomas. He'll walk fast.

thirty-five
The Fall

The sleet, rain, and snow have merged to form inky pools along the street, and Cohen hops lightly through them, the hem of his pants gathering water, darkening, getting heavier. Duke Street is mostly empty, although an occasional car drifts south past him. It's late. He feels guilty having left his father.

He feels something strange in the air, something he doesn't recognize right away, and he stops at the corner of Duke and Walnut, looks up into one of the small trees. A strong wind kicks up, moving the gray clouds across the sky, sending a shower of stray drops from the branches. The streetlights still drown out the stars, but he imagines he can see them up there, pinpricks of light coming from so far away.

He is struck with the thought of how long it takes the light to reach him. How much has changed in the universe since that light left its star and traveled through the darkness, illuminating everything. It saddens him to think that some of those stars, perhaps many of them, no longer exist, but their light goes on shining as if nothing at all has happened, as if nothing is wrong.

He realizes what it is he senses, what it is sweeping through the alleys and moving the small tree limbs until they bob like little kids' fishing poles: it is the slightest hint of spring. Some stream of warm air has found its way from another part of the earth to that very spot on Duke Street. In the glare of the streetlights, he realizes the tree beside him has buds, minuscule bulges of life preparing to unfold. He reaches up and holds a cold tip in his fingers, the earliest beginning of a flower.

By springtime, his father will be gone.

The waters are separating. The waters of the sky are blowing away in the wind and the waters of the earth lay before him, and he walks through them to the church and up the sidewalk ramp. The door is unlocked. He lets himself in.

Nothing is different. Everything is the same. The Christ is still on the cross, his downward-facing eyes the gentle disappointment of a parent whose child cannot quite get it right. Cohen looks nervously away. He sees the confession screen still standing.

A shadow shifts behind it, a subtle movement of darkness hovering behind darkness, and he tenses. Two words leap into his mind and send a panic shivering through him: *The Beast.*

"Father James? Is that you?"

"I'm sorry, Cohen," the priest says, and there is mild amusement in his voice.

"You scared me."

"You entered rather suddenly yourself."

"Why are you here?" Cohen walks over and sits in the chair on the near side of the screen. It's almost like talking to himself.

"I couldn't sleep. And I thought you might come back again tonight."

"What if I hadn't?"

There is a gentle movement on the other side of the screen, an obscured shrug, a barely audible chuckle. "I'm a priest. I'm always waiting for something. Usually I'm waiting for God, but sometimes other things, or people."

"How long have you been waiting?"

The priest sighs. "I am always waiting, Cohen. I will always wait for you."

Something about the priest's words or the way he says them brings tears to Cohen's eyes. He clears his throat unsuccessfully, clears it again, louder this time. He sniffs, wipes those seeds of tears from his eyes with his index fingers.

"I'm sorry. Okay." He takes a deep breath, and the words come out shaky, hesitant. "Bless me, Father, for I have sinned."

"The Lord be in your heart and mind, Cohen, and upon your lips, that you may truly and humbly confess your sins: In the Name of the Father, and of the Son, and of the Holy Spirit. Amen."

"Amen," Cohen says, and even though he

stares at the black screen, he is envisioning so many other things: the pallid look of his father on the bed, the trail of shadows the Beast left behind when he was a child, the young man whose grandfather is dying in the neighboring hospital room. He thinks of Kaye and Ava and the police detective who obviously thinks he killed his father, a charge Cohen finds difficult to dispute. He remembers the blood he wiped off his shoe and then onto the sycamore tree. He remembers every Sunday school story he ever heard, and the obtuse angle of Miss Flynne's feet as they stuck out from between the pews on that afternoon so long ago.

"I confess to the Almighty God, to his Church, and to you, that I have sinned by my own fault in thought, word, and deed, in things done and left undone, but especially in regards to . . ." He sticks in the same spot once again. He licks his lips. "But especially in regards to the death of my father."

"Cohen," Father James says, and the sadness is so heavy in his voice that it threatens to grind everything to a halt. He says every word as if it is his last. "Cohen. What are you saying? I implore you, tell me the truth, so that your confession may be acceptable and your absolution complete."

Cohen nods absently, still staring at the screen. "The doctor has said we have to remove him from life support."

"I'm sorry to hear that."

Cohen gives a cynical smile. "Me too. You know, Father, my dad and I, we've not been great friends through the years. I've seen a lot of things a kid should never see."

He feels like he can't catch his breath, as if he is the little boy staring at his father drunk and asleep on the couch.

"My father's accident, all of this, it's not anything I ever wanted. Not really."

"But you are . . . involved?" Father James says quietly in a voice that is barely a question. "You were involved in his accident."

"I am concerned that something I said may have led him to try to take his own life. I don't know, I can't be sure. But I have to be involved now. That's the point. My sister and I have to decide about taking him off life support." Cohen clears his throat. "For these and all other sins which I cannot now remember, I am truly sorry. I pray God to have mercy on me. I firmly intend amendment of life, and I humbly beg forgiveness of God and his Church, and ask you for counsel, direction, and absolution."

There is silence. Not even the heater kicks on to stir the pages of the open Bible. The Christ in the painting does not move, does not even breathe.

Perhaps death has already come.

Father James is motionless behind the screen, like the dark cloud in space, the one inside a supernova left behind after a star explodes. And because Cohen cannot see his mouth through the screen, it is a shadow speaking. It is a voice coming out of nothing.

"Cohen, I will be here waiting."

The silence eats its way inside of Cohen. He cannot bear it. "Father."

Silence.

"Father," he begins again, falters.

Silence.

"Father, are there things that cannot be forgiven?"

"From Romans: 'For I am convinced that neither death nor life, neither angels nor demons, neither the present nor the future, nor any powers, neither height nor depth, nor anything else in all creation, will be able to separate us from the love of God that is in Christ Jesus our Lord.' "

"What about the blaspheming of the Holy Spirit?"

"Ah, yes. From Mark: 'Truly I tell you, people can be forgiven all their sins and every slander they utter, but whoever blasphemes against the Holy Spirit will never be forgiven; they are guilty of an eternal sin.' "

"What do you think that is, blaspheming the Spirit?"

Cohen expects a straightforward answer, something directly from a book, but Father James surprises him. He gives a kind laugh, a laugh full of curiosity and hope.

"There are many interpretations," he says quietly, and Cohen can tell by his voice that he's still smiling. "Is this what you've come to talk about this late at night? The blasphemy of the Holy Spirit?"

"No, Father. I already know what that is."

"You do?" the priest asks, surprise in his voice.

"Yes. The only things that cannot be forgiven are things done to a child. Those sins go on and on; they plant their seeds and wreak their havoc for generations. These things done to children, that's the blasphemy. That's the unforgivable sin."

For a moment it feels like the screen has been removed. They are one person, knowing everything that has ever happened to the other.

"I'm sorry, Cohen."

Cohen feels a stab of surprise. "So you know," he says.

"I do not know," the priest replies, and his voice slides out of a man weighed down by too many confessions. "But I have known . . . many things. I can imagine. Maybe that is enough."

"Maybe."

Cohen looks out through the small windows toward the city street. A single car goes by, the sound of it so far away. The empty late-night moments come, one after the other, one after the other, and he wishes he could sit here for the rest of his life.

"Very well. I will absolve you of the sins you have confessed."

"What of those I have not?"

Another silence. Another age. Father James does not answer his question.

"Our Lord Jesus Christ who has left power to his Church to absolve all sinners who truly repent and believe in him, of his great mercy forgive you all your offenses; and by his authority committed to me, I absolve you from all your sins." Father James pauses, then reiterates, "All your sins." He pauses again. "In the Name of the Father, and of the Son, and of the Holy Spirit. Amen."

"Amen," Cohen whispers.

"The Lord has put away all your sins," the priest says.

"Thanks be to God," Cohen says.

"Go in peace," the priest whispers, "and pray for me, a sinner."

Cohen stands and hurries out without looking back. He has been away from his father for too long. What if he's gone?

PART THREE

Wednesday, March 18, 2015

*Whose seed
is in itself...*

Genesis 1:11

thirty-six

The Visitor

Cohen's walk turns gradually to a fast walk, then to a slow jog. Anxiety pushes him. He never should have left his father alone. He knows this now. There's an aching sort of foreboding at the edge of his mind, something he can't get a good look at, but it's still there, still gnawing away. He shakes his head to clear the fog, the weariness. Sleep. He needs to sleep.

He jogs for a block or two and gets close to the hospital—he can see it rising, a shining tower, the white lights and layered parking garage—but he has to stop jogging. He's not in shape. His lungs burn. He leans against the streetlight while waiting for the signal to turn.

Inside the hospital, Cohen walks the long, dim hallways and rides the elevator up. *Ding.* He walks out into the hallway and sees the night nurses on duty. They glance up, recognize him, smile or nod or look away. The same anxiety rises again as he gets close to his father's room. What if he died while Cohen was gone? What if his sister came back and found him missing? What if the doctor was able to take his father off life support without the family's permission? He never should have left.

The door to his father's room is wide open, and he rounds the corner quickly. Where has the time gone? It's two in the morning. Of what day? Wednesday. Or Tuesday? No, Wednesday. He's almost positive it's Wednesday morning. He'll check on his father, and he decides if everything is okay he'll go down to the cafeteria, see if he can dig up some coffee, maybe a donut.

He walks into his father's room and stops. His heart races. There's a strange red haze gathering in the corners of his vision, a humming in his ears that started far away and now resembles the approach of a crashing wave.

"Cohen?" a voice says, and he realizes it's Kaye and she's standing over by the window. But he cannot look away from the woman there in front of him, standing at the foot of his father's bed, taking in his father. She looks old, but sharp and hard as he remembers her.

"Cohen? Where were you?" Kaye says, concern creeping in around the margins of her voice. "We were worried."

He does not, cannot, reply. He must focus on breathing. Inhale and let the air out. He squeezes his eyes shut. Opens them. She is still standing there.

He's tired. So tired. And the exhaustion moves through him like a chill.

When Kaye speaks again, there is a slight shaking in each word, the way teacups rattle in their saucers when an earthquake begins. "Cohen? Aren't you going to say hello to Mother?"

thirty-seven

The Ice in the Shadows

Than, Hippie, and Cohen walked back and forth along the sidewalk outside the funeral home for a long time that night, and if someone had seen them, they would have been intrigued by the scene: three children, sometimes walking, sometimes crawling, sometimes swiping their fingers along the cement as if trying to swab something from a crime scene with their own skin. Cars drove past but no one stopped. The streetlights watched, and the bony trees shushed them in a cold wind. A dead branch high in the sycamore tree hung precariously by a thread of sinewy, torn wood, and it knocked, knocked, knocked against the trunk, trying to break free. Cohen went inside, up the stairs, and put on a coat. He stared at his father sleeping on the couch again. He didn't stay there long, only long enough to wish yet again that his father cared where he was going.

It took his eyes a minute to adjust when he got back outside, and at first he couldn't find Than and Hippie. They had wandered down the street. Than was on his hands and knees, staring hard at the sidewalk, his gaze sweeping side to side.

Hippie, as usual, stood with her hands deep in her pockets, staring up at the night sky, waiting.

Cohen walked quietly toward them, not wanting to arouse the ire of Than. When he was still a little ways off, he reached out his hand absently and let his fingers skim the side of the building. He felt the roughness of the brick, the grit of the mortar, the specks of dust that crumbled and fell to the ground in the wake of his movement. At the corner of the building where it went back into the alley, his fingers slowed on something sticky.

"Ugh," he groaned, pulling his hand away, nearly wiping it on his coat. He stopped.

"Hippie!" he shouted, turning his hand toward the light. Before Than and Hippie got there, he knew what it was, not because he could see it clearly in the dim glow of the streetlights but because of how it felt on his fingers. There was a coldness to it that spread inside his skin, infiltrated his blood, spread up almost to his wrist, as if the shadow were inside his blood and pumping itself toward his heart. For a moment he panicked, frozen in place.

Than grabbed him by the forearm and twisted it so he could see Cohen's fingers in the light. "Where?" he asked, looking closer.

"The corner," Cohen said, still afraid of what the strange substance was doing to him. The tips of his fingers, where the black tar stuck, ached with cold, as if liquid ice had been spread along his hand. He couldn't bend his fingers at the knuckles. His wrist felt slightly swollen. And he couldn't tell if it was his imagination or not, this sensation that the cold was creeping farther up, farther in. The bone in his arm felt brittle, like a long icicle hanging from the eaves.

Than dropped Cohen's arm and stared at the corner of the building where he had wiped his fingers.

"Here," Hippie said in a quiet voice. She held out a white handkerchief, tinted golden in the streetlights. He reached for it, then paused. It looked so clean. He didn't want to mess it up.

"Go ahead," Hippie said, reaching out farther, and he took it. He wiped the shadow from his fingers quickly, and most of the cold evaporated as he removed it. But there was still a residual sense of numbness. He shook his hand to try to restore circulation, squeezed it into a fist over and over as if that was the problem, as if his hand had only fallen asleep or lost feeling after he'd played outside in the snow. He handed the handkerchief back to Hippie, and she folded it in on itself.

She moved in closer. "You didn't get it all," she said in a chiding, motherly voice. She held his hand in hers and gracefully, slowly rubbed each finger with the clean side of the handkerchief until all of the shadow had been removed.

"Thank you," he whispered.

"Are you two lovebirds finished?" Than shouted from somewhere in the alley.

"What?" Cohen protested a little too vehemently.

"Than!" Hippie shouted, happiness in her voice.

The two of them wandered through the dark toward Than. Behind the funeral home, where the backs of city homes lined up like forgotten faces, they found Than, and he pointed at the ground. Another swipe of darkness, this time a broad stroke like paint from a wide brush. They stared knowingly at each other and went deeper into the alley, walking closer together now, feeling a bond in the uncertainty of what might happen. Than led the way.

They went through the alley to the next street over. This was a busier street, a main thoroughfare from the north end of the city to the south. It was better lit, and they could see the black splotches and dashes plainly, like Morse code.

From there, the Beast seemed to have wandered aimlessly through the city, circling blocks and cutting through alleys before finding its bearings on New Street and shooting straight out of town, into the country. They followed the Beast's shadow tracks, and the night watched them. Soon they all knew where the tracks were leading.

They stared at the path through the woods,

the one that led over the train tracks, meandered through blackberry brambles, and ended with melted children's toys and a blackened, burned-out trailer. Eventually the three of them stood at the top of the bowl-shaped valley, side by side, and the blackberry stems weaved this way and that in a middle-of-the-night wind that tried to bring back winter. Cohen pulled his shoulders up, withdrew deeper inside his coat. Hippie took a deep breath and let out a steaming stream of hot air. Only Than seemed unaffected by the temperature, the wind, how dark the night was.

"Let's go," he said quietly, starting down the circular path through the thorns, bent at the waist, trying to stay low.

Hippie glanced at Cohen as if she wanted to tell him to go home. But she didn't say anything. Finally she nodded at him and followed Than. Cohen watched them go. He looked up at the stars, bright in a sky that the wind had swept clean. He shook his head, taking one step after another, following the other two down, winding closer to the trailer and finding it hard to believe this person walking willingly toward the Beast was him.

The trailer's windows were dark like gaping wounds.

thirty-eight
The Kite

"Hello," Cohen's mother says, looking away from him and back down at his father.

He can't tell for sure who she is talking to, him or his father. He stands there, unsure what to do. He wants to turn and leave, walk out the door. He hasn't seen her for years. Decades? Yes, decades.

But something holds him there in the doorway. He wonders what it is. He knows it's not love that keeps him there—he feels nothing for the woman at the foot of his father's bed, the woman with white hair, the same piercing green eyes, the same rock jaw, and the same mist of firm opinions swirling around her head like clouds around the upper reaches of the world's highest peak. He knows if he stays he will be subjected to them, their lightning crashes, their thunderous rolling. But still he stays.

"Hi, Kaye," he says, not knowing what else to say, and Kaye seems to take his words as a peace offering. She comes all the way from the other side of the room, all the way from where the dark night spills in through the window, all the way to him. She wraps him in her arms. He returns the hug and holds her for an extra moment, if only to give himself more time to think about what to do, how to respond to the presence of this other person.

Kaye pulls away and looks up at him.

He sighs. "I'm sorry."

She nods, looking like she might break.

"How is he?" Cohen asks.

She nods again, her mouth twitching. She raises her hand to cover it, shaking her head back and forth.

"I talked to the doctor," Cohen says, looking into her eyes, then away, then back at her. He thinks she might be the most beautiful thing in his life. "They want us to consider taking him off life support."

Kaye gasps, turns, moves to their mother's side. She covers her face with both hands and cries in absolute silence. Cohen feels strangely unmoved, and he glances at his mother to see how the news affects her, how the weeping of her daughter affects her, but she stands there stoic as ever, and he wonders if she's even heard him.

"These places always smell the same," his mother says in a firm voice. Cohen's not sure if he's ever heard her speak so quietly. Maybe this news has struck her deeper than she's willing to show. "You'd think they could spray something that smelled better. You'd think they could make use of those plug-in air fresheners. They charge enough for everything else. A candle wouldn't kill anyone."

"Mother," Cohen says, and he doesn't know what to do with the taste of the word in his mouth, but he says it again. "Mother, what are you talking about?"

She looks at him. "I'm talking about hospitals."

"Did you hear a word I said?"

She stares at him with that same old look, the same old manipulating confusion, as if nothing he said would ever be worth listening to so why would she start now?

"Dad is dying. They want us to take him off life support."

She stares. Unflinching. Cohen presses the heel of his hand against the center of his forehead, as if the pressure will change everything. He closes his eyes and digs in deeper, his sinuses aching. He reaches down and pinches the bridge of his nose, the pressure soothing something far beneath the surface.

Kaye has quieted. She moves back over to the window, and he follows her, staying far back from his mother as he passes behind her.

They both stand there, looking down at the nighttime city far below them. Kaye has one hand on the glass.

"Where were you?" she asks, her voice pained. "How could you leave him here alone?"

"I had to get out."

"Where?" Kaye asks again.

He shrugs. "The church."

She reaches over and holds his arm. "You've always gone back. After Mom and I left, we tried to find a church. Here and there and everywhere." She smiles. "Eventually we quit trying. But you, even after everything. You always went back."

Her comment seems to find some deep mark. He nods, but it's not meant for her or anyone else, it's simply meant as a placeholder while he tries to figure out what that says about him. He has always gone back. It's true. Time and again. Even after his father, a pastor, betrayed his family in the sanctuary, Cohen has always gone looking for God.

"I guess so," he says.

"Well," she says, "right now? Cohen, I need you here. I need you—here."

He nods again. "Why did you bring her?" he asks without looking at Kaye.

"Mother?" she asks, as if he could be talking about someone else.

He looks at her and raises his eyebrows.

"You want to talk about that here?" she asks, her words crossing into a different place, an area of disbelief. "Maybe because they were married once upon a time." She's trying to whisper, but frustration or disbelief or even anger gathers momentum behind her words, edging the volume up. "Maybe because she deserves to know what's going on. Maybe because she's our mother."

"She's not my mother, not anymore, hasn't been for a long time."

"She'll always be your mother. You are half her. Whether you want it or not."

He shakes his head but doesn't say anything. Kaye walks back toward her mother and stands at the foot of the bed beside her. Cohen looks at the object of their gaze, his father, his bald head shining, though the stubble grows. His large features. His fading.

"We had good times, the four of us," their mother says, almost a plea to see things differently. She has never done that before. She has never pled for Cohen to see things the way she does—she always assumed everyone would come around in time.

"It's true," Kaye says. "It's true."

"Remember when he brought home that kite and added string?" their mother says, her voice incredulous, and Cohen cannot separate the amazement in her voice from the insinuation of his father's stupidity. This is the mother he remembers. "The three of you flew it and let it out until it was just a speck."

Kaye smiles. "I ran inside and told you to come out."

"I didn't want to, but you begged and pleaded. When I came out, it fell from the sky, probably killing some far-off person or animal, and the three of you went traipsing after it, through the woods, through the fields, the mud and the muck. You didn't come back until after dark, and you all had to shower. I had to wash your manure-covered clothes." She shakes her head at the naivete, at the innocence of trying to find lost things that have fallen that far away.

"We found it," Cohen says, as if that is argument enough.

"Yes, you did," she says, but her voice is not an admission that Cohen is right as much as it is a statement that finding it wasn't even remotely close to being the point.

"Remember when Dad brought home that telescope?" Kaye says, laughing now.

Her mother frowns. "That thing cost him a week's pay. It took us months to recover from the expense."

"We could see the rings of Saturn," Cohen says quietly, without emotion. "We could see details of the craters on the moon."

"He hooked up a flat white board to the eyepiece so we could watch the eclipse. Remember how the round shadow moved across the sun?" Kaye asks enthusiastically.

"I have to use the restroom," their mother mumbles, moving toward the door.

"He was a good father," Cohen says.

"There's a bathroom here in the room," Kaye says. "You can use this one."

"These places always smell the same," their mother says, disregarding Kaye and walking out of the room.

thirty-nine

Through the Veil

"I thought that went well," Cohen says wryly to his sister while walking over to his father's hospital bed.

"You didn't give her much of a chance," Kaye says, sitting in one of the chairs at the foot of the bed.

"You didn't give me much of a chance. That was quite a surprise, Kaye."

"True."

"And to think she's as sweet as I remember."

Kaye gives him a playful shove, but soon the two of them are staring down at their father again. He is like a black hole in the room, and the sheer force of his presence, his dying, always brings them back around to him.

Cohen glances over at Kaye. "You know we're going to have to make a decision about Dad," he says, glancing at the window, where it is still the middle of the night. He looks up at the clock. "The doctor will be back here in the morning, three or four hours. What are we going to tell him?"

Cohen stares at her and she returns his gaze. He grows uncomfortable and looks away.

"What happened, Cohen?" she asks.

"What do you mean?"

"I mean, what happened? To Dad."

"It was a trocar."

"I know that, Cohen!" she says, suddenly animated. Loud. She stands, grips her stomach with two hands, and paces short, swaying steps. "You keep saying that, but how did it happen?"

"I don't know, Kaye," he says, running his hand through his hair, shaking his head. "When I went down there with the police yesterday, they showed me where it happened. It must have been an accident. He must have fallen while he was carrying it to the sink to clean it. I don't know. I don't know what else to tell you, Kaye. I wish I knew."

Kaye glances at the door to make sure their mother isn't coming in. "Do you think he . . . committed suicide?"

Cohen takes a deep breath. "I hope not. I don't mean to be crass, but if he did, we won't see a cent of his life insurance, and without that we lose the funeral home."

Kaye closes her eyes and tries to take a calming breath. "Do you think that's what happened?" she whispers. "Do you think Dad tried to kill himself?"

"It needs to be an accident, Kaye."

"It needs to be?"

He nods. "It needs to be. And maybe it was."

The words make Cohen even more tired. How many more things have to be said? How many more hours of this endless watching, waiting?

"We have to let him go, Kaye. Look at him. This isn't Dad anymore. He's gone. We have to let him go. He wouldn't want to live like this."

Her eyes are still closed and she covers her face with her hands. "I know, Cohen. I know."

He puts his arm around her. "Are you still growing?" he asks, trying to lighten the mood.

She laughs through her tears. "I think so. Feels that way." She puts a hand on her stomach, turns her face away from him, and takes in a sharp breath.

"Contraction?"

She waits, exhaling slowly, a stream of air through pursed lips. "Yeah." Her words come through a thin veil of surprised pain. "Yeah, that was a strong one."

"They want out?" Cohen asks, raising his eyebrows.

"Soon," is all she says. "Soon."

Their mother comes in, walking as if she herself is the doctor and she has a cure for Calvin, one that only she can bring about.

"How cute," she says in a monotone voice that is almost some kind of accusation, looking at Cohen still hugging Kaye. He drops his arm. He looks at Kaye and shakes his head in disbelief.

"Hi, Mom," Kaye says.

Cohen drifts away from his mother, back toward the window. Kaye sits in her chair. Their mother stands vigil over Calvin. She speaks to Cohen without even looking at him.

"Is that how you always dress when you come on visits to the hospital?"

He thinks of ten different replies, all varying degrees of sarcasm or sincerity, but he settles on not saying anything. It feels good, as if in his silence he has somehow neutralized her ability to tear him down.

"And neither of you brought fresh clothes for your father? What is he going to wear when they finally let him out of this smelly, disgusting place?"

"Mother," Kaye says before following Cohen into silence.

They remain like that for hours, three people so far away from each other. Cohen wonders how other children and parents go on through their lives, choosing what to forgive, what to ignore, what to become embittered by. He wonders if everyone feels this way in the presence of a parent.

At some point in those early morning hours he sits on the floor, leans against the wall, and falls asleep. Later he wakes, and a hint of morning light comes through the window. His mother hasn't moved from where she stands at the foot of the bed, staring, waiting—for what? His sister sleeps in the chair, all belly, arms dangling down both sides, legs reaching for some unattainable comfort. He pretends to sleep. He does not want his mother to know he's awake.

But a face peeks in around the door. It's Thatcher, the boy from next door, still wearing the same John Deere hat, still flaunting the same unruly teenage stubble.

"Is Mr. Cohen in here?" he asks Cohen's mother. She doesn't look at him.

"Hey!" Cohen stands, stretching the ache out of his body. "How's it going?"

"Can I talk to you? Out here?"

"Sure, sure," Cohen says, walking slowly past his sleeping sister, past his mother who doesn't move, even though he must brush against her in order to pass by.

forty

The Flash of the Gun

Their walk through the brambles took longer than Cohen thought possible. He began to imagine he could see the light gathering in the east, the sun preparing to rise, but it was a trick of his mind and the sky stayed dark, except for the moon that hung at the tree line.

"What if it's in there?" Cohen whispered at one point when the three of them stopped. They were at the edge of the hollow, and his eyes went from window to window to window. Even in the dark, he could see the blackened parts of the trailer, the melted playthings.

"We need to finish this," Hippie whispered, looking over at Cohen. He glanced at her, then at Than, and in Than's eyes he could almost see the long dark hall, the room with the desk, the gun hidden in the air duct. Cohen swallowed hard, nodded. Than nodded back. The three crept toward the front door.

Cohen's heart beat in every part of his body: his chest, of course, but also in his hands, his head, his ears. Each moment, each step, sent a sharp sensation through him. At the empty front door, he reminded himself to breathe.

Hippie crept up into the trailer on all fours. She disappeared inside. Than crouched at the steps and motioned furiously for Cohen to follow her. The burned carpet was brittle under his fingers, and a scent like burned hair came up off it where his hands crushed the fibers. He tried to move without making a sound as he followed Hippie deeper into the ash. He reached up and itched the corner of his eye, and his hands smelled charred. Behind him, he sensed Than coming inside.

They were in the hall faster than he had hoped. Hippie was silent as a shadow. Than was so quiet he might have been behind him, or he might have been floating above him, or he might have fled, leaving them alone. Cohen was too scared to look over his shoulder, terrified that he would look back and see nothing, or see the Beast.

As they moved through the hallway, his hands and knees grew icy cold, and he thought water had gotten into the trailer, soaking into the carpet, and they were crawling through melted ice. The cold worked its way under his skin, pumped deeper with each beat of his heart, and he realized they were crawling through shadows that had leaked from the Beast. Another surge of panic jolted him—what would it do to him if he didn't wipe it off right away?—but it was too late for running.

Sometimes as they crawled, his hands came down on the soles of Hippie's shoes. The three of them were close together again, and he could hear Than's breathing, feel the floor creaking under his weight. They were being too loud. Of that he was certain.

The bedroom door was on their left, and they passed it without giving it a second glance. Outside, even at night, it was brighter than inside the trailer. Maybe the moon had reversed course, maybe the stars were brighter, maybe morning was approaching. Cohen felt a sharp desire to be out there, out in the lung-burning cold and the wind, running through the path that wound up the hill, blackberry brambles grabbing at his coat. But he crawled forward.

At the door to the room with the small desk and the heat register that had swallowed the gun, Than tapped his leg and pulled on his jeans to tell him to go into that small space. Cohen grabbed Hippie's foot. She turned. He raised a finger, telling her to wait. What he could see of her face in the dark looked confused, but she nodded. He went a few crawls into the room, a few silent movements, and there was the register. He lifted it, trying to stay silent, willing it to come up without a scrape or a bang. And it did. It slid out soundlessly, like a secret.

He reached down, and there it was: the gun. He lifted it, and it was heavy, and it was death. Than was right there with him, taking the gun from him, taking the sock full of bullets.

Than leaned in close, so close Cohen could feel his breath tickle the folds of his ear. "It's loaded and ready to fire," Than whispered, handing the gun back.

Cohen nodded nervously. The two of them crawled back into the hallway. Than grabbed Hippie's leg and pulled her back. He pushed Cohen forward and Cohen balked. Than put his hand on Cohen's back and nudged him forward again.

The door to the back bedroom had been pushed up against the frame by whoever or whatever had gone in last, but it had not been closed so that it latched. There was a narrow space of darker than dark that Cohen tried to look through to get a glimpse into the room, but he could see nothing. The windows were covered with something. The room was pitch-black.

Cohen leaned back and stuck his head in between Than and Hippie. "I can't see anything," he whispered.

The three of them stayed there for what felt like a long time, waiting. What happened next, happened fast.

The creaking sound of steps moved from the back of the trailer to the bedroom door. The door opened. The Beast saw them, even in the darkness, and it roared, charged. There was a ferociousness to it, and Cohen knew it was coming for them. He stared into that heart of darkness, a cold cloud of shadow, and the numbness in his hands and knees was nothing compared to the cold that emanated from the Beast and descended on all of them in that moment. Cohen didn't think. He raised the gun. He pulled the trigger.

He had never felt anything like it. The sound of it, the flash and the smell, the kick of the gun, and the scream of Hippie who did not know there was a gun—all of it pushed back the darkness. There was a roar, a wounded bellow, and the cloud of darkness gathered in on itself and swept away from them, crashed through one of the bedroom windows in a tangle of black curtains and glass, and was gone.

The three of them sat there for a long time, listening, shocked, not saying a word: Cohen with his back against the hallway wall, Than lying on his back, looking up through exhausted eyes at the ceiling, and Hippie beside Cohen, her head on his shoulder. The gun was on the floor in between Cohen's feet, his forearms resting on his knees.

"It's okay," Hippie said quietly, reaching up and putting her hand on his head, the way a traveling preacher might touch someone's head before they're baptized. "It's okay."

Cohen looked at her. He shivered violently. She took out a new, clean handkerchief, and again she cleaned the icy shadows from his hands. He put his head on his forearms and wept.

Light came through the bedroom windows as the sun rose in the east, but there was no warmth in the light. Spring felt distant. A winter wind blew through the window, nudging pieces of glass that had broken but didn't fall, sweeping over all three of them. They eased their way to their feet, and no one said another word as they slipped from the trailer.

The stars were still there, barely, fading as the pale sunrise leaked through the naked trees.

forty-one

Missing

Cohen walks out into the hallway and feels that sober sense of cautious hope that seems to wander hospital hallways early in the morning, when those who are still alive breathe easier. The sun will rise again soon. He wants to put his arm around the boy and say, "We have all survived another night." Instead he asks him a question.

"Everything okay, Thatcher?"

"Yeah, yeah, I think so."

"Is your mom around?"

Thatcher shakes his head. "No, she still hasn't come back."

"What's she afraid of?"

As if on cue, the banging sound of a dropped food tray comes from Thatcher's grandfather's room, followed by a string of profanity.

"Dad's still mad."

Cohen nods. "Want me to talk to him?"

"No way!" he says, incredulous. "No. I wanted to see if you might help me look around for my mom. I think she's here, in the hospital."

"What makes you think that?"

Thatcher looks over his shoulder. "Pretty sure

I saw her leaving Grandpa's room when I was coming up the hall."

"Did you go after her?"

"I wasn't sure if it was her. And she was far away, and she walked through that door really quick. I don't want my dad to find her."

"Yeah. Sure. I'd be happy to help you look. Can we start in the cafeteria? I need a coffee."

The boy smiles, and Cohen is surprised at how happy he can look. He has a nice smile with straight, white teeth and shallow dimples.

"You drink coffee?" Cohen asks.

"Sure."

They go down the elevator to the main level and walk to the cafeteria. It's quiet, and nurses walk by in soft shoes and doctors wander the halls staring at clipboards, their eyes ringed by dark circles. The kitchen in the cafeteria is not open yet, but there are canisters of coffee and one lone girl standing at a register. Beyond that, the cafeteria is empty except for one person: Ava.

"Morning, mister." The girl at the register punches a button, yawning.

"Hi there. Two coffees."

She tells him the total and takes his money, gives him change.

"How long has that woman been here?" he asks.

"Oh, her? She came in maybe five minutes ago. You know her?" The girl sounds suspicious.

"She's a friend. That's all."

"Oh." She doesn't look convinced. "Well, enjoy your coffee."

Cohen leads Thatcher back toward the small round table where Ava is sitting. She stares out the window, distracted, and her coffee sends up smoke signals.

"Good morning," he says, reluctant to bring her out of her reverie.

She turns, and for a moment he isn't sure she recognizes him. "Oh, Cohen! I'm sorry. I was . . . very far away." She laughs and pats the table. "Join me?"

"Sure, I was grabbing a cup of coffee when I saw you."

"And is this your nephew?" she asks.

"No, no. This is my friend Thatcher. His grandfather is in the room next to my dad."

"Oh," she says, concern slowing down her voice. "I'm sorry. Is he okay?"

"No, ma'am," Thatcher mumbles.

"I'm very sorry."

They sit down, Cohen beside Ava and Thatcher on the other side of him. They sit quietly while the cafeteria wakes up around them. Three employees walk past, all the way to the entrance to the kitchen. One of them comes back out to take up a post at the other register. The shutter at the tray drop-off rises. Soon Cohen can smell bacon.

"So, you two met in the hallway?" Ava asks with a gentle smile.

Cohen returns her smile. "Something like that."

"How do you know each other?" Thatcher asks.

Cohen looks at Ava and motions for her to answer.

"Well, let's see," she replies. "Cohen and I went to school together for many years. We went to the same church for a short while. We played baseball together."

"Really?" Thatcher asks.

"Yes, girls play baseball," Ava says sarcastically.

"I know that," Thatcher protests.

"I'm just giving you a hard time."

"She was very, very good. Best player on the team," Cohen says, looking at Ava.

She laughs. He likes the way she laughs. It's the same laugh she had when she was a girl, the same smile she gave him from her spot at first base, the same grin she had when they sat on the sidewalk outside the funeral home, and it takes his mind off of everything.

"Well, maybe. I don't know about that. But I did love it."

"Now she's a detective," Cohen says. "So watch yourself."

"Seriously?" Thatcher asks, eyes wide.

Ava nods, taking another sip from her coffee. "That's right."

"Maybe she can help us," Thatcher says to Cohen in a quiet voice.

Cohen shrugs.

"With what?" Ava asks.

"My mom is missing."

"Your mom is missing?"

"Yeah."

"For how long?" Her voice becomes more businesslike with each question.

"Maybe a day or two."

"Have you reported it?"

"Dad doesn't want to. Says she'll be back when she's good and ready."

Ava's eyes go wide and she stares at Cohen as if to corroborate the story.

Cohen grimaces and nods. "I know it doesn't sound good, but it's true."

"Are you serious? Why haven't you reported this?"

"He's seen her around," Cohen says, raising his hands defensively. "Or at least he thinks he did."

"You did?" she asks Thatcher.

"I don't know. I think so," he says nervously. "I actually think she might be hiding in the hospital. I hope that won't get her into any trouble. Maybe forget I told you that."

"What's she hiding from?"

Cohen sighs. "Okay, here's the deal. Thatcher's grandpa is dying. Thatcher's dad is a rather violent man—sorry, Thatcher—who will take it out on anyone who's within striking distance, and the doctor basically killed his grandfather by giving him the wrong medication. I think Thatcher's mom still wants to sit with and take care of her father-in-law, so she's holed up somewhere here in the hospital and comes out at night when her angry husband isn't around. That's my theory. But I'm no detective. Sound right?" He looks at Thatcher.

"I'd say so." Thatcher shrugs.

"What do you want my help for?" Ava asks.

"Maybe keep your eyes out for her?" Thatcher says. "I just want to know she's okay."

"After we drink our coffee," Ava suggests, "maybe we can take a wander around the hospital?"

Thatcher seems relieved.

"I'll check in on my dad, and if everything's okay I can join the search party. Speaking of my dad," Cohen says, turning toward Ava, "they want Kaye and me to give them the okay to take him off life support."

"Oh, Cohen." She stares into her coffee, then back up at him with sad eyes. "I'm sorry." She pauses, glancing at Thatcher. "I really shouldn't be talking about this with you, but I think you're in the clear. There's no evidence suggesting foul play or suicide. I'm pretty sure it's going to go down as an accident. That's all I'm saying. And you didn't hear it from me."

Cohen nods. "Thanks." He stands up, pushing his chair away from the table. He stops, stares at the windows, then looks back at Ava. "Thanks."

forty-two

The Cave

Than was outside the trailer waiting for them, but he wasn't facing the trailer. He was looking up into the woods, and when he spoke, his words were flat.

"We should go around back and make sure it's dead."

Cohen shuddered at the thought and the cold and the dread of facing it again. It wasn't until that moment that he realized he had picked up the gun again. He looked down at it the way a child looks at a fresh injury.

Hippie led the way, starting for the other side of the trailer without a word, without waiting to see if the boys would follow her. The experience with the Beast in the doorway to the bedroom seemed not to have diminished or intimidated her. If anything, she had grown somehow, become more fierce.

Than followed her, looking first at the ground, then up at Cohen, and immediately Cohen could tell things had changed between them. Than's look held respect, confidence, and a kind of equality Cohen hadn't felt from him before. Than nodded, walked past, and followed Hippie around the corner. Cohen steeled himself and went after them, glancing over his shoulder, always feeling that something was coming up behind him.

By the time Cohen came around to the back of the trailer, Than and Hippie were turning from the broken bedroom window—it was covered in the black pitch—and moved over to the brambles where it looked like someone had rolled a large boulder up the hill. The Beast had cleared a path, everything flattened, trampled, broken. Sporadically along the path were splotches of the shadow, thick and unmoving in the cold, clinging to rocks and thorns and low branches like thick mucus.

"What next?" Than asked, and Cohen sensed the shifting of leadership. Something had changed. He couldn't figure out why or how or even exactly what, but something had changed.

"We need to get some rest," Hippie said. "Then we come back here and follow the trail."

"Won't it get away?" Cohen asked, surprised at the sound of his own morning voice, raspy and dim.

Hippie shook her head.

Than took a few steps into the trail the Beast had left behind. "Nah," he said without further explanation.

Cohen looked over at Hippie.

"All of this?" she said, pointing at a nearby

bramble covered from top to bottom with liquid shadow. "It's dying. It's going to run until it feels safe. We'll let it get settled. It might even be dead by the time we find it."

"Because I shot it?"

"We need to get some rest," Hippie said again. "C'mon."

"Where are we going?"

Hippie looked at him, and there was compassion in her eyes, and concern. "To where Than and I always go when we need to hide."

Cohen followed them. They went to the front of the trailer again and walked up the meandering trail through the brambles to the top of the hollow. He looked back at the trailer at the bottom, now distant and empty.

When he turned back around, Than and Hippie were up the trail, and he hurried to catch them. The sky was icy blue without a single cloud, the previous days' rain long gone. The air was still one minute, so still the trees looked frozen, and blustery the next, whipping branches and leaves at his face. When they got to the train tracks, Hippie turned and walked along them.

"Where are we going?" Cohen asked again, pausing.

Than looked over his shoulder for a brief moment, turned away, kept walking.

Hippie walked back to Cohen. "We're going to a place where we can rest. Someplace warm.

Then we'll come back here and track the Beast once it's dark. It won't be long now."

For a moment Cohen stood there on the tracks, weighing his options. He stared down at the gun still in his hand. He had held it for so long it felt like his old hand had fallen away and been replaced with a barrel, a hammer, a trigger, bullets. Lifting the gun, he nearly handed it to Hippie and walked straight back into the city, back to the funeral home and his own bed. They both looked down at the gun, and it stood between them like an offering.

But it fell back to his side. He nodded. She reached out and put her hand on his shoulder, gave him the slightest of tugs, and without thinking anymore he followed her, walking along the train tracks.

Hippie took the lead, and they walked for ten minutes, fifteen minutes, thirty minutes, like silent apparitions looking for a way out of the world. At an unmarked point, Hippie veered from the tracks and plunged into the thickest part of the forest, bent over, nearly crawling on all fours. Than followed her. Cohen copied them, too tired to ask any more questions.

Soon the trail opened up and they could walk upright, but they were going up and down steep hills so that Cohen had to hold on to small trees to keep from sliding to the bottom. Hippie and Than vanished into a glade of evergreens with low, sleeping boughs, trees that lined a sort of cliff. Behind the green branches, nestled in among the soft needles, was a shallow cave in the rock.

Cohen went in among the shadows. It was dark there despite the morning. He placed the gun on a ledge. Than had already gone to the back and lay on a flat slab covered in leaves. Hippie worked up a small fire in the middle of the cave, and the smoke rose, drifted out into the woods. She placed a few large logs on the fire, sat with her back against a wall, and closed her eyes.

Cohen sat down beside her. He thought he would never be able to fall asleep, not there with his back against a hard wall, but the heat and the slowly rising smoke mesmerized him. He wondered what his dad was doing, if he had woken up yet, if he realized Cohen wasn't at home. He wondered what his dad would do if he realized he was missing, if he would care.

He fell asleep.

forty-three
The Nurse

"So, what can you tell me about your mother?" Ava asks Thatcher as the elevator rises through the center of the hospital. "Where would you be if you were her?"

"I don't know," Thatcher says, shrugging.

"Didn't you tell me she's a nurse?" Cohen asks.

The boy shrugs again, nods. His eyes are bloodshot from lack of sleep, and his baseball cap lists farther and farther to the side as the morning goes on.

"So, what you're saying is, we're looking for a missing woman who's a nurse and she's hiding in a hospital?" Ava asks.

Cohen smiles.

Ava looks at him, then at Thatcher. "Does the term 'needle in a haystack' mean anything to you two?"

She finally gets a smile out of the boy.

"What kind of a nurse is she?" Ava asks.

"I don't know. A regular old nurse, I guess."

"If I were a nurse, where in a hospital would I hide?"

"Maybe where there are a lot of nurses, so you could blend in?" Thatcher asks.

Ava looks over at Cohen playfully. "Why didn't I think of that before?" she says. "This boy's going to be a detective someday."

Thatcher tries not to smile, scratches the back of his neck, and yawns without covering his mouth, a long, exaggerated yawn that makes Cohen rub his own eyes and wish for a few hours of sleep. The elevator arrives at their floor and they walk out. The hospital is awake now, with nurses walking here and there, orderlies serving breakfast, doctors going from room to room.

Thatcher looks at Cohen. "I'll catch up with you soon."

"Okay," Ava says. "Well, Thatcher, should we go floor by floor?"

"There are a lot of floors," he says, sounding hesitant.

"We'll do one at a time, and you can check in with your father in an hour or two to see how your grandfather's doing. I'll stop by later, Cohen."

"Thanks, Ava," he says, glancing at Thatcher. "Hang in there."

Cohen watches as they walk away and stop to talk to a few nurses, Ava asking questions. They glance into a few rooms, open the door to a storage closet, and are confronted by a nurse. Cohen smiles. He walks into his father's room.

Calvin is in his bed, looking exactly the same. Cohen's mother stands at the foot of the bed like an ancient stone statue. His sister sits in the same chair she always sits in, both hands on her stomach, eyes glued to their father. Dr. Stevens is there.

"Ah, Cohen, I'm glad you're back. I've been talking with your sister and your mother."

"Hi."

"Yes. Well. Can we talk?" He takes a few steps to the back of the room, beside the window. The sun is already well above the buildings, and the sky is an enchanted, oil-painting blue.

Cohen follows the doctor. Kaye rises up out of the chair with a groan, a hand on her back. Their mother never moves, never blinks.

"Your babies have dropped since yesterday," the doctor says to Kaye, smiling.

"Yeah," she replies with a grimace. "I feel like they're ready to fall out."

"Are these your first?"

"No, I have a son."

"Okay. Wanted to make sure you knew the signs of impending labor. Do you have a C-section scheduled?"

Kaye nods.

"Good." He pauses as if searching for a good transition. When nothing seems to come to mind, he beckons for them to move a little closer. He gives a sad smile, lays his clipboard down on the windowsill, crosses his arms, and leans back against the glass. "I'm sorry to say there's nothing more we can do. Your father is no longer responding. There's no reason to expect he'll recover."

Cohen looks over at Kaye, and she does not respond the way he expects—no hand to the face, no tiny whimpering sounds. In fact, she barely responds at all. Her eyes glaze over, her lips remain slightly apart, shallow breaths coming and going. She licks her lips. She swallows. That's all.

"I am recommending that we remove your father from life support."

Cohen does not take his gaze off Kaye. She nods, and now her eyes are moving from one thing to another—from the window to the doctor's face to her mother to her father and back to the window.

"Kaye?" Cohen asks.

She closes her eyes and takes a deep breath. "No," she says. One word.

"I'm sorry?" Dr. Stevens asks.

"I said, 'No.' "

"We need to talk about this, Kaye." Cohen's voice comes out quiet, gentle.

"There's nothing to talk about."

Cohen looks at the doctor, who does not look surprised.

"Take your time," Dr. Stevens says. "I think it would be good if the two of you spend some time talking together. I'll be back this afternoon. If you have any questions, please let me know."

"Thank you," Cohen says. "We'll . . . yes. Thank you."

Kaye has gone back inside herself, staring at Cohen through empty eyes.

The doctor walks past their mother and through the door. She watches him walk out, takes a deep breath, and comes over to the window. "Kaye," she says, as if calling her out of some deep place.

Kaye looks at her as if she is only now realizing her mother is there in the room with them.

"Kaye," she says again.

"Yes, Mother."

"You have to let him go." Her words are clipped, demanding, emotionless.

Kaye blinks twice in quick succession.

"You have to let him go," their mother says again.

Kaye shakes her head. "No. Mom. Only yesterday you were talking about him having fresh clothes so he could walk out of here!"

"Kaye," their mother says a third time, reaching out and putting both of her hands on Kaye's shoulders. "You have to let him go."

"No, Mom. No." Kaye is shaking her head frantically, back and forth, back and forth, and the tears that were dammed up all morning spill over. "No." She keeps saying it in between sobs, the word muffled from behind her hands, which she put up to shield her face. "No."

Cohen finds himself crying. It's the first time since he saw his father lying on the floor of the funeral home that he feels moved to tears, and it's Kaye's childlike insistence that her father not die that gets him. They are children again, and their parents are telling them they're getting divorced and that Kaye will go with their mother and Cohen will stay with their father and this is how it will have to be—their parents will still be friends, there will be nothing in between them except a little distance, and they will still be a family, a kind of family.

"No," Kaye had said that afternoon. The country house's windows were wide open, and the breeze came so deliciously through the screens that it was as if the world itself was in denial about the destruction taking place. "No, Mom. No."

Cohen rubs his eyes with both hands to try to push the tears back up where they came from.

forty-four
There Is Evil

Cohen woke in the cave with Hippie and Than. They were still asleep, and he felt an ache for them. He wondered why they had to find the Beast, why this responsibility was theirs. He leaned forward and looked at Than for a long time, the way he slept, melting into the rock, hidden in the shadows at the back of the shallow cave. He stared down at Hippie, his eyes following the softness of her cheeks, the round slope of her nose, the pitch-black of her hair. He sighed, leaned back against the rock.

"You okay?" Hippie whispered.

She caught him off guard, and he looked down at her and nodded. He looked over at Than. "What exactly are we doing?" he asked in a low voice. "What is this Beast? Where did it come from? Why are we killing it?"

He looked back at Hippie, and her eyes grew sad. She looked away, and for a long time he thought she wasn't going to answer, that she would go on staring at the ceiling of the cave until the end of time. He looked out through the evergreens and could see light falling in slants through the needles. The smell of pine was

299

intoxicating, and the safety he felt there, hidden away from the world, was something he hadn't felt for a long time. He wondered if they would have to leave. Couldn't the three of them stay there, hunt for food, keep the fire going, make the cave a little more comfortable? No one had to find them.

"The Beast," Hippie said quietly, "is a killer, Cohen. It has already taken the lives of children, and it will not stop."

A chill moved slowly through Cohen's body when Hippie said "the lives of children."

"There is evil in the world," she continued. "Did you know that, Cohen? There is evil, and most people live their lives content to ignore it. But someone has to do something. Someone has to stop it."

He tried to nod, but his neck seemed suddenly inflexible, as if a metal rod had replaced his spine. He swallowed hard.

Hippie looked over at Than. "We'll stay here until it gets dark. We'll rest and eat. After the sun sets, we'll track down the Beast. By the time the sun rises tomorrow, all of this will be over."

"Then what?" Cohen asked, but Hippie didn't answer. She rolled over so that her back was toward him and fell back to sleep.

forty-five
The Nightmare

Cohen thinks it might take him some time to find Ava and Thatcher, wandering as they are through the entire hospital looking for Thatcher's mother, but he pushes the button for the elevator, the doors part, and there they stand.

"I was on my way to find you two," he says.

Ava smiles in surprise. Thatcher takes off his hat, scratches his head. He looks tired.

"We went down a few floors but didn't see her," Ava says. "So we thought we'd check out the floor above us."

Cohen steps inside. The back of the elevator is lined with mirrors while the sides and front on either side of the door are stainless steel. There are small sections of mirror around the buttons, so that when he looks at them he sees mirrors of mirrors on into infinity. One thousand Thatchers. One thousand Avas. One thousand versions of himself, all of them Cohen Marah, all of them about to help the boy look for his mother, all waiting for Calvin to die.

"Any leads?" he asks Thatcher, pushing the button.

"A few nurses think they've seen her."

"Where?"

"Mostly around my grandfather's room."

"Recently?"

"Yeah, but mostly at night."

"So she's holing up during the day?"

Thatcher nods. "I guess. That's what Miss Ava seems to think."

"Shouldn't we sit somewhere quiet and wait for nighttime? Sounds like it would be pretty easy to find her in the evening."

"Thatcher's father is in the room right now," Ava says hesitantly.

Cohen gets the message. "Alright. Well, let's keep looking."

The doors part and the three of them walk out onto the tile. They're on the floor directly above the one where his father and Thatcher's grandfather are both taking their last breaths. But this floor is different. Cohen can't figure it out at first, what it is about this floor that feels so far from all the other ones. But then he realizes.

It's a wing only for children. Many of them have bald heads, wear medical masks, and carry stuffed animals. The nurses bend at the knee and talk to them on their level, smiling, their voices soft, an octave higher. A blue soccer ball bounces toward them and Thatcher instinctively snags it.

A tiny voice cries out from down the hall. "Hey, man, over here!"

Cohen spots the owner of the voice, an eight- or nine-year-old boy with light brown hair and dark eyes lost in sunken sockets. He pulls himself along on a walker, determined. "C'mon, kick it back!"

Thatcher glances at Ava, drops the ball, and kicks it in the direction of the boy.

"Thanks, man!" the boy shouts. He turns and swings his foot at the ball, sending it flying to the opposite end of the wing. A nurse protests and the boy laughs, a weak chuckle, before scooting down the hall.

The walls in the reception area are covered in drawings and paintings and sketches created by a hundred hospitalized children. Cohen is drawn to them like a moth to the flame, and Ava and Thatcher fall in behind him. He makes his way from one end of the display to the other.

He sees a picture done in almost all orange, and the searing brightness of it draws his attention. He steps closer. There's a house in the middle of the orange paint, a house made of thin brown lines, and inside it is a stick figure, a little girl. Beside the little girl is a baby. The girl has a tear in her eye, and the baby has been colored in all black.

Farther down the wall is a picture in crayon: green grass, a brown tree with no leaves, and puffy clouds outlined in blue. Under the tree is a little girl who appears to be waving. In the clouds are small houses, and beside one of the houses is a person waving down at the little girl.

There are finger paintings of families and pencil sketches of houses and trees and rivers. There are crayon drawings in their speckled wax, faces and snowmen and one that looks like the hospital.

Close to the opposite end, after he has looked at nearly all the drawings, Cohen sees one that makes him stop: it's a well-drawn colored-pencil sketch of evergreen trees. In the middle of the evergreens is a round hole, and in the hole is a little girl. Beyond the trees, high on a mountain, is a black smudge, terrible in its ambiguity.

The Beast.

He shakes his head. It can't be. He looks closer.

"What does that look like to you?" he asks no one in particular.

"What?" Ava asks.

He points at the black smudge in the picture.

"That's a boulder," Thatcher says.

"A boulder?" Cohen asks skeptically.

"A shadow?" Ava guesses.

"I guess. Maybe."

"What do you think it is?" Ava asks.

Cohen traces the dark smudge in the mountains with his fingers. It is the size of his thumbprint.

"A nightmare."

They walk the hall and feel the weight of emotion floating in that sea of sick children, the desperation, the lightness of hope being lost and found, given and taken. They're on the top floor of the hospital, and there are large windows at each end of the hall, and through the windows Cohen sees light and sky and the city. Again he feels the relief that comes with morning, as parents wake up and find their children still with them, as breakfast is served and children eat, as doctors make the rounds and nurses check vitals. The wing grows louder in the time it takes them to walk from one side to the other.

"Anything?" Cohen asks Thatcher.

He shakes his head. "Naw," he says, trying to rebuild his tough exterior in the face of disappointment. But when Ava puts her arm around him and gives him a squeeze, he doesn't shrug her away. He sighs, takes off his hat again, and pushes his hair to the side.

"Wait," Cohen says, looking over Thatcher's shoulder. "Is that your mom?"

Ava and Thatcher look down the hall. A small crowd of children have come out of an activity room and are milling about, waiting for nurses and parents to demand they go back to their rooms. The outside light grows brighter, and the lights in the ceiling dim to compensate. Beyond the children, halfway down the hall, a woman dressed like all the other nurses holds a clipboard, writing. She hangs the clipboard up on the wall beside one of the rooms and turns to walk away.

"Mom!" Thatcher shouts, but his voice gets lost in the sound of all the children. "Mom!" he shouts again, louder this time.

The woman stops. She seems to consider turning around, but instead she walks away, walks faster.

Thatcher starts after her, trying to navigate the constellation of children.

"C'mon," Cohen says, but Ava is already ahead of him, and then she's ahead of Thatcher.

They make it through the children, and the woman, still off in the distance, ducks into a different stairwell. Ava runs in after her, with Cohen and Thatcher right behind.

"Mom!" Thatcher shouts, and his voice echoes off the painted cinder blocks. The sound of it vanishes along the endless cycle of stairs that fold back on each other and down, down, down. Cohen peers through the opening between the handrails and can see Thatcher's mother running down. Ava is behind her.

Floor after floor, Cohen and Thatcher and Ava chase the woman. The stairwell goes darker the farther they descend, and Cohen's legs start to burn. He stops to catch his breath, waiting for Thatcher. He leans back against the wall and puts his hands up on his head, looking back up the stairs. But Thatcher is nowhere to be found.

"Thatcher? Are you coming?"

No answer. His voice floats up the stairs, comes

back to him, floats away again. The light is so dim that when he peers in between the handrails he can only see up a few floors.

"Thatcher!" he shouts again. Nothing. He looks down. Strange—it's completely dark and he can't see the bottom, but he can still hear Ava and the woman running farther and farther away. He runs down one more floor and looks around. There are no doors leading out of the stairwell. How many floors down has he gone?

He hears a bellowing sound far below, and he freezes in place, everything in sharp contrast. His ears strain to hear it again. His heart rate soars, and it takes everything in him not to turn and run back up as fast as he can.

Where is he?

The stairway seems endless. He continues down, but now he's not going so fast, and the sound of the women's footsteps fade below him, replaced by another sound. He stops at each floor, looking down as far as he can into the darkness, waiting, listening.

He reaches the bottom, the stairs end, and he arrives in a long, narrow room that's dimly lit. The floor is concrete, the ceiling pale white, the walls dark and shimmering like heavy curtains. He shakes his head. What is going on?

The air is heavy, cool, and damp, like the air in a cave. He walks slowly through the open space, preparing himself to run in the opposite direction.

Ahead of him, at the other end of the room, someone is waiting for him. He gets closer and realizes it's Ava. She is facing him, not saying anything.

"Ava," he says, but she doesn't answer. She doesn't blink. She doesn't move. There's another woman in the shadowy corner of the room, but she won't come closer, and she doesn't answer when he calls to her. Why did she lead them all the way down here? Why did she run from them?

"Who are you?" he asks. Nothing. "Ava, we should go. I don't like it here."

Ava nods, still without blinking, but she doesn't move to join him.

"Ava," he says again. This time the fear is thick in the back of his throat. "Ava. Come on."

The shadows from the corners gather together, and the Beast rises, bearing down on them.

forty-six

What We Deserve

Cohen wakes up.

"Well, look who decided to come back," his mother says without looking at him.

Come back? At first he thinks she's talking about coming back from that dark, dank room with Ava and the Beast and the woman in the corner. Was his mother there? But dreams fade quickly, and he finds he can't remember. Was she in the other corner? Had she gone down with him? Was she in the dream at all?

Kaye sits up straighter in her chair, and it looks like she has been sleeping too. He glances at his father and an ache splits him in half, a gnawing in the pit of his stomach, a deep desire to go back in time and do things differently.

"Anything new?" he asks Kaye.

"No, nothing new," she replies, looking at the clock on the wall. "Actually, the doctor should be back here soon." She pulls herself up out of her chair in that ponderous movement only pregnant women make, the simultaneous leaning back and rising.

He moves over and helps her stand. "He doesn't look good," he says.

"That's because he's dying," his mother hisses.

"His skin looks grayer," Cohen says, always looking at Kaye, trying to pretend his mother is not there.

"He's on his way out," Kaye says.

"You look absolutely exhausted."

Kaye smiles, and somehow it makes her look even more tired.

"You should go home," Cohen says. "Get some sleep. Take a warm bath."

"Is it that bad?" Kaye jokes.

"You're always thinking I'm making disparaging comments."

"Aren't you?"

He smirks. "Well, all the nurses are complaining about the smell."

Kaye laughs. "I'm not going home. But I could use a walk. I think I need to stretch my legs. Want to come along?" The way she asks, the way she looks at him, he can tell it's not a question. It's a plea.

"Sure, sure. Of course." He turns to look at their mother. "Think you can handle this assignment?"

She rolls her eyes, grunts, shakes her head as if in disgust that she hadn't been here to fulfill her role earlier.

"Okay," he says, looking back at Kaye. "I'm going to assume that series of prehistoric sounds was a yes. Let's go."

The hallway is quiet, rustling in the doldrums

between the breakfast hours and the beginning of lunch.

"Why's it so dark around here?" Kaye asks, waddling down the hall.

Cohen laughs. "You sound like Mom."

Kaye gives him a frown. "I'll never be that bad." She stops abruptly, puts one hand on the wall, and leans hard against it. The other hand clutches her stomach. She closes her eyes and breathes forcefully through her nose. After ten or fifteen seconds, she stands up straight, gives Cohen a look that says, "Don't ask," and keeps walking.

Cohen disregards the look. "What was that all about?"

Kaye looks at him, and he can see she's trying to decide whether or not to tell him the truth. "Cohen," she says, her voice faltering. "Cohen, I think these babies are coming."

"What?"

"I know. Bad timing, huh?" She laughs nervously.

"Have you called Brent?"

She shrugs. "I don't want to bother him unless I'm completely sure."

"But it will take him a few days to get home."

She nods. "He can't cut this trip short anyway. It's too important."

"Should we talk to your doctor? Let them know what's going on?"

"I'm going to give it a few hours and see if the contractions keep going. They'll probably fade. I'm sure they'll fade. It's far too early."

She holds her stomach and winces. They stop walking. She takes a deep breath, sighs, and looks at him apologetically.

"Fading, huh."

She smiles, forces a small laugh. "I guess so."

"Listen, Sis, Dad can hold on for you. Okay? I don't want you risking these babies."

"I'm not risking anything, Cohen. I'll be fine. I'm in a hospital." She says the last sentence with such sisterly reassurance he can hardly bear it.

"Sis."

"Co."

They get to the end of the hallway where the wall is mostly glass looking out over the city. Cohen finds it remarkable how green the city looks from that high. The streets are almost all lined with trees, so that when you're driving you see trees and buildings, but when you're up at the top of the hospital the high branches of the trees all but cover the city. It's like a forest with a few buildings poking through.

"It really is a beautiful city," Kaye says.

"Even more beautiful when Mom's not in it," Cohen said in a wry voice.

"It's nice of you to call her Mom."

Cohen laughs. "Big sis. Always finding the silver lining."

"Don't say anything, okay? About the contractions?"

"I don't need an excuse not to talk to her."

"I'll go to the doctor if they pick up."

"It's okay," he says, putting his arm around her. "It's all going to be okay. I trust you."

"Now who's being the optimist?"

They turn and start walking back toward the room.

"Seriously, though, why'd you have to bring her here?" he asks.

"She deserved to know what was going on."

"Deserved? I can think of a million things she deserves, and none of them involve being told that her long-ago husband is dying."

"We don't all get what we deserve, Cohen."

He lets that sink in. "You got me there. That was below the belt."

They walk up to the room and stand outside.

"I'm going down to the cafeteria," he says. "Would you like something?"

"You're going to have to talk to her at some point, Co. You can't pretend she doesn't exist."

"Coffee? A cookie? A candy bar for the twins?"

Kaye shakes her head and walks into the room as if the whole world is about to be born from her. He turns to go.

His mother's voice shouts from the hospital room, abrasive and terse. "I'll have a coffee. Black."

forty-seven

Back into the City

The light faded in the cave. Night came early there. Cohen stood up, pushed his way through the thick evergreen branches, and looked around the woods. Stars appeared even though the sky was not completely dark, and clouds caught the last light, bathed in it, their edges silver and shining. Cohen bent over and picked up a few pine cones, threw them absentmindedly into the forest.

He heard the sound of branches rustling apart, and he turned to see Hippie pushing her way out from under the evergreens, followed by Than. The three of them stood there for a long time, not saying anything, watching the sky grow dark.

"I wonder if my dad's looking for me," Cohen said to no one in particular.

"Do you still have the gun?" Than asked.

Hippie glanced at them with pursed lips, disappointment. Cohen nodded and patted his coat pocket.

"It gets dark around here fast," Than said. "We should go down to the tracks." He didn't hesitate but walked away with unwavering steps.

At first Hippie and Cohen stood there without

following. "I'm sorry we dragged you into this," Hippie said, her voice fragile and hesitant.

"Someone had to kill it," Cohen said before correcting himself. "Someone *has* to kill it."

"It's probably dead by now. We need to find it and make sure."

"Yeah. Probably."

But Cohen's words felt as empty as Hippie's sounded. He didn't believe the Beast was dead.

"You don't like the gun?" he asked.

She sighed. "No, not really."

"How else would you kill a Beast?"

"I don't know." She reached over and grabbed his hand. "Do you remember in the funeral home how you jumped on its back? You didn't have a gun then."

"That's true. But it almost killed us. You think the three of us could take it down on our own, without the gun?"

She looked over at him, and he felt a surge of whatever it was he had felt when he first saw her wandering through the woods with her brother. Her eyes, her skin, her mouth.

"Probably not." She sighed again, this time a sigh that sounded like a final breath. "Probably not." She let go of his hand, not in the way you drop something but in the way a boat drifts from the dock.

He followed her through the woods, down the steep hill to the tracks. They joined up with

Than and the three of them walked in single file, no one saying a word. Filling the silence far behind them, a train whistled. Above, the clouds scattered. The stars shone, those faraway stars, their light only just arriving.

It seemed too fast, but there Cohen was, staring down into the bowl-shaped valley, down at the mobile home. The darkness pooled there as if it were a liquid running to the lowest place, gathering, something they would have to wade through. The three of them moved through the blackberry brambles and Cohen wondered when they would get their leaves, when the berries would come.

They walked around to the back of the trailer and the crashing path the Beast had made through the brambles. Than took out a flashlight and looked around the trailer one last time, the beam bobbing up and down, swaying from this side to that. Cohen peered into the darkness, straining his eyes to see what might be there. The night grew cold.

"Nothing new," Than concluded, coming back over to the two of them. "Nothing's changed. You ready?"

Hippie nodded, Than aimed his flashlight at the crushed path, and they followed along.

The trail wasn't hard to follow—the Beast had obviously not been concerned about leaving evidence behind. It careened from here to there, trampling everything in its way and leaving large swathes of black, sappy shadow. Black tar. Cohen avoided it. He didn't like the coldness it put inside of him, the way he couldn't shake it off. He remembered Hippie wiping down his hands, how warm she had been.

The trail meandered more or less back the way they had come the night before, and soon they took their very first steps back onto a sidewalk. Streetlights rose ahead of them. It was late, the middle of the night, and buildings loomed like ancient outer walls.

The Beast had gone back into the city.

forty-eight
There Is a Mender

"Bless me, Father, for I have sinned."

Cohen sits comfortably in the chair. At each night's confession, he has felt more at ease. He has not looked up at the crucified Christ. He's afraid he will see the same thing he always sees.

Behind the screen, Father James is a vapor, a mist, a temporary gathering of particles that will soon move farther and farther apart, dissipating into the universe. He clears his throat. "The Lord be in your heart and mind and upon your lips, that you may truly and humbly confess your sins: In the Name of the Father, and of the Son, and of the Holy Spirit. Amen."

The chapel is silent. Outside, night has a firm hold on the city.

"Thank you, Father James."

Cohen looks closely at the screen separating them, wondering where it was made, what it's made of. There is something comforting about it being there, something necessary about having that thin barrier between them, between his confession and the person who will hear it.

"I confess to the Almighty God," Cohen says, his voice barely above a whisper, "to his Church, and to you, that I have sinned by my own fault in thought, word, and deed, in things done and left undone, but especially, again, in regards to the death of my father."

At first Father James does not speak, and the silence gathers around them like an invisible crowd pressing in for a closer look.

"I have absolved you of this sin," Father James says in an even voice. "Why do you keep confessing it?"

"My father is not dead yet. His death is ongoing, and I feel like I can't experience true absolution until after he has died. I'm sorry. I can't shake it. I know it's not proper of me to dwell on sins that have been forgiven."

"I understand, Cohen."

I understand. Cohen cannot remember the last time someone said that to him.

"You're pretty quiet back there." He tries to chuckle, managing something quite a bit less than that.

"There is no true confession without someone who is willing to listen, Cohen. A confession is a thing flung into the silence."

"Silence. Yes. I wonder about that."

In the silence, while he considers what to say next, he can smell the old carpet, the winter turning to spring, Father James's cologne or aftershave.

"Father, has God ever seemed silent to you? He

seems silent to me. Actually, this is one of my troubles. I used to believe God heard us. I used to believe he intervened."

"And now?"

"I don't know. I don't like not knowing. What do you think? But you're a priest—of course you believe."

"Being a priest is not the same thing as always believing. Yes, God is sometimes silent. God is often silent. It is into this silence that I throw myself daily, trusting there is something more waiting for me there."

"More? More than what?"

"More than what I can see. More than what I can taste, touch, hear, or smell. Something more."

"Still, it's a lonely thing, a world where God does not intervene."

"Yes. And sometimes the silence is unbearable."

Cohen sighs. "I was about fourteen years old, I think. I've managed to block it out pretty well since then. Haven't thought about it much. We never talked about it, my dad and me. Never. I never processed it. I don't think we did that kind of thing in the eighties—processed stuff. Only crazy people went to a shrink. But now with my father's death, you know, it's been coming back to me in pieces."

The chapel seems to grow smaller during his confession, as if the entire universe is pressing in for a closer look.

"What are you thinking, Father?"

The priest stirs, seems to uncross his legs and cross them again. "We are all broken, Cohen. We are all reeling from the things that have been done to us in the past or from the things we have done. We have all killed, all destroyed, all hated. There is nothing new in what you have done or what you are remembering, nothing new under the sun. This is confession: remembering and bringing something into the light so that it can be seen, held, and let go of, into the silence."

"Yes," Cohen says. "Yes."

"We cannot let go of that which we have not grabbed on to."

"Yes."

"Who or what did you kill, Cohen, when you were a boy?"

"It is the great secret of my life, Father," Cohen says, trying to figure out how to tell it.

My God, my God, why have you forsaken me? The sentence runs through his mind over and over again. He remembers Miss Flynne giving the lesson for that one, the wooden cross, the crucified Christ sticking to the flannel board, falling off, being put back on. A little girl—what was her name?—always cried at this lesson. He remembers staring at the flannel-graph Jesus, wishing he could cry.

"This girl, Ava, she was there. She's here now. She's the agent who opened the investigation into my father's death. It's like everything is converging. I feel emotionless. I feel like I'm a helpless observer forced to watch my past happen over and over again."

He stops. There is too much to tell. He knows that now.

"I don't know where to begin, Father. I don't know how to tell it. It's all tangled in my mind, some of it here, some of it there. I killed someone when I was a child, not on purpose. Not really. I didn't know what I was doing. This person, they deserved it, if that's possible. And I'm angry at my father for never talking to me about it. It's the one thing he could have done for me when I was young. He could have listened. He could have asked how I was. But he didn't. And now he never will."

Father James sits rigid, listening. Cohen does not know what else to say. He stumbles into the rest of the confession.

"For these and all other sins which I cannot now remember," Cohen says, and there is an ache in his voice, a sadness at the thought that he might never be able to tell it, might never be able to confess the right way. "I am truly sorry. I pray God to have mercy on me. I firmly intend amendment of life, and I humbly beg forgiveness of God and his Church, and ask you for counsel, direction, and absolution."

"I will speak with my fellow priests in this

parish to determine if I should take any further action, but Cohen . . ." There is compassion in Father James's voice, and sadness. "We are all broken. Hope remains. There is a Mender."

Cohen stares down at the floor. He wishes he could believe that, even if only for a short time.

"Our Lord Jesus Christ who has left power to his Church to absolve all sinners who truly repent and believe in him, of his great mercy forgive you all your offenses; and by his authority committed to me, I absolve you from all your sins: In the Name of the Father, and of the Son, and of the Holy Spirit. Amen."

"Amen," Cohen says.

"The Lord has put away all your sins," the priest says.

"Thanks be to God."

"Go in peace, and pray for me, a sinner."

PART FOUR

Thursday,
March 19, 2015

*To divide the light
from the darkness . . .*

Genesis 1:18

forty-nine
Followed through the Dark

Cohen walks out of the chapel a few minutes after midnight on Thursday. Could it be Thursday already? Could it be he came to the hospital on Monday afternoon, that his father is still alive, that Ava has returned, that he has seen his mother, that his sister will give birth to twins at any moment? So many things that were incomprehensible only four days before are now spinning his reality into something he can barely recognize.

Confession has left him feeling both lighter and sadder. It's as if some invisible weight has been lifted, but now that it's gone he misses it. Perhaps it was the chat he had with Father James about the absence of God. He's not sure. He's been thinking those things for a long time—months? years?—but this is the first time he's ever spoken them. Speaking them felt right.

He has the strange sense he's being followed. But Duke Street is the same as it has been on nearly every late-night walk he's taken that week—the streetlights are still, the sidewalks cracked, the air some fresh mix of far-off cigarette smoke, exhaust, and trees moving into this new spring. The sky is as unobservable as ever, lost above the light pollution. The hospital rises a few blocks ahead, the randomly lit windows a modern constellation.

He looks behind him, stops, and listens for footsteps. He turns at the last minute and takes a few quick steps down a narrow alley that's belching steam from someone's boiler exhaust. Standing in the quiet darkness and waiting to see if his tail will make themselves known, he wonders if this is what it feels like to be a private investigator, or a criminal. He remembers ducking down an alley like this one so long ago, tracking the Beast.

First there's a shadow sliding along the pavement. The sound comes next, someone with a light walk, someone quick. He sees a young man with a ball cap.

"Thatcher?"

Thatcher jumps as though he's been shot. "Oh, man! Mr. Cohen! You scared me to death! What are you doing?"

"What are *you* doing?"

"I was trying to catch up to you." Thatcher ducks his head, clearly embarrassed. "I followed you to the church."

"You what?"

"I know. I was bored and curious. I stayed back pretty far, and when you went inside, I sat on the street around the corner. I was going to say something when you came out, but I fell asleep."

Cohen laughs and shakes his head. Thatcher grins.

"How's your grandpa?"

"Not good. Actually, my dad came back—that's why I was kind of itching to get out of there. But they don't think Grandpa'll make it through the night."

"I'm sorry."

Thatcher shrugs, doesn't say anything. His mouth quivers and he clears his throat to chase off the emotion. "What about your dad?"

"Same, I guess. My sister still doesn't want to take him off life support."

"Is there a chance he'll come back?"

"I don't know, Thatcher. I really don't know. It doesn't seem that way."

The two of them go the rest of the way without speaking, Cohen thinking about death, its approach, the losses to come.

The sound is the first thing Cohen notices.

It's like a roar that goes on and on, a roar and a sob and a cry all in one, and at first Cohen thinks it's coming from his father's room. The first thought he has is that his father has come out of his coma and is in terrible, unrestrained pain. He knows how silly this is even before he arrives at his father's barely opened door and looks inside. The room is dark. His mother is asleep in one of the armchairs, looking as prim and in control as she does when she's awake.

His sister is standing at the window, staring into the night.

He moves to speak to her but the roar erupts again, and now he realizes it's coming from Thatcher's grandfather's room. Thatcher has already gone in and walked around the bed, and he's standing at his grandfather's side, crying softly. The roar fades. There is a moment of silence, the kind that drapes over most nighttime hospitals, and then the sound comes rushing back.

It's coming from Thatcher's father. He's on his knees at the foot of the bed, wearing jeans and a flannel shirt, the sleeves rolled up. His ball cap is crumpled in his hands, which are covering his face. His mouth, even in between cries, remains open, saliva escaping in long threads like sap oozing from a tree.

"Ahhhhhhhhhh!" he cries again, bending further under the weight of his anguish. There's a nurse at the grandfather's bedside and a nurse behind the father, appearing unsure of what to do. Two more nurses, drawn by the awful shout, nudge Cohen aside and enter the room. A doctor follows.

One of the nurses, the one beside the bed, uses her stethoscope to check for a heartbeat, listening at his wrist, his chest, here and here. She bends down close and listens at the grandfather's open mouth. She straightens, looks at the man as if saying farewell, makes eye contact with the nurse standing behind Thatcher's father, and shakes her head, a subtle back-and-forth.

"I'm sorry, young man," she says quietly to Thatcher. "Your grandfather has died."

Thatcher nods through tears that fall faster than he can wipe them away. His father begins another roar, but this one—whether due to exhaustion or a lost voice or despair—reaches only the volume of a loud moan. Thatcher looks up at Cohen still standing in the doorway and tries to grin, perhaps to let Cohen know everything will be okay, but it rises lopsided and choked.

The nurses leave one at a time, and Cohen senses their relief. Thatcher's father radiates an aura of anger and pain. Who knows what this man will do now that the full weight of grief has been lowered on him? Cohen would walk over to Thatcher, except he would have to step over the back of the man's legs, and it's not something he wants to do. He wants to keep his distance.

The doctor has somehow managed to remain mostly invisible in the corner, holding a clipboard to his chest—the same doctor Thatcher's father had charged with killing the old man. He seems smaller somehow, as if all of his authority has been stripped. He seems like a child waiting for discipline to be meted out.

The doctor starts speaking multiple times, and each attempt ends before a sound comes out of his mouth. He adjusts his glasses. Finally he speaks.

"Mr. Nash, I'm very sorry for your loss."

He takes a step toward Thatcher's father. Cohen wishes the doctor would walk out. He is willing him to do it, to leave. The air is full of charged molecules waiting to explode, threatening to combust at a wrong word, a sudden move.

Cohen thinks of leaving, only to glance at Thatcher's face. It's for Thatcher that he stays.

"Mr. Nash," the doctor says quietly, "is there anything I can do for you? Anything at all?"

He takes a few more steps so that now he stands beside the grandfather, looking down at Mr. Nash. If someone were to walk in without knowing the situation, they would think Mr. Nash is begging the doctor for forgiveness.

Please get out, Cohen thinks. The words *while you can* also come to mind.

Mr. Nash lifts his head slowly. "For my loss?"

His eyes are so full of hate that Cohen glances quickly at the doctor, expecting to find him dead, or at least mortally injured. But he's unhurt, if frozen in place.

"You," Mr. Nash says. "For my loss?"

The doctor stammers.

Thatcher's father breathes faster. "You are dead to me."

The words "to me" come out so quietly that at

first they don't register with Cohen. At first he thinks the man has simply said, "You are dead."

The doctor nods, a strange signal of assent in the face of those piercing words. He takes an unsteady step toward the wall, as if he's lost, as if he cannot find the door. Or perhaps he also only heard, "You are dead." He grabs the door handle and walks out, leaving the room behind.

The presence of death is strong after the doctor leaves, lingering in the corners, hovering below the ceiling. Cohen feels that rush he always does in its presence: first the rush of the funeral director to do what must be done before time beats him to it, but then the rush of awareness at his own mortality. Someday that will be his body lying there, still, no longer breathing, growing cold. Someday. And where will he be?

His body will still be there, but where will he be?

Without thinking, he moves into the room, ignoring the questioning glare of Mr. Nash, steps behind him, and walks around to the other side of the bed. Thatcher glances up at him, and Cohen puts his arm around the young man who now looks more like a boy. He squeezes his shoulder. The two of them stand there staring down at Thatcher's grandfather.

He is a handsome man even in death. He's large but not overweight, sturdy from a lifetime spent in open fields. His fingers are thick, his hands coated in cracked calluses. His fingernails are broken, fractured, and cover bruised fingers. He has a gash on the back of his left hand, the shape of a scythe's blade, deep red. The man's face is kind and at peace. His white hair congregates in three main tufts: one on each side and one at the top. His false teeth have been taken out, so his mouth is shrunken and powerless.

"Who are you?" Mr. Nash asks, barely opening his mouth with each word.

"Cohen. Cohen Marah."

"What are you doing here?"

"I'm a friend of your son. My father is in the next room."

For a moment Mr. Nash thinks about softening. Cohen sees it, the consideration of retreat, the closing of the mouth, the unfamiliar practice of thinking before speaking. Perhaps he thinks of Cohen as an unlikely ally, someone who can join him on the side of the patients in their war against the medical field.

When Mr. Nash seems to think of no immediate reason to be angry at Cohen, he turns back to Thatcher. "Where were you, boy?" he asks, blame in his voice.

Thatcher looks up, surprised. He doesn't say anything.

"Don't look at me like that. Where were you?" The anger is rising, and Cohen knows it's anger at the doctor and at death and at a life that slips through our fingers so smoothly without leaving a trace. But none of those things are present or tangible—not the doctor, not death, not life—so Mr. Nash's anger latches on to Thatcher.

"I was out," Thatcher says, and he has hardened too, in the way a young man will harden when struck too many times. All of his softness has evaporated.

"Out where?" Mr. Nash comes around the bed, now having to peer around Cohen to lock eyes with Thatcher. Without realizing it at first, Cohen has pulled Thatcher closer to his side.

"Out," Thatcher says.

"With him?"

"No."

"Then with who?"

"No one. By myself."

Cohen closes his eyes. For a moment he is a child again and Mr. Nash is the Beast, its hot breath on his neck, its icy shadows clinging to his shoulder and to his hands and knees from where he crawled through the trailer. He feels a strange courage rising in him, something that does not reflect his normal middle-aged complacency. He slowly begins releasing Thatcher. His heart races and a thudding resounds in his throat, his rib cage, the tips of his clenched fists. He opens his eyes.

Mr. Nash is gone. Thatcher stands there, staring up at him.

"Where'd your father go?"

"Out. I don't know."

"Any sign of your mother?"

Thatcher's face crumples. He glances back at his grandfather's body and shakes his head.

fifty
You Don't Know Us

As they walked into the city at night, trailing the Beast for the final time, it began to snow. At first the flakes were light, the weight and consistency of fine ash, but as they walked into the city and the night passed, the flakes became thicker, falling like the particles in a snow globe, swirling and difficult to see through. The roads remained wet, not allowing the snow to accumulate, but it created a white coating everywhere else. It lay gently on Cohen's shoulders and head and didn't quite melt, forming an icy skin.

"Isn't this splendid?" Than muttered, constantly brushing the ice from his shoulders.

Hippie didn't seem to be affected. She never was. She continued walking, and for a little while she took the lead, putting some distance between herself and the two boys.

Cohen watched her walk. There was something of a cat about her movement: smooth, graceful, and balanced. But she was also on the prowl, looking here and there, touching every tree she passed, searching for the shadow sign left behind by the Beast. He was amazed again at the translucence of her skin, the artistic curve of her fingers, the shape of her.

"Don't even think about it," Than said with a harsh laugh.

"What do you mean?"

"You know what I mean. Don't even think about it."

Cohen paused, giving in to the fact that Than knew what he was thinking. "Why?" He watched as Hippie approached a dark alley.

"Why? Why?" Than parroted the sound of Cohen's voice, darting his arm out and holding it up like a security measure, stopping both of them. He stared at Cohen with a confused look. "You don't know anything about us. Not one thing."

"I know your names," Cohen said, taken aback, scrambling to think of all he knew about the two.

Than shook his head.

"Those aren't your names?"

"Yes, they're our names," he said as if Cohen had completely missed the point.

"So what's . . ."

"Anyone can tell you their name. That doesn't mean you know the first thing about them."

Cohen glanced nervously up the street at Hippie. She was at the dark alley. She stopped and looked into its shadowy depths.

"So, who are you?" Cohen asked, accusation in his voice. "If I don't know anything, tell me."

A seriousness descended on Than, a kind of thoughtful weight, and when he spoke Cohen couldn't tell if Than was talking to him or to himself.

Than lowered his arm, took a step back, and leaned against a telephone pole. "I can't lie to you. But I can't tell you everything."

"What are you talking about?"

"Ask me. What do you want to know about us?"

"I don't know. Where do you live? And don't say in that cave."

Than shrugged. "It's dry. Usually warm. We used to live in that trailer, until the Beast burned it down."

"Parents?"

"No mom." He paused.

"And your dad?" Cohen asked.

Than twisted his mouth to the side as if he wasn't sure how to answer, as if the answer was a riddle. "Yes," he said slowly. "And no."

"Whatever. This is pointless." Cohen turned to walk away, but Than grabbed his shoulder.

"You don't know us," he said, glancing up the street to where Hippie was taking a piece of paper down from a light post.

"Whatever," Cohen said again.

Hippie interrupted them. "Guys. You should see this."

Cohen trotted up to where she stood in the

shadow of the alley, glad to put some space, even temporarily, between him and Than. Still, they both arrived at about the same time and looked at what Hippie had in her hands. A siren sounded somewhere in the distance.

It was a photocopied picture of Cohen, growing wet as snowflakes rested on it and melted. Above it was the word "MISSING." Below it was the phone number for the police and the funeral home.

The handwriting looked like Ava's.

fifty-one
Waking Up

Cohen goes back to his father's room. The lights are out, and it's in the middle of those morning hours when two a.m. turns to three a.m. turns to four a.m. His mother is still sleeping in the chair, back straight, mouth a flat line. His sister has fallen back to sleep as well, lying on the hard floor with various cushions and pillows tucked around her, supporting her neck and sagging stomach. He notices a boy in the corner.

His nephew sleeps in his baseball uniform. Cohen must have missed him when he peeked in earlier. His baseball cleats sit beside him, he uses his glove as a pillow, and one of the thin hospital blankets is twisted around him like a toga. His baseball hat is half on, half off, turned slightly to the side. His eyelids flicker, a dream passing.

Cohen realizes he has become callous to the situation. Maybe it's because of the strained relationship he's had with his father. Maybe it's the endlessly repetitive nature of days spent in the hospital, days blurring in on each other, days and nights that seem not to move forward but round and round, one leaving, one arriving, always through the same revolving door.

Maybe it's because he's a funeral director and death is an everyday occurrence. But Cohen feels numb.

An empty chair receives him. He sinks into it as far as it's possible to sink into a shallow wooden chair with thin cushions. He wedges his elbow between the armrest and the wall, braces his head against the palm of his hand. The last things he sees before sleep takes him are the swirling prints and deep wrinkles in his palm, wrinkles that will only get deeper and longer until someday he is lying there in the bed.

Even in his sleep, Cohen senses the hospital waking around him. The sky brightens before the sun can lift up over the city. Kaye and Cohen and their mother wake without speaking, everyone staring at Calvin.

Time has stopped. Johnny sleeps on. The city wakes. The nurses come and go and still everyone in the room remains unchanged. Cohen wonders what it will take to rouse them from that strange stupor.

"I think it's time," Kaye says without moving from the floor, without moving anything but her mouth, which Cohen cannot see from where he sits. Her pronouncement might as well have come from someone outside the room.

"Certainly," his mother says. "Certainly. Past time."

Cohen takes in a deep breath and savors it as he

exhales. This air. This breath. "When did Johnny come in?"

"I told the sitter to bring him. She's been so good to us, but she needed a break. I could tell when we spoke on the phone. So he had a game and then he came in."

"A game? In this weather?"

Kaye doesn't reply.

"I think you're right," Cohen says. "It's time. I'll tell the doctor."

Kaye rises with monumental effort. The pillows fall away from her. As she straightens, she stops, grabbing her stomach with both hands. She turns gingerly away from their mother, and Cohen can tell she's trying to hide the contraction.

"Are you having a contraction?" their mother asks.

"No. It's only indigestion, Mom."

"Indigestion?" She sounds offended at the idea that one of her children would suffer from a weakness like indigestion.

"Yes."

"Are you sure? What have you been eating? You've never been a good eater."

Kaye breathes out through pursed lips, closes her eyes. The contraction passes. She opens her eyes, turns to her mother. "I think I know the difference between contractions and indigestion," she says.

"I'm rather sure you do," her mother says with

suspicion in her eyes and a charge of impropriety in her tone. But she is not able to follow that scent any further because at that precise moment the door opens.

Dr. Stevens enters. "Good morning," he says, and Cohen wonders what it's like to monitor so closely the mortality of strangers, to watch as death gathers them up, sometimes slowly, stretched out over days or weeks, and sometimes in a moment, before anyone can catch their breath.

Cohen yawns and stands up, Kaye nods her head, and their mother replies, "Good morning to you, Doctor." She communicates simultaneously a deep respect and a profound mistrust.

The doctor doesn't take his hands out of his deep pockets. He doesn't move to look at his clipboard, the one tucked up under his arm. It seems there is nothing more to check, to monitor, to hope for.

"Have you come to any decisions?" he asks, sympathy heavy on his face.

"Yes," Cohen says, glancing at Kaye and his mother. Johnny stirs on the floor behind him. "It's time."

"So, you're ready to remove life support?"

Cohen nods, and the nod feels monumental to him, as if he has nodded to the man holding the lever to release the platform under the gallows. The doctor looks from Cohen to Kaye. She nods, wiping her eyes.

"I'll have some paperwork for you to fill out," Dr. Stevens says. "I'll stop by in an hour. In the meantime, don't forget to take care of yourselves. Have some coffee. Eat some breakfast. Okay?" He pauses. "You're making the right decision. There's nothing more to be done here. Your father is at peace, and his body is ready."

The three of them sit, frozen in place. Their mother picks absently at an imperfection in the chair. Kaye holds her face like the character in the painting *The Scream*, but her mouth is not open. The weight of her hands pulls downs on her cheeks.

"Thank you, Doctor," Cohen says in a hoarse voice. He clears his throat. "Thank you. We'll be here."

Outside the window, the sun rises above the city, a brightness that feels like a deliberate offense to what is happening in the room. It glares off the wispy clouds that are simultaneously winter and spring. Cohen walks to the window and pulls down the blind.

fifty-two

Run

Cohen took the "Missing" flyer from Hippie's hands. It had been nearly thirty-six hours since they had tracked the Beast from the funeral home. The poster was wet through, wilted by the still-falling snow. He balled it up into a tight sphere and stuffed it in his pocket where it bulged, a lump against his thigh. He thought of his father. He wondered if he was out looking for him, or if the despair of a lost son had driven him further into a drunken stupor.

Cohen thought of Ava too, wondered at her friendship, the constancy of it, the persistence. He had been so obsessed with Hippie and Than that he had been avoiding her, not returning her calls. But she was still out there. She might have been the last person on earth looking for him, concerned with his whereabouts.

The siren whined louder, and the three of them stepped into the shadow of the alley, waiting for it to pass. A police car screamed by, its flashing lights pushing back the dark, but only for a moment. In a flash it was gone, and the darkness washed back over everything, thicker than before.

Hippie pulled her hand away from the brick

wall of the house lining the alley, raised it into the slanting light they had withdrawn from. Her fingers were coated in black, and with her other hand she gripped her wrist. The look on her face was pure anguish.

"Are you okay?" Cohen asked.

She grimaced, bent over at the waist, still clinging to her wrist. She moaned, and it was a low, mournful sound, like an animal giving birth. Something was wrong.

"Hippie?" Than asked, moving closer. "What's up?"

"It's different," she said, the words barely emerging. She wrenched her torso around, twisting as if that was the only thing keeping her from crying out.

"The Beast's shadow?" Than pressed.

She nodded without speaking, not looking at them, not wanting them to see the mounting pain on her face.

A sense of panic rose up in Cohen. He paced out onto the sidewalk, back again, out, back. "What are we going to do?"

"I don't know," Than said in a grim voice, holding up Hippie's hand to peer at it.

She moaned again when he moved it, pulling away. "Than, careful," she whispered. "I think I have to sit down."

Another police car flew past them, siren on, lights flashing.

"What is going on?" Cohen asked no one in particular. "When it was on me before, it was cold, it hurt, but not like this."

A flash of light caught his attention and he looked up at a second-story window in a house across the street. An old woman had pulled back the curtain and looked down at them. She had a round face and her gray hair radiated out around her head like a wiry halo. When she saw Cohen looking up at her, her eyes went wide and she threw the curtain closed.

"I think we should go," he said.

Than muttered something.

"I can't, I . . . don't . . ." Hippie gasped when she spoke, unable to get a full sentence out.

"Why is this happening?" Cohen aimed his confusion at Than, demanding answers.

Than shook his head. "Something about the Beast has changed. Maybe it's dying and its shadow is more powerful. Maybe . . ." He paused. "Maybe Hippie is more vulnerable. I don't know. It's like acid on her."

"We have to wash it off," Cohen said.

They left her there at the edge of the light, and she seemed to be losing her mind. She sat down and moaned and rocked back and forth, side to side, as if the movement kept the worst of the pain at bay. Both scoured the alley for something, anything they could use. Cohen found an empty five-gallon paint bucket. He tripped over it before he saw it, sending it clattering through the alley, its metal handle pinging against the sidewalk.

"There's a faucet back here," Than said. They turned on the water and it came out ice-cold. The bucket filled slowly, the water gurgling and rushing. It had a crack in the bottom, and the water leaked out almost as fast as they could fill it.

"That's good," Than said when the bucket was only half full. He carried it to the edge of the alley, water slipping through the bottom, and set it down beside Hippie, raising her to her knees. When Hippie lifted her hand, the one that had been covered in the shadow, Than paused. Her skin seemed wilted under the tar, as if it had eaten its way inside and corroded her flesh.

When Cohen realized Than was frozen in place, he crept forward, reached out, and took her blackened hand in his own. "Here," he whispered. "I'll do it."

He rested the top of her wrist on the edge of the bucket so that her palm faced upward. He had to coax her fist open—at first it was clenched in pain, and as he slipped his thumb under her fingers and gently eased them back, Hippie clenched her teeth and screamed through her closed mouth.

"It's okay," Cohen whispered over and over again. He reached down into the icy water, drew out as much as he could with one cupped hand,

and let it drip down. He touched the tar. It sent needles of cold into his own hand, but he kept rubbing and rinsing and scrubbing.

Soon Hippie went limp, her back against the brick wall. She had passed out. Than sat beside her, propping her up. The water in the bucket was gone, so Cohen went back and refilled it. When he returned, he continued cleaning her hand, whispering the entire time. "It's okay. It's okay."

In some places on her hand, like the wrinkles at the base of her fingers and the bent sections of her knuckles, he had to use his fingernail to peel back the Beast's sludge from her skin. This scraping seemed to disturb her even deep in that unconscious state, and she gave a heavy, hoarse sigh, her head listing from one side to the other. After what seemed like a very long time, he had removed almost all of it.

What remained in him were questions. Why this effect, when before Hippie had seemed immune to the Beast's residue? And what if she accidentally bumped against more of it? How would she survive?

More sirens. Police cars approached. This time there were three of them. They stopped directly in front of the alley, parked in the opposite lane of the one-way street. Than and Cohen watched, trying not to move, as the three officers crawled out of their patrol cars and walked to one of the doors across the street. Two of them stood back as the third knocked loudly, a thudding they could hear where they sat. Any sound they made seemed suddenly amplified. Everything else on the street was silent except the police officer knocking on the door and the beating of their own hearts and the raspy breath of Hippie regaining consciousness.

The police officer waited. He peered through the glass and knocked again, even louder this time. The other two officers turned and looked up and down the street. They seemed bored, preoccupied, looking for something out of order. The police officer raised his hand to knock again, stopped, peered through the glass, and took a half step back. The door opened.

Cohen looked closer. It was the woman from the window, the one who had looked down at them and thrown the curtain shut.

"We should go," Cohen said.

"Why?" Than asked. Hippie stirred.

"C'mon," Cohen hissed, rising carefully. "That woman saw me in the alley. I think she called the police on us." He felt the grit of the bricks scrape the back of his coat as he pushed himself up. He tried to get farther back into the shadows.

The woman was nodding to the police. One of the officers took out a small notebook and scribbled some things. The woman pointed across the street to the alley where they sat.

Than grabbed Hippie's face between his hands.

"Hippie," he said. "Hippie, get up. Wake up. We have to move, now."

She tried to open her eyes, but her lids seemed to weigh a million pounds. Cohen saw the whites of her eyes, two crescent moons. They closed, she shook her head, and her body went limp again.

Cohen bent over and put his arm under her back. "Help me."

Than came in close, and they picked Hippie up, arranged her so that she was between them with one arm around each of them, and started waddling down the narrow alley, her feet dragging beneath her. They got to the back alley and Cohen looked over his shoulder. The three police officers had left the woman at her front door—she peered curiously into the night, craning her neck. They were coming across the empty street, walking toward the alley, and three flashlight beams winked on.

Cohen and Than dragged Hippie across the narrow street that separated the backs of the houses and farther into the alley, over a grate, past a telephone pole, and into the shadows behind a dumpster.

A burst of cold air swept through the city. The police officers came deliberately through the shadows.

"C'mon, c'mon, c'mon," Cohen hissed.

Hippie started reviving. Her feet weren't dragging anymore. She was walking, albeit with their help. They made it out the other side, all the way to the neighboring street. They turned right and walked quickly, still helping Hippie along.

"Hey!" a voice shouted. "Wait!"

Cohen looked back. One of the police officers had come out of the alley, now a block behind them. He motioned for the other two to hurry, and the three of them started jogging lightly in and out of the streetlights. Darkness, light, darkness, light. Their shoes made thudding sounds on the sidewalk. They had not turned off their flashlights, and they made glancing, stabbing beams that bobbed against the houses and the street and the sky.

"Run," Cohen said calmly.

fifty-three

Singing

The nurse moves like a spirit, without touching anything, without making a sound, so that Cohen doesn't realize she's there until he sees Kaye sit up straight in her chair. She does that when people come into the room, even though it makes her uncomfortable. She doesn't last long in the chair, so she stands and walks loops around the room, circling past the window that looks out over the bright afternoon, out over the city. She steps gently over Johnny, who has been sleeping off and on. She passes Cohen and arrives at the foot of the bed where their mother has been sitting all these long hours. Kaye rests her hand on her mother's shoulder.

"How are you?" Kaye asks the nurse.

The nurse gives her a kind smile, and immediately Cohen thinks she has lost someone recently. He can always tell. Maybe it's from his job, but he can always see it in the eyes. There is something calm there, something placid, as if a great disturbance has passed by but now the surface has regained its balance and is even more calm for the trouble it has gone through.

"Good morning," the nurse says. She wears

tan slacks and a white collared shirt. Her graying brown hair is pixie short, and her dark eyes are full and round. "I know you've signed all the paperwork, but I'd like to talk you through what I'm doing, if that's okay?"

Kaye nods, her hand fleeting once again to cover her mouth. Cohen swallows hard. Their mother sits up, an almost imperceptible straightening.

"First I'm going to remove your father's breathing tube. This will disconnect him from the ventilator and alleviate any discomfort the tube may be causing him."

Cohen stares at his father, at his chest rising and falling, lifting the sheet and lowering it. It's a movement so predictable, so monotonous, that it seems like it could go on and on into eternity. Cohen remembers coming into the living room late on a Saturday afternoon when he was a child, before his parents divorced, before everything that happened. His father was asleep on the sofa, his fingers still green from cleaning out the lawn mower, shards of grass clinging to his scalp, his ears. He was wearing a white T-shirt and dirty jeans, and his socks were on the floor beside him. His bare feet were a ghostly white. Cohen had stood beside his father for a long time, watching his chest rise and fall.

"Will he stop . . . breathing?" Kaye whispers from behind her hand, as if she does not want her mother to hear the question.

"He might," the nurse explains in a kind voice. "Or he may go on breathing for some time."

Kaye nods a jerky okay, wipes a lone tear from her cheek. It leaves a wet mark, a glistening smudge. Cohen covers the distance between them, reaches up, and wipes away the remnants of her tear. Kaye puts her hand on his shoulder, gives him a half smile, and looks down at their mother sitting in front of them.

That's when he hears it: music. Is it singing? Is it coming from the television? He looks over his shoulder, but the TV is off. He looks around the ceiling for speakers but doesn't see any. He realizes his mother is singing softly to herself, barely moving her mouth. He turns his head so that his face is toward Kaye and his ear is closer to his mother. What is she singing?

"While we walk the pilgrim pathway
Clouds will overspread the sky,
But when traveling days are over
Not a shadow, not a sigh.

"When we all get to heaven,
What a day of rejoicing that will be!
When we all see Jesus,
We'll sing and shout the victory."

Kaye looks over at him and they lock eyes. He mouths a question silently. "Do you hear her?"

Kaye leans closer, nods, smiles, more tears rising.

"Okay," the nurse says. "Your father is disconnected from the ventilator."

Kaye's glance changes quickly to panic. "He is?"

"Yes."

Cohen and Kaye move as close as they can to their father. This is it. This is the end.

Seconds go by. Minutes pass.

"Is he still breathing?" Kaye asks.

The nurse bends down close to Calvin, placing one hand on his chest. She turns her ear so that it's only inches from his mouth. "He is still breathing, yes, and he doesn't seem to be labored by it."

Kaye looks at Cohen. He smiles and nods at her.

"I'm also going to remove his feeding tube." When the nurse says this, Cohen's mother's voice seems to go up a level in volume. Barely noticeable, but louder.

"I know this has been a difficult decision for you," the nurse says quietly, her hands busy. "But it won't put your father in any pain. Often, receiving food in your last days or hours can only cause more discomfort."

"We are dead to the world and its
    pleasure,

357

Our affections are centered above,
Where we own such a wonderful
  treasure,
'Tis a home in the city of love."

Cohen clears his throat gently and looks at
Kaye, hoping she'll say something to their
mother, maybe ask her to quiet down a bit. He
knows she won't listen to him. But Kaye is
staring at their father, lost, somewhere else.

"When we get home we'll shout and
  sing
The praises of our Redeemer and King,
And make the heavenly arches ring
With the songs of home, sweet home."

Cohen glances at the nurse, embarrassed that
she might hear. He puts his hand on his mother's
shoulder, hoping to stir her out of her singing
reverie, but when his fingers find the soft fabric
of her shirt, a pulse of memory and sadness
works its way through him. He can feel her
slender collarbone, the hollow in the cleft of it.
She is fragile. He has never realized this about his
mother before, never once seen her as anything
besides steel and iron and cold, hard rock.

And then, as he becomes more and more
conscious of the feel of his mother's clavicle
under the pads of his fingers, another realization

comes. She will die. Her stony countenance will fade into a placid resignation. And it will be only him and Kaye.

He is not a middle-aged man anymore, not in that moment—he is a little boy comforting his mom. His hand, which he first lifted to chide her, remains there, and instead of embarrassment at her singing, he feels a certain acceptance, as if for the first time in many years she is giving him a gift he has the ability to accept.

"Yes, we'll gather at the river,
The beautiful, the beautiful river;
Gather with the saints at the river
That flows by the throne of God."

fifty-four
Back to Where It Started

"Stop right where you are!" the police officer shouted, and in that moment, in that precise moment, as the night looked down on them and no one came outside and no one drove by, fourteen-year-old Cohen remembered he still had the gun in his coat. Instinctively he found the flapping slit of his pocket and reached inside. He and Than ran with Hippie laboring on between them. Clouds rolled in from the southwest, swallowing the moon and taking on a threaded silver lining.

"Stop!" the police officer yelled again, and this time, for some unknown reason, Cohen stopped. Both of his hands went into his coat pockets. He could feel the smooth, cold metal of the handgun, out of place in a world with so many rough edges. The trigger was there too, though he didn't let his finger remain on it. He was afraid of what might happen if he did.

Than and Hippie's running petered out when they realized Cohen had stopped. Than bent over, breathing heavily. Hippie fell to the ground and sat, drawing her knees up to her chest, resting her forehead on them. Cohen wasn't sure, but he thought she might be crying.

"Put your hands where I can see them!" the police officer shouted. His voice seemed to be the only thing on the street, the only sound in the world.

Cohen watched as Than rotated with slow steps, still bent at the waist, still gasping for breath. Hippie slid around on her backside until she faced the police officers. She was holding her hand again, as if the pain hadn't completely gone away.

Cohen was about to turn around, was practically in the act, when he stopped. He saw something on the ground.

"I said, put your hands where I can see them!"

There. Between Than and Hippie. He had missed it at first because he thought it was a shadow on the sidewalk, but he could tell it wasn't. It was a mark left behind by the Beast. This was its trail. This was where it had gone.

He glanced at Than. They made eye contact. Cohen looked quickly at the shadow-trail, and Than's glance followed. Hippie did not look up. Her forehead stayed on her knees.

Cohen glanced over his shoulder, surprised at many things. The police officers stood much farther away than he had originally thought, nearly a block behind. They pointed their weapons at him and Than and Hippie. He was surprised to see that some neighbors had woken up and come out onto their porches, and now they stood there, watching. Snow started falling from the clouds that had eaten the moon, a snow that first fell lazy and meandering, spaced so far apart.

That's when the storm blew in. Thick snow swirled on a north wind, blowing the blizzard into the faces of the police officers. The one in front, the one who had done the shouting, hid his face in the crook of his hand and yelled something, but Cohen couldn't understand it.

"I think we should run," Than shouted through the storm. Hippie stood to her feet.

"Okay," Cohen said. He could barely see the officers through the falling snow, but they seemed to be walking closer.

"Ready, Hippie?" Than asked. "On three. One. Two. Three."

They ran, the shouts of the police officers following them, faint and ineffective in the wind and the snow. Cohen overtook Than and Hippie and led the way, darting down a side alley, nearly slipping on a wide, deep puddle of black. He slowed for a moment, staring. It was the Beast's shadow-trail. He kept running. He didn't look back.

They came to a wide street. The wind was stronger there in the open, and the snow stung his face. Hippie was behind him somewhere.

"Hippie!" Cohen shouted into the storm, but the wind swallowed his voice. Then he saw her.

She stopped, disoriented, weak, her arms hanging limp at her sides. He could tell she was about to sit again. He ran back, grabbed her arm, and dragged her along. The three of them walked forward together, slowly, through the blizzard.

All the running, the turning back on their own trail, the cutting through alleys, the low visibility, had turned Cohen around and left him confused as to exactly where in the city they were. But in a moment, when the storm slowed and there were spaces between the snow, he looked up ahead and recognized the street. It was Duke. They were coming up on the funeral home, back to where it had all started. And as they drew closer, he saw smears of black tar on the glass doors.

"You said it was probably dead by now," Cohen said quietly. There was no anger in his voice, no bitterness or blame. He looked at Than. Than nodded, a weary gesture. The two looked at Hippie. She blinked, and her eyes stayed closed for a moment.

There was nothing else to say. The three of them pushed open the doors and walked into the funeral home, their own shadows melting into the darkness.

fifty-five
Who Will Make It through the Night?

"Is she still singing?" Cohen asks Kaye as she joins him in the cafeteria.

She nods. He looks through the floor-to-ceiling windows, the ones that look out onto Duke Street, and notices the sky is growing dark yet again. The moon is off to the north in sharp relief, barely visible, tangled up in the sycamore branches. The days keep coming and going, the earth keeps spinning.

"What day is it, anyway?" he asks, taking a bite of an apple, staring into his coffee.

Kaye laughs. "Good question. I can only remember the days because of Johnny's schedule. Today he had practice, which means it's . . . Thursday night, I think?"

"Sounds about right. What are you eating?"

"I think it's oatmeal," she says, laughing again in a light voice.

"What's she singing now?" Cohen asks.

Kaye takes a bite of oatmeal, her mouth taking its time with the food, her eyes staring absently at the table. "What isn't she singing? That's the question. 'Amazing Grace.' 'How Great Thou Art.' 'Great Is Thy Faithfulness.' "

"The classics."

"I guess so. But also hymns I never heard before, songs I never knew existed."

"It's amazing she remembers it all," Cohen remarks. "She's never been back to church, has she?"

"We went a few times, you know, after we left. But since then? Not that I know of. I think she would have told me. But a lot of those hymns, as soon as she starts singing, I remember the words too."

"Yeah, me too."

"Do you sing them at Saint Thomas?"

"Not most of them. They're a different set of hymns, a different history. That stuff she's singing, it comes straight from that old church, when Dad was preaching fire and brimstone."

"The sermons Mother wrote for him," Kaye says.

"The sermons Mother wrote for him," Cohen repeats. His words bear the weight of an echo, the way things shouted into a mountain come back to you deeper, slower. He sips his coffee, considers his next sentence. "Honestly? I think it sounds kind of nice."

Kaye looks at him in surprise. "You do?"

He nods, takes another sip.

"Me too," she says.

"Don't tell her I said so." He laughs quietly. "And Dad?"

Kaye looks up at him as if he has charged her with something. Talk of him seems to make her nervous. "Dad?"

"Is he"—Cohen pauses—"still breathing?"

She nods, and Cohen thinks about his own breathing, becomes acutely aware of the movement of his rib cage, the expanding, the contracting, the feel of air moving in and out of him, the coolness of it on the back of his throat, the warmth of it going out. He wonders what it will be like when that stops.

"Have they said anything?"

"Who?"

"The doctors. The nurses."

"About him dying?" Kaye asks with unusual directness.

"Yeah."

"No. Without food and water, without the ventilator, they said he probably won't last the night."

The night, Cohen thinks. *The night.* Making it through the night seems to be the goal of everyone there. Make it through the night. See another sunrise. Watch all the light from those distant stars fade and witness the morning creep up over the city, glaring off the cars and the windows and the puddles on flat rooftops.

Who will make it through the night?

fifty-six

The Painting

"Bless me, Father, for I have sinned."

The air in the chapel is as still as water not quite frozen. There is the smell of incense burned long ago. Cohen looks up over his shoulder and sees the unobtrusive clock spinning off the seconds, the minutes, the hours crawling toward midnight. He wonders if his mother is still singing, if his father is still breathing, if his sister is still contracting.

He feels an urgency—he needs to get back to his father's bedside. There's a desperate desire in him to be there when his father dies, to be present when his father takes his final breath. He hopes it will bring him closure, or peace, or maybe something else, something he can't quite identify. Something in him is missing, he knows this now, and he thinks it might be filled if he can be beside his father when he dies.

Yet equally powerful, perhaps more so, is this desire to confess. It has become an important addition, the quiet walk to the church in the middle of the night, the somber entry into the chapel, the relief at seeing Father James behind the screen, waiting for him, sitting still, as if receiving Cohen's confession is the sole purpose of his life.

"The Lord be in your heart and mind, Cohen, and upon your lips, that you may truly and humbly confess your sins: In the Name of the Father, and of the Son, and of the Holy Spirit. Amen."

"Amen." The word passes Cohen's lips, but some part of it stays behind, like a pinpoint of light. It feels like a word from a foreign language—new, like a word he has never said before. *Amen.*

"Amen," he says again, glancing away from the confession screen and up toward the painting. Something about it doesn't seem right, and then he realizes—it's not the same picture.

"When did you change out the painting?" he asks Father James.

"I'm sorry?"

"The painting. When did you replace it?"

The priest pauses, and his confusion seeps through the screen, so that Cohen can feel it like a mist.

"I don't know what you mean, Cohen. That's the same painting that's always been there."

Cohen has the feeling that he's in a dream or is perhaps losing his mind. "I'm sure it's not," he says. "I'm sure of it. Before, the face of Christ was, I don't know, disappointed somehow. Not looking directly at me, but definitely thinking of me. He looked down to the side, where I always imagined John and Mary stood, or someone else he knew, but his disappointment was never directed at them. His disappointment was somehow for me. In me."

The father gives a subtle laugh. "What do you see now?" he asks, and there is still a smile in his voice, always kind, always hopeful.

"You can see it," Cohen replies, frustration grabbing at the edges of his words. "The face of Christ is looking at us, directly at us. His eyes, those green eyes with dark brown flecks, they're almost real." His voice has dropped to something barely above a whisper.

"What is the crucified Christ saying to you in this moment through that painting, Cohen?"

Cohen continues staring at the eyes, the way they blend with Jesus's dark skin, the way the background is an infinity of space and time and sky. The disappointment is no longer there, but what is it that he's seeing? What is that expression?

"I don't know," he replies. His voice trails off.

"I think you do."

The two men sit. One is old and at peace. The other is middle-aged and torn. Cohen feels the same confusion arise in his mind about the past, the present, what is separating them, what is keeping them intertwined in his head.

"Are you sure that's the same painting?" Cohen

asks, his voice full of doubt, rising almost to an indictment.

"I am sure," Father James says quietly. "I know that painting well. I have spent many, many hours contemplating it during my decades here. Cohen, the painting has not changed. But what you see has changed. Or perhaps you have changed, are changing. This is miracle enough. If you're seeing something new, then you will soon hear something new. The seeing and the hearing do not always come at the same time, but they move together, like thunder and lightning."

Cohen takes a deep breath. The change in the painting disconcerts him. When he walked into the chapel, he felt a great sense of peace. Now he isn't so sure.

"I confess to the Almighty God, to his Church, and to you, that I have sinned by my own fault in thought, word, and deed, in things done and left undone, but especially in regards to removing my father from life support and hating my mother." The words come out of him in a careless manner, light and thoughtless, but they end with a kind of sob and hot tears.

Father James does not respond.

Cohen continues to the end, talking at a fast pace, his words clipped. He fights the tears with an uncharacteristic cynicism. "For these and all other sins which I cannot now remember, I am truly sorry. I pray God to have mercy on me. I firmly intend amendment of life, and I humbly beg forgiveness of God and his Church, and ask you for counsel, direction, and absolution."

"I am sorry to hear about your father," Father James says after a brief silence. "May you find peace in such deep loss."

Cohen almost speaks. He almost explains how small a loss it actually is, how badly his father hurt him in the past, how simple life will seem when he can walk away from the funeral home, the business, the constant death, death, death. But he doesn't say any of it, because inside of him is the deep desire to be present at his father's death, and this desire seems to contradict everything else he thinks he feels.

"Our Lord Jesus Christ who has left power to his Church to absolve all sinners who truly repent and believe in him, of his great mercy forgive you all your offenses; and by his authority committed to me, I absolve you from all your sins: In the Name of the Father, and of the Son, and of the Holy Spirit. Amen."

"Amen," Cohen whispers.

"Why do you hate your mother, Cohen, when it was your father who betrayed her?"

When he said he hated his mother, he had thrown the words into the air without thinking about them, the way a child will say he hates broccoli or rainy days. But when Father James asks him the question, when he takes Cohen's words and hands them back in a way that forces him to consume them, they make his breath catch in his throat. He can't reply.

"Do you know what I think, Cohen?"

Cohen leans forward and slightly to the side, away from Father James. The heat in the building switches on, and a rush of warm air swirls through the chapel. It smells of dust and ancient things. When Cohen doesn't reply, the priest speaks slowly.

"I think you hate her because she's not your father. I think you've loved your father because, in a strange kind of way, you realize you are your father. You have the same weaknesses, the same faults, the same possibilities. This is frightening for a son to consider, that he may be inclined to make the same mistakes his father made. But most of all, I think you hate your mother because she was the one who left."

Again Cohen remembers the day the car pulled away, Kaye in the back seat, growing smaller, their car speeding away, kicking up dust, belching exhaust, the tires screeching around the distant bend. His father stood there for so long in the middle of that unlined country road that eventually Cohen stopped waiting for him, went back inside on his own.

The sound of Father James's voice brings him back.

"I'm sorry. That was improper of me. I should

give you space to discover your own answers to these questions. I suppose I'm not as patient in my old age as I would like to be."

When Cohen doesn't reply, he continues. "The Lord has put away all your sins."

"Thanks be to God," Cohen replies, standing.

"Go in peace, and pray for me, a sinner."

PART FIVE

Friday,
March 20, 2015

*Let the waters
bring forth abundantly
the moving creature
that hath life.*

Genesis 1:20

fifty-seven
There's a City of Light

Cohen walks up Duke Street from the church to the hospital, against traffic, the shadows lengthening and shortening while the headlights pass. The windows are dark. There is not a single person walking the sidewalks, crossing the street. Only cars, few and far between, sweeping south on Duke, their headlights dazzling his vision.

The air is much warmer than when he had walked south toward the church only twenty minutes earlier. There's a light breeze, but it has lost its winter's edge, and it carries the hint of spring moisture, the smell of seeds. The smell reminds him of the shallow ditch that lined the road between their country house and the narrow road, the one that, in the spring, filled with wriggling tadpoles. Those waters teemed with life, the miniature sea creatures swam, and day by day their tails shortened and their stumpy legs grew. Then one day they were gone, slapping their sloppy, halting jumps across the street toward the creek or burrowing deep in the long grass.

Could that kind of transformation happen to him?

Another car, another line of light, another wake

of darkness. It's strange, these competing desires. When he's in the room with his father, he feels caged, as if he must get out, do something. But when he's away, a sense of panic wells up inside of him that he might not be there when his father dies, that he won't be standing beside the bed when his father takes his last breath.

He walks faster.

Inside the hospital, he can hear his mother from down the hallway, the sound of her voice clear and unwavering. He wonders if she stopped even for a moment while he was gone, if she has taken a drink, eaten anything, used the restroom. She has certainly gotten louder. He turns into the room. She doesn't look up at him or even seem to be aware of his gentle arrival into the room. She starts a new song.

"A mansion is waiting in glory,
My Savior has gone to prepare;
The ransomed who shine in its beauty
Will dwell in that city so fair.

"Oh, home above,
I'm going to dwell in that home;
Oh, home of love,
Get ready, poor sinner, and come.

"A mansion of rest for the weary,
Who toil in the vineyard of love;

O sinner, believe, and be ready
To enter that mansion above.

"Oh, home above,
I'm going to dwell in that home;
Oh, home of love,
Get ready, poor sinner, and come."

The words move around inside his head, and he remembers once, long ago, really believing that there was something beyond this, something out there more ancient than the stars and their faraway light. An ache fills him, a sadness for the belief he lost somewhere along the way. He wants it back. This is why he has been going to confession, and he realizes it there, listening to his mother sing: he wants to find that belief. He wants to rediscover it. Would he ever feel that way again about God, the way he felt when he was a child?

Cohen looks for his sister and finds her standing by the window, gazing out over the nighttime city. To him, she looks like a queen, grand and majestic, on the verge of birthing the first inhabitants of a new world. It's the beginning of time and they are somehow there, nothing in front of them except all the ages to come.

His father remains unchanged, although his breathing is so shallow that at first Cohen thinks he has died. He moves closer, bends over him, and then hears it, or perhaps senses it. The light breaths, the ins and outs, spaced apart and slow as if each is its own effort, each disconnected from everything else. It brings tears to Cohen's eyes. He has trouble pulling himself away. What if this breath is the last? Or this one? Or this one?

A nurse comes in and squeezes past him. The nurses have less and less to do now, but they continue to stop by, mostly as a courtesy.

Cohen straightens up. "How will we know when he's died?" he asks her. "What if he takes his last breath and we don't realize it?"

Her face is sympathetic and soft. "Sometimes people slip away without their loved ones realizing it at first. It's not always a sudden, dramatic thing. This gradual slipping away is a process. I think it's a blessing to have these quiet moments with him."

Cohen nods, but he's not so sure. These quiet moments have brought up more from his past than anything else he's ever experienced. These quiet moments have dug deep, pulled away calluses, disturbed the living skin, so that he feels a constant ache.

In the silence left behind by the nurse, he notices his mother's voice again.

"There's a city of light 'mid the stars,
    we are told,
Where they know not a sorrow or care;

And the gates are of pearl, and the
   streets are of gold,
And the building exceedingly fair.

"Let us pray for each other, nor faint by
   the way,
In this sad world of sorrow and care,
For that home is so bright, and is almost
   in sight,
And I trust in my heart you'll go there."

"Is this allowed?" Cohen asks. "Shouldn't she quiet down? I can ask her to." After a pause he adds, "I don't think she'll listen to me."

The nurse gives a kind smile and offers a barely noticeable shrug. "None of the nurses on this floor mind it, and we haven't had any complaints from other patients or guests. It's okay with me."

"Do you think she's disturbing my dad?"

The nurse glances down at his father. "He's fine. I'm sure he can hear her. Do you know of any reason the sound of her singing might be disturbing to him?"

Cohen looks away from her, toward his father. There is somehow less of him than there was before, and what remains is haggard and weary and weighed down in the bed.

"I'm sure it's fine," Cohen says.

Again he remembers those old days in the

revival church, lying on the floor on hot summer nights, the sound of people fanning themselves, the simultaneous creaking of pews when they stood to sing. He would lie there in the shadow of the pew, feeling the summer breeze come in through the long windows, listening to his father's emotional plea for the eternal salvation of one more soul. From there he watched the feet of people on their way to Calvary, shuffling their way past the standing crowd, gliding up the center aisle to the stage. He could hear people wailing. Under the pews, between all the feet, he could see them kneeling.

And the crowd would start in with a new hymn.

All those old hymns with their images of battles and rivers and homes over there—they were the soundtrack to his childhood. And hearing his mother sing them—at first he finds it hard to believe this is true—he realizes his disdain for her is retreating. There is a new softness there. If he doesn't look at her hard eyes, her unyielding forehead, he can remember the love he once had for her.

As if she can read his thoughts, she starts a new song.

> "Just as I am, without one plea,
> But that Thy blood was shed for me,
> And that Thou bid'st me come to Thee,
> O Lamb of God, I come! I come!

"Just as I am and waiting not
To rid my soul of one dark blot;
To Thee whose blood can cleanse each
   spot,
O Lamb of God, I come, I come!

"Just as I am, though tossed about
With many a conflict, many a doubt;
Fighting within, and fears without,
O Lamb of God, I come, I come!"

Kaye comes over and stands beside him, reaching her arm up to him.

"Where's Johnny?" he asks her.

"I sent him home with the sitter. He needed to get out."

"I know that feeling."

"Remember in the old house, how Mom would sing while she did the dishes? Dad would sit in that old recliner watching the news and we'd all end up in there with him. I'd be reading and you'd be playing on the floor and Mom would come in and sit in the corner reading her Bible."

He nods, but it's more a robotic movement than anything resembling assent, because something uncomfortable has lodged in his chest, something sour. For every quiet memory like that of his mother, he has ten harsh ones, and capping them all is the one of her driving away, leaving his father standing in the middle of the road.

Hours pass, and they remain there, place-holders. Cohen paces the room, Kaye falls asleep, Cohen sits down, Kaye paces the room, Cohen falls asleep. All the while, their mother sings.

Cohen wakes in the chair. Morning approaches. He realizes Kaye's hand is on his shoulder, and he reaches up as if to hold her hand, but instead he lifts it, sliding out from under her half hug. Without looking at her or his mother, who is still singing, he edges his way toward the door and walks out into the almost-morning hospital. The lights are low. He finds his way to the stairwell and pushes open the door. He clears his throat, only to hear the echo of it travel up and down through all the floors.

He walks down, down, down, aimless and wandering. The stairwell is empty except for the yellowish lights that buzz on each landing and beside each door. He stops, not sure where he is, not sure what floor he's on, and he sits in the corner, wedging his body in the right angle of two cement block walls. The tiles under him are cold. There are no windows. There is nothing.

Where did his life go? His belief? His father? Where did they all go? How could it be that so many things have been lost?

Cohen sits there and weeps.

He hears a rhythmic buzzing, some kind of alarm. He wipes his eyes and stands up, drowning in the yellow light. He hears a scream. He walks onto the closest floor and sees people running. There's the sound of rapid tapping in some far-off place.

Rattattattattattat.

Rattattattattattat.

A voice comes over the intercom. "This is an emergency. This is not a drill. I repeat, this is an emergency. There is an active shooter in the hospital. Please go into the closest room and lock the door."

There's an explosion and the building shakes. A panel falls from the hallway ceiling.

Cohen turns and sprints back into the stairwell, taking the stairs two at a time until he arrives at his father's floor. It is already vacant, all the doors closed, ruled by an eerie silence.

The same recorded announcement issues calmly from the intercom speakers in the ceiling. "This is an emergency. This is not a drill. I repeat, this is an emergency. There is an active shooter in the hospital. Please go into the closest room and lock the door."

He reaches his father's door and turns the handle, but the door is locked. He bangs on it. "Kaye! Mom! It's me!"

There's no answer. He bangs again.

"Kaye! Are you in there?"

fifty-eight
The End of Things

Cohen led the way into the funeral home, and a strange authority seemed to transfer from Than and Hippie to him. It happened as quickly and subtly as the breath of wind that stirred the sycamore branches. They fell in behind him, and he could sense them there, their presence, their eyes looking over his shoulder.

He held the gun in his hand. It seemed to go from heavy to no weight at all, a nothing sort of thing, and he had to look at it and look at it again to make sure it was there. And it was, the cold steel glinting in the glare of the streetlights shining through the glass doors.

The storm grew heavy again, and swirling snow crowded frantically against the glass. Outside, the sound of the sirens was distant. Than aimed the flashlight around Cohen without walking in front of him, and the light caught Cohen's body, projected his shaky shadow across the room and up onto the walls and the ceiling. He was a giant walking. Standing behind the flashlight, Hippie and Than left no shadows, no mark of themselves.

"Wait," Cohen said.

Hippie paused without making a sound. Than took a few extra steps so that he was almost beside Cohen, and the three of them stood still, their breath rising around them. The room was cold, colder than it should have been. The coffins sat quietly in the darkness. The door at the back, the one that led into the stairwell and up to the apartment, was slightly open. The door at the right side of the funeral home's main level, the one that led into the chapel, was closed.

Than stared straight into the shadows, leaning his head to the side as if straining his ears to hear something, anything. Cohen glanced at Hippie. She gave him a kind look, the shadow of a smile, and he nodded back at her. Behind her, a single car drove south on Duke through the snow, moving at a turtle's pace, but the sound of it didn't pass through the glass. Only the light. Only the image of it moving, like in silent movies. Everything else was resting under a heavy stillness.

"Look," Than whispered, aiming his flashlight over at the door to the chapel, keeping the beam low. There was a light under the door, thin as a piece of yellow thread on a black suit.

Cohen nodded, filled with fear and uncertainty and a strong desire to get to the end, whatever that might mean. He was ready for the search to be over. He was ready to get rid of the Beast and see Than and Hippie out and climb back into his bed. He wanted to sink into the mattress, pull up the covers, and sleep until evening came the next day, then roll over and sleep another night through. But there remained this one thing.

"Let's go."

The light under the door didn't fade, and it took them only a few moments to glide over to it. They stood there for a long time, and Than turned off his flashlight. They stared down at the glow, the light that seemed to reach out toward their feet. They looked at the black tar on the frame around the door, the trail the Beast had left behind. Cohen clenched his jaw, raised his hand to push open the door. This would be it. This would be the end of the thing.

Cohen paused. He looked at Than and felt an unexpected friendship there. Another car went by, and the speckled light slid over Hippie's face. He stared hard at her. She reached up and touched his face with two fingers, running them down along his jawline. They were cold, and her touch was so slight. He closed his eyes for a split second, sighed, and turned from both of them. He opened the chapel door and walked in.

There was an unexpected brightness to the room, and at first Cohen couldn't look directly at it. A light at the front of the chapel—one of the overhead lights above the pulpit—shone down like a spotlight.

The shadows in the room started to gather,

pooling together, running like liquid from every corner, until out of the floor at the front of the room rose the Beast, as tall as the chapel, a shimmering, moving space of nothingness.

Cohen raised the gun, pointed it at the center of the darkness. His hand trembled. The room smelled like someone had vacuumed it recently, and Cohen also caught the scent of the pine cleaner, but the Beast brought its own smell, metallic and primal.

That's when Cohen heard Than shout, "Cohen!" followed by a short, piercing scream.

Hippie.

Cohen looked back through the door, back into the display room, but they were gone. He raised the gun toward the darkness.

"Where are they?" Cohen said, his voice wavering.

The Beast seemed to turn to face Cohen, and he could tell it was tired, haggard, drawn down. The Beast seemed to expand for a moment, filling the front of the chapel, and Cohen wasn't sure, if he decided to shoot, where exactly he should aim.

They are gone.

He realized these words were coming to him from inside his head. He somehow knew the words originated from the Beast, but they weren't connected to any voice. They were pieces of information that sprang up out of nowhere.

The Beast didn't talk, not out loud, but he communicated with Cohen, and those three little words came through clearly.

They are gone.

Cohen's hands trembled, the gun shaking up and down. "No, they're not."

They are gone.

"No!"

His voice echoed over the empty chairs, against the front chapel wall, and back to him again. The wall of darkness that was the Beast seemed to diminish for a moment. It seemed to pull in on itself, and that was when Cohen noticed the pooling shadows at its feet. A rivulet of it crept toward him, a narrow thread of the purest darkness he had ever seen. It shone like oil.

Yes. There was mourning tangled up in the Beast's words, and anger, and a seismic fissure that went all the way down. *Yes. They are gone. They died in the fire. I did it. It was me. I came here because I wanted to see them one last time. But they are gone.*

"No," Cohen whispered. His hands holding the gun lowered ever so slightly. In the silence between their words he could hear the accumulation of small things, the buzz of the light above the pulpit, the stirring of the air as the heat turned on. Behind the Beast there was nothing, at least nothing to be seen, but Cohen could feel what was there behind it, in the great shadow it left: eternity and darkness and death.

Cohen was suddenly cold. His clothes were wet with melted snow. His feet were heavy, his toes numb at the tips, and whether it was from standing in a pool of the Beast's darkness or simply from running through the cold night in the city, he didn't know.

The Beast teetered from one side to the other, bumping the pulpit, knocking over a chair. It was a boat taking on water, listing in the storm, further with each wave. Then it was down.

They are gone. This was the last thing Cohen felt from the Beast. The words came like sobs, and the Beast began to diminish faster, somehow shrinking and taking a more solid form. Cohen watched, horrified, as the darkness and the shadows and that huge, tilting thing transformed into a dead man lying there, flat on the floor, his head leaning against the side chapel wall at a sharp angle. He had a week's worth of beard on his face and disheveled, graying hair and a tired, mean face. The black shadows were suddenly a deep red, and Cohen knew the wound was where he had shot the man the night before, in the trailer, with Hippie and Than.

"Cohen!" a voice shouted. "Is that you? Are you back?"

Behind him the door creaked open. He turned,

and there stood Ava in the doorway, her mouth gaping.

"Ava," he whispered. "What are you . . ." But the look on her face stopped him. She was staring at the dead man, at the pools of blood. Even in the dim light, she could see it all. She could see the man's stubble, his stained clothes. Even in the darkness, she could see the glint of metal in Cohen's hand. The gun.

She backed away, the look on her face never changing. Cohen moved to follow her, and he would have, except for Hippie and Than.

Hippie and Than.

He threw the gun to the floor and it was absorbed by the carpet. He fell to the floor and screamed their names.

"Hippie! Than!"

But they were not there, and he no longer expected to find them. He crawled on all fours to the Beast, now only a man, and stared at him. With every ounce of bravery that remained he moved in close and checked for breathing—a moving chest, air stirring from his mouth—but there was nothing. The man's skin was still warm, and his jaw was loose and pliable, and Cohen couldn't hate him anymore, even though he tried. How he tried!

He thought back through everything, every little conversation and moment he had spent with them, especially with Hippie. He thought of the day they first met, the day they fought the Beast in the funeral home, their hike along the train tracks and sleeping in the cave. He thought of how she had reached up and touched him only moments ago, her cold fingers on his jaw. He reached up and rubbed that spot, tried to feel any part of her she might have left behind. He had loved her, he knew that. How could this be?

He thought about Ava. He imagined her searching for him in the city, her eyes shining in the light, lifting those "Missing" posters and stapling them to each and every pole and tree, the staples sometimes catching and sometimes bending on staples already there from other signs posted by other people.

He imagined his father, maybe walking the city, staring into Cohen's printed eyes. He thought of his father waiting in the funeral home, perhaps drinking, perhaps falling back to sleep, but always waiting.

Waiting for him.

Cohen stood. He was soaked through from sweat and the snow, and there was blood on his clothes, he knew that now. He paused. Had the snow fallen on all of them? Had they left footprints in the mud, in the snow? Or had it been only him all along? He wanted to go out and look, but he was scared of what he might find. Or not find.

Weariness pressed on him like a lead blanket.

He walked back through the dark funeral home, all the way to the stairs, and up he went one step at a time, his dirty soles making gritty sounds on the floor. He climbed up out of the dark into the lesser dark, and there he sat in the apartment, staring out the window onto Duke Street. A far-off siren wailed. The snow no longer fell. The sky was dark and clear.

fifty-nine
Something New

"Is that you, Cohen?" Kaye's voice trembles through the door, far away, lost, like a voice from the afterlife.

"Yes!" he hisses, looking over his shoulder. "Let me in."

The lock clicks and the door swings open.

"Kaye! Did you hear what's going on?"

"We heard. The nurses are all in other rooms. I'm scared, Cohen."

Cohen closes the door quietly, locking it. When he turns back around, Kaye is bent over, facing away from him, her hands on her knees. She is holding her breath, and a quiet groan escapes, ending in panting.

"Are you . . . ?" Cohen asks, panic rising in him. For a quick moment he wants to run back out the door, down the stairs, away from this pain, away from this fear. But he doesn't. Kaye can't run from it, and he can't leave her to face it alone.

Kaye nods without looking at him, without taking her hands off her knees, without standing up straight. "They're coming."

"They're coming?"

She nods. "The twins are coming."

"Now?"

She nods again and stands up straight, putting one hand on her back and pressing, closing her eyes, sighing.

"Can you stop them?"

She looks at him, eyebrows raised. "Are you serious?"

"I mean, I don't know, slow it down?"

She turns away and paces the room. Their mother is still singing.

"Does she know what's going on?" he asks Kaye, motioning toward their mother.

Kaye shrugs. "I don't know. She started singing quieter when I asked her to."

And the singing was quiet, barely discernible even in the silence. Cohen stared at his mother.

> "Nearer, my God, to Thee, nearer to
>   Thee!
> E'en though it be a cross that raiseth
>   me,
> Still all my song shall be,
> Nearer, my God, to Thee.
> Nearer, my God, to Thee,
> Nearer to Thee!"

"Mom, stop it," Cohen hisses. When she doesn't, he gets down closer to her. "Mom. Seriously. Stop. It."

She looks up at him, her eyes clear and shining, but she doesn't say anything. She just keeps singing.

"Mom!" he shouts.

"Quiet!" Kaye shouts at him. "Are you serious? You're really going to do this right now? Argue with her? In this moment?"

There is a knock at the door, barely audible. It sounds more like a gentle scratching, the nudge of time or fate pressing in, asking for an audience. Kaye and Cohen freeze in place, instinctively holding their breath. Cohen hears the person shuffle around outside and slide down the door. He hears palms hit the cold tile floor. He realizes the person is probably looking under the crack in the door, trying to see who's in the room. He looks down at his own feet, wondering if they're visible. He puts his hand on his mother's shoulder, hoping that will quiet her, but she goes on singing in her whispering way.

A voice hisses under the door. "Cohen?"

Cohen looks at Kaye. Again the voice comes in under the door, a message in a bottle.

"Cohen? Are you in there?"

Cohen creeps toward the door, walking on the balls of his feet, staying clear of the bed and the discarded IV rack. He gets on his knees, bends all the way down, and peers under the door. There's an eyeball on the other side, a cheek pressed to the ground.

397

"Cohen. It's me. Thatcher."

Cohen jumps to his feet and opens the door. "Get in here," he says, pulling the boy through. "What are you doing in the hallway?"

"I came to see you guys, see how your dad is doing, and then everything happened."

They all look at Calvin. He is at peace, knowing nothing of what goes on around him. Or at least that's how it appears. His eyes are closed, his bald head now bristling along the edges with one-week-old stubble.

"Is he . . . ?"

Cohen shakes his head. "No, he's not dead. Not yet."

They go on staring. Outside, the sun rises, light coming through the window, a fresh light. Kaye walks to the glass and stares out into the morning. It's only when she is halfway through the contraction that Cohen realizes what's going on. Her fingers grasp the hard sill until they're white-knuckled. She presses her forehead against the cold glass. She manages to remain silent until the end, when her voice rises in a scratchy kind of low scream.

Cohen walks quickly to her side. "They're coming?"

She nods.

"We have to find a nurse."

"I know a good hiding place, a safer place," Thatcher says. Cohen looks at him. The young man lost his hat in the chaos, and his swirling, matted hair reminds Cohen of the top of a calf's head. "We should go now."

"Put your arm around me," Cohen says to Kaye, pulling her arm around his shoulder, helping her walk.

Kaye winces and breathes exaggerated breaths. They pass their mother at the foot of their father's bed.

"Mom," Kaye says in a whisper. "You have to come with us."

> "To God be the glory, great things He
>   has done;
> So loved He the world that He gave us
>   His Son,
> Who yielded His life an atonement for
>   sin
> And opened the life gate that all may go
>   in."

"Mom, what is wrong with you?" Cohen hisses. "Get up! We have to get out of here!"

> "When we walk with the Lord
> In the light of His Word,
> What a glory He sheds on our way!
> While we do His good will,
> He abides with us still,
> And with all who will trust and obey.

"Trust and obey, for there's no other
   way
To be happy in Jesus, but to trust and
   obey."

She doesn't look at them. She doesn't stop. Her voice grows louder, though, somewhat defiant, and Cohen can see the mother of his childhood there—the mother who mouthed the words to all his father's sermons, the mother who stormed out onto the baseball field and threw the sock at his father's feet.

"Wait," Kaye says, her entire body tensing.

"Another one?" he asks.

She nods, grabbing her stomach with her free hand, and her knees go slack. Cohen bears up under her weight. She tries to moan quietly, but at the tail end of the contraction her voice elevates again.

"Not so loud!" Thatcher says.

Cohen looks up in surprise and glances quickly at Kaye who has somewhat regained her footing. "I wouldn't say that if I were you."

"C'mon. Hurry," Thatcher says.

Cohen pauses. Kaye walks away from him, limping along on her own, following Thatcher into the hall.

"Faster," Thatcher insists, and there is genuine terror in his voice, as if he has spotted the gunman at the end of the hallway. Cohen sees the boy as if for the first time, and he realizes he has come to love him in such a short time.

But Cohen cannot leave. He looks at his dying father. He hopes his soul is far, far away. He hopes his hearing—*"That's always the last thing to go"*—is long gone. But what if it's not? Cohen doesn't want this to be the last thing his father hears: the shuffling feet of his fleeing children, panic-stricken voices, his daughter moaning through frightening contractions.

"Father," Cohen says, darting to the head of the bed. He touches his father's bald scalp, something he has never done in all these long years. The stubble is prickly. "Father, I'm sorry. For everything. For taking that sock, for not being everything you needed me to be. If you think of me somehow after you're gone, think of us playing catch, Dad. That's it. I promise that's how I'll remember you."

He thinks of all the long years stretching ahead of him, all of those long, fatherless years where he will no longer have Calvin to look for, to find.

He backs away, into the doorway where Kaye and Thatcher were moments before, then runs out into the hall. He sees them walking, waddling along the hallway. It's eerie and empty. Cohen thinks of everyone barricaded in their rooms, everyone listening to them make their way down the hall, everyone hoping they are not the gunman.

There is the distant sound of gunfire. Screams come up at them through the floor, through the air vents. Cohen thinks of all the children above him; he hopes they're not afraid. He hopes they don't someday wrestle with the question burning him up from the inside.

Where is God?

"Where are we going?" Cohen asks, catching up to Kaye and Thatcher. The boy has one of Kaye's arms around his shoulders. Cohen lifts her other arm around himself so she's supported on both sides.

"She's been hiding up here, in this closet. She's been here the entire time."

"Your mom? You found your mom?"

Thatcher nods, gives a half smile. He stops walking and at first Cohen keeps going. Why stop here? But then he sees a utility closet, the door painted the same color as the wall, with air vent slats along its bottom half. Thatcher turns the handle and the door clicks. It takes Cohen's eyes a moment to adjust to the darkness inside.

The closet is fifteen feet deep, narrow from one side to the other. Pipes and electrical conduits line the ceiling and terminate at the back in a series of panels and switches. On the floor is a sort of bed made up of white hospital sheets and pillows. Thatcher's mother stands there like a ghost, like someone who no longer exists. A naked bulb hangs above her, glowing.

Thatcher pulls the heavy door closed. It does not have a lock on the inside.

"She's in labor," he whispers to his mother. "Twins. They're coming."

The young man's voice crumbles at the end, folds in on itself, and he bites his knuckle but that doesn't stop a whimper from escaping.

Kaye gives a heavy exhale and starts rubbing her stomach. She bends over and Cohen reaches to support her, but this time she pushes him away. She shakes her finger at him but doesn't speak, simply hums. She hums her way through the contraction, a monotone kind of buzzing that grows steadily louder.

"Ma'am, they'll hear us," Thatcher whispers.

Kaye glares at him, moaning louder. Thatcher's mom holds out a towel, and Kaye puts it against her mouth, muffling the sound.

"It's happening fast," she says in a hoarse voice after the contraction passes. "The twins are coming. I can't stop it. They're coming." She starts to cry.

"Honey, honey," Thatcher's mother says, and her voice is soothing like warm milk, but also somehow solid, reliable. "You can't stop it, so don't even try. You are going to do this because you can do this. And I'm going to help you. I'm a nurse. I've delivered thousands of babies."

"And calves!" Thatcher chimes in, trying to be

403

helpful. A low round of chuckles spreads through the closet.

"Yes, and calves," she says.

"Twins?" Kaye asks, her eyes desperate.

"Plenty."

"Here comes another one," Kaye says, her voice timid, as if asking for permission to have another contraction.

"Okay, go into it with strength. You walk or pace or squat or hang from the ceiling, whatever it takes to get through each contraction. Or squeeze this man's hand. Make sure he's not wearing any rings."

"He wishes," Kaye says, grimacing as the contraction grows closer. The other three stand there wincing with her, holding their breath. Cohen is in awe of what he's seeing, what Kaye is capable of.

Again he hears the rapid spit of gunfire, closer this time, either on the floor below them or in the stairwell. Cohen looks at Thatcher, then at his mother. *Where are the police?* The light bulb winks quickly off and back on. The announcement sounds again through the hospital's public address system.

"This is an emergency. This is not a drill. I repeat, this is an emergency. There is an active shooter in the hospital. Please go into the closest room and lock the door."

Cohen stares at Kaye. He wonders if she heard

it—but of course she did. Does she comprehend it? He wonders if she's thinking about their father only a few doors down, or their mother, who won't stop singing. She doesn't appear to be thinking about anything except the gathering wave of the next contraction.

"Here comes another one," she says, grimacing again. "I can't breathe. I have to take off my pants."

"Go ahead, honey."

Thatcher looks horrified. He turns and faces the wall, arms crossed, while Kaye rips her pants off. They fall to the floor, and she crouches into the next contraction, moaning, muffling her moans with the towel.

"There you go, there you go," Thatcher's mom says while the contraction fades. "Honey, how long have you been having contractions like this?"

"A few days," Kaye whispers.

"A few days? Oh my. Can I check you?" She motions for Kaye to lie down on her back. Kaye nods and gingerly spreads out on the floor, and now it's time for Cohen to look away. A wave of light-headedness spreads from his eyes, a kind of numbness.

"Dear," she says, "you are going to have these babies any minute. You're almost there. I can see the hair of the first child!"

Kaye starts crying again. Cohen feels like he

might faint. Kaye does not get up off the floor for the next contraction—she simply turns over onto all fours. With each one, her moaning is louder, longer, escaping the towel she has balled up and crammed into her mouth, the towel she now bites in anguish.

"Good, good," Thatcher's mom whispers, and for a moment they're all still: Kaye on the floor, naked except for her top, eyes closed between contractions; Thatcher, facing the electrical boxes; Thatcher's mother, on her knees at Kaye's feet; and Cohen, facing the door, eyeing the ventilation slats, holding his breath as he hears voices coming out of the stairwell.

"This it?" one of the voices asks as the door to the stairwell slams open. Cohen gets closer to the slats, tries to see through, but they're angled down so he can only see the floor tiles outside.

"Yeah, this is the right floor," a second voice says. It sounds like Thatcher's father.

Thatcher turns toward the door, skirts Kaye where she lies, and joins Cohen, listening. He reaches up and turns out the light, and all Cohen can see are the white lines of the light coming through the vent.

"Is that your father?" Cohen asks in a breathless whisper, more a mouthing of the words than an actual saying of them.

Thatcher's eyes are wide, suddenly terrified. He nods.

"Who's with him?" Cohen asks.

"Sounds like my uncle."

"Your uncle? He never came when your grandpa was dying, did he?"

Thatcher shakes his head. Outside the door, the men walk farther away, down the hall.

"But he's willing to kill people over your grandpa's death?"

"My dad's family," Thatcher whispers without looking at Cohen, "his whole family, they don't need a reason."

The uncle's voice comes to them, loud and abrupt. "You think that doctor's up here?"

"Wasn't in his office, was he?" Thatcher's father growls.

"Didn't mean you had to shoot folks," his uncle mutters. "I thought we were here to scare 'em."

"What was that?" Thatcher's father hisses. The men stop walking. For a moment the hallway is silent again, but there is something distant, something rhythmic. Something foreign.

"It's a helicopter," Thatcher's father spits out, laughing. "A helicopter. It's serious now. Stay away from the windows, boy, unless you want to get picked off like a groundhog." He laughs again, the sound of it echoing through the empty hall, creeping in through the vents.

The uncle mutters a stream of profanity. "How we getting out of here, Jim?"

"Oh, I know a way."

"With a helicopter out there?"

"Tunnels," he says, and the way he says it, it sounds like that one word is the solution to every problem. "Tunnels under the hospital, under the street. I saw 'em myself. Now, room by room. Room by room. We'll find him. Then we'll get out."

Cohen turns away, glances in Kaye's direction. Her face glows white from the lines shining through the slats. She looks at him, a pleading expression bearing down on her face as the next contraction squeezes in. It seems strange to him in that moment how little control Kaye has over her body. In nearly every other instance, he thinks, a person decides what their body will do: eat or run or prepare for sleep. But Kaye has lost the controls. Her body is moving on without her—it has decided what will happen next. She's only along for the ride.

But no, she's not along for the ride anymore—he can see it in her face, something new, some kind of fierce determination. He can't describe how he knows this, what it is about her expression or her posture that communicates it. He simply knows. She no longer cares about the shooter or where she is giving birth. She doesn't care who is there in the closet with her. It's only her and this labor, her and these babies.

He moves to her side. She twists until she's on her hands and knees again, and when the next contraction comes, she arches her back. The towel is in her mouth like a horse's bit, and she moans loudly into it, bites the cloth. Fluid leaks from her, and blood, and feces. Thatcher's mother presses on Kaye's back for the duration, and in another moment Kaye is spent, heaving, gasping for air. Thatcher's mother is saying soft, kind words while cleaning her legs and replacing the sheets and pillowcases, and Kaye is someone else entirely.

She's from another world, Cohen marvels, staring at her closed eyes. Her hair is wet from sweat, and muscles have appeared out of nowhere in her arms, firm as a twisting ripple in the trunk of a tree.

He glides back over to the door, listening for the men. Thatcher is there beside him.

"Where are they?" Cohen whispers.

"He won't shoot us. He won't."

"Are they still on this floor?"

Thatcher looks at Cohen. "He won't shoot us." He keeps saying the same thing, but his words hold no conviction.

"Where are they?" Cohen asks again, gently.

"They walked to the other end of the hall. I can hear them opening doors, asking about the doctor. But they haven't shot their guns."

Cohen looks at him. Again he sees himself in the boy. His love for a father he does not understand. His certainty crumbling.

"They haven't shot anyone yet. Have they?" the boy asks.

Cohen reaches over and messes up the boy's hair. It's soft and matted out of place.

"We're going to be okay," Cohen whispers. "All of us."

sixty

In the Beginning

"Okay," Thatcher's mother says quietly. "It's time, Kaye. I need a few good pushes and the first baby will be out."

The look on Kaye's face is that of someone who has finished a marathon only to be told they must start another one immediately.

Cohen looks over his shoulder at Thatcher still standing by the door. "Anything?" he asks.

Thatcher shakes his head. Cohen looks at Thatcher's mother.

"Now's the time." She nods.

"Here it comes," Kaye whispers through gritted teeth. "Someone hold my leg."

Cohen grabs her leg and she lies on her side. Between her legs emerges the crown of a head matted with dark hair, streaked with white vernix. Only the top. Kaye's moan turns into a pushing groan and then a scream, muffled poorly by the towel she is nearly biting through. Cohen has one hand on her heel and one hand on the inside of her knee. It takes everything he has in him to hold it in place.

The contraction passes and the baby's head slips back inside. Cohen sits there holding Kaye's leg. The seconds pass in silence. Kaye looks like she's fallen asleep. Thatcher's mother rests her hand on Kaye's shoulder and hums a song Cohen cannot recognize. But her humming reminds him of his own mother down the hallway, behind the closed door of his father's room, singing those old songs, singing a piece of Cohen's past that will never come back.

He sees it all again while he kneels there beside his sister, knees aching, waiting for the next contraction. He sees the inside of the old church, the swaying congregants, the flash of light on his father's head, the abrupt way he pulls the handkerchief out and wipes the sweat from his forehead. He sees the ushers hovering around the back, waiting for cues to turn down the lights or open the windows. He sees their old piano player slipping onto the piano bench from the dark corner where he waited the entire service. His fingers tickle the keys, so quietly that at first Cohen can't hear it, but the sound grows louder and louder until he feels his emotions coming and going with the sharps and the flats.

"Here it comes," Kaye says, and she sounds hopeless, lost in a maze of pain, afraid that she will never find her way home.

"You can do it, Sis," he says, his voice sounding more confident than he feels. "You can do this."

She braces herself. Her body shudders and her stomach turns to rock. The little head emerges, and her screaming groans cannot be contained by the towel. The head comes farther, nudges out so that it's free all the way to the neck, and there's the little face, bunched up and folded in wrinkles, eyes still closed, bright pink lips and a face somewhere between red and purple.

"One more good push," Thatcher's mother says.

Kaye cries with despair, but she pushes and out the baby comes, suddenly slippery, shoulders and arms and belly and bottom and knees and feet and finally the trailing cord.

"Thatcher, a towel."

The boy listens to his mother and passes the white fluffy towel to Cohen. Thatcher's mother hands him the baby, so alive against the whiteness, its mouth open, gums wide, eyes watery and still closed. Then it cries, at first a little bleat like a lamb, but then it turns into a longer sound, a kind of whimpering scream.

Kaye is a heap on the floor, weary and limp as if she has no bones. "What is it?" she gasps.

"A boy," Cohen says, tears breaking his voice and blurring his eyes. "A boy."

Kaye laughs a sob and still doesn't move, and Thatcher's mother leans in.

"Rest while you can, honey. You've got one more coming, but the second one is a piece of cake. Here." She takes the baby from Cohen, pulls out a hospital blanket, and wraps the tiny, wriggling thing tighter. Already he is sucking on his bottom lip and his eyes open in tiny slits, like a closed door with light sneaking out the bottom.

Cohen wonders if this baby boy will remember this somehow, if this moment in time in a hospital closet will lodge itself in the deepest place of his mind and emerge someday—images of these people, this light bulb, this darkness with the slats of light breaking through. Will he remember the metallic smell of blood and the edge of fear everyone else was feeling? Can he sense how desperately they all want him to remain quiet?

They stay very still, taking Kaye's lead. She's on her side, waiting. Thatcher's mother is standing, holding the baby, swaying back and forth, bumping up and down. Thatcher sits down beside the slats again, the light making lines on his face.

"You okay?" Cohen asks Kaye in a whisper.

She nods without opening her eyes.

Cohen glances up at the bundle of baby, smiles at Thatcher's mother, moves from beside Kaye to the door, and sits beside Thatcher. "You okay?" he asks the boy.

"What's taking the police so long? Where are they?"

"I'm sure they're evacuating the building. They're probably making their way up floor by floor. They'll be here any minute. Hang in there."

"Is your sister okay?"

"She's doing great. Almost there."

"I've seen cows give birth, but I've never seen anything like that."

"Me neither," Cohen says. "Pretty intense."

"Why do you think he's doing it?"

"Who?"

"My dad. Why do you think he's doing this? Shooting up the hospital?"

Cohen pauses, sighs. "I don't know, Thatcher. I don't know."

"The thing is, my dad, my grandpa, they never even got along. Sometimes I thought they hated each other. They never stopped fighting about the farm, the animals, how things should be. I thought Dad would be relieved when Grandpa died. Not this. I never thought he'd do something like this."

Cohen nods. When he speaks, the words come out measured, and his eyes are looking off to a different place. "Fathers and sons, I don't think they ever really know how to be with one another. My own dad is over there in that room, dying, maybe dead by now, and for the last week I couldn't even figure out what I'd say to him if he came back for one minute. It's been a long time since we've known how to speak to each other. We never fought, or rarely anyway, not like your dad and grandpa, but . . . I don't know, I wonder if fathers and sons ever know how to be to each other."

"I hate my dad," Thatcher says, a questioning look on his face, seeking confirmation or rebuke.

Cohen purses his mouth. "I guess a lot of sons hate their dads at different times."

"Do you hate your dad?"

Cohen shakes his head. "No. I do not."

"Did you ever hate him?"

Cohen thinks for a moment. "I don't know. I don't know if hate is the right word." He thinks back on the nights his father slept drunk on the sofa, never waking. He thinks of how his dad stood in the middle of the road when his mother left. He remembers playing catch with him in the green grass at the old place in the country, the sky blue, the smell of summer, the heat bearing down. "I know I loved him, a lot of the time. But then we lost each other. Maybe he lost me. Maybe I lost him. I don't know. Maybe that's the problem with fathers and sons—they lose each other."

"What if you want to lose your dad?" Thatcher looks away from Cohen, staring into a dark corner of the closet.

"Everyone loses their dad. It doesn't matter if you want to or not. It's finding him again that's the hard part. I don't know if that happens very much."

The two of them sit there, Cohen listening to the sound of his own breathing. His sister takes a deep breath and sits up, leaning to one side. Thatcher's mother brings the baby over to Thatcher, hands the bundle to him, and makes small adjustments to how he's holding him. She's found a blue hospital pacifier and the baby sucks it rhythmically.

"There you go," she whispers. "You keep being good and quiet, little one."

"Maybe Mr. Cohen should hold him?" Thatcher says, his voice hesitant.

"No, he needs to be ready to catch the next one." She smiles and her voice is light and airy—there's nothing in her world except the arrival of the next baby. No shooters, no lack of help or clean equipment. She moves like a breeze back to Kaye, again finding towels and various things to use to clean her up.

"How long will it be? How long does it usually take for the second one to come?" Kaye asks.

"It could be five minutes. Or it could be an hour."

"I don't think it's going to be that long."

"Listen to your body. It will tell you when."

Kaye nods, a grimace full of pain and fear wrinkling her face the way fire wilts paper from behind.

"Do you feel a contraction coming?"

Kaye nods again, moving back to all fours. Cohen wonders how she can survive another splitting, another push, another human emerging. She seems to share his doubts, and now she moans without the towel, her voice humming like an electric transformer about to explode. But her cries are weaker, as if she has lost the strength to even feel pain.

The contraction passes. "Cohen, come hold my leg." She moves onto her side again.

"They're coming this way," Thatcher hisses. "I can hear them. Quiet!"

Cohen can hear the men's distant approach in the silent closet, their voices hollow as if coming from the other end of a long tunnel. The words aren't clear, but they grow louder. A ventilation fan turns on in the closet, numbing all other sound.

"Another one." Kaye's words are clipped and hard. The leg Cohen holds grows tense, and she presses her heel into the palm of his hand. She cries out again. He holds her knee up and another head appears, another head of dark hair. This time it does not pause at the opening but rushes straight out. Thatcher's mother guides the screaming baby onto a towel and rests the baby on the floor before grinding at the umbilical cord with a paper scissors. Blood is flowing out of Kaye now, pulsing. Thatcher's mother encourages her onto her back and presses on her now-gelatinous stomach, and more blood and fluid ooze out.

"Is this normal?" Cohen asks, feeling woozy. "Isn't that a lot of blood?"

Kaye lies there, one arm up over her eyes.

Thatcher's mother doesn't answer Cohen. There is an urgency to her movements. "She still needs to pass the placenta. After that, we're home."

The words are barely out of her mouth when the door swings wide, and there stand Thatcher's father and uncle, their weapons raised.

"What in the . . ." Thatcher's father begins, taking in the scene: Thatcher sitting in the dark corner, hunched over a baby who has now begun to cry; Thatcher's mother bundling up baby number two, a girl, and handing her to Cohen as if nothing out of the ordinary is happening; Kaye, eyes closed, naked from the waist down and indifferent to the presence of the two armed men.

The uncle's eyes nervously scan the puddles of blood on mats, on towels, on the floor. Where they expected to find a few people hiding, they find life bursting forth, and towels stained, and miracles.

"So, this is where you've been hiding," Thatcher's father spits out, and hate rises in his eyes. He looks at Thatcher. "How long did you know about this?"

Thatcher stares hard at the baby, bobbing him up and down, trying to quiet him.

"And you. You just can't leave my family alone."

He's talking to Cohen now, but Cohen is

419

oblivious to everything. He has forgotten his father dying, his mother singing, his sister bleeding. He has forgotten Thatcher holding the other child or even the two armed men or the smell in the closet. He has forgotten everything that has come before and every worry he has about the future. Because there in his hands, the second baby opens her eyes.

The baby's face is unnaturally calm, her tongue rising to curiously feel her own lips, tasting the air. It's the movement of a trout gently touching the surface of the water, wondering at this strange other world. She strains to move her arms, but she doesn't fight. Thatcher's mother has wrapped her snug, and she resettles into that tightness. She lets out a kind of yawn without opening her mouth. And still Cohen stares at her eyes.

They're green with flecks of dark brown. They're peaceful and loving. They're the eyes he saw at his last confession, the eyes in the painting of the crucified Christ. Cohen cannot look away.

"I'm talking to you."

Cohen barely hears the voice. He is captivated by the love and inquisitiveness he sees in those eyes. He keeps his face close to the baby because he knows her early vision is blurry, shortsighted in these first hours. Perhaps she can't even see him. He moves closer until his nose touches the baby's. Her eyes are so close. Inside of them he sees another universe, stars being born and dying, galaxies revolving, light moving from one end of everything that exists to the other, lonely comets streaking icy paths through empty space. Everything that has ever been is caught up in the matter of that universe, and it is all there in those eyes, inches from his own.

How long! he marvels. *How long it takes the light to reach us!*

"I said, I'm talking to you."

He looks up and feels nothing but elation, nothing but absolute intoxication at the growing understanding that he is alive. He is here. He exists. Nothing about the scene around him can deaden this new sense. Not the frantic nature of Thatcher's mother's movements as she continues soaking up more blood. Not the white translucence of Kaye's skin or the way her limp arm falls from her eyes and drifts aimlessly, unconsciously, to a resting point on the floor. Not even the gun held by Thatcher's father as it turns toward him, the black hole at the end of the barrel something he will look into, a future he is no longer afraid of.

He stares up into the man's eyes and sees the vacancy there, the loss, the anger. He gives him a smile that, without the benefit of knowing Cohen's recent realization, could easily be interpreted as a sad smile.

Cohen looks away, back into the eyes of the baby in his arms, and waits.

There is the volley of gunfire.

Thatcher's mother screams.

Thatcher shouts, but it's more like one of Kaye's long, unending moans. He turns his body to shield the twin he's holding.

Cohen is surprised. He feels nothing. He looks around the room. In the doorway he sees the bodies of Thatcher's father and uncle. The father is motionless, moaning, but a fading moan, one that sounds like the release of every last thing. The uncle's leg twitches once, twice. A shudder runs through his arms.

Cohen hears the sound of a dozen or more boots, their scuffing unmistakable, loud in the silence. There is the clatter of weapons being kicked out of lifeless hands, spinning across the waxed hospital floor, and colliding with the wall. Shouts. Shadowy figures in black body armor staring into the closet.

One of the men lifts his hand and raises a visor-like mask. "Hold your fire," he says in a firm voice. "Hold your fire."

Ava's face appears in the doorway, filled with concern. She scans the scene, taking it all in, and when she sees Cohen, her mouth opens slightly. "Cohen," she whispers, clearly not knowing what to say next.

Cohen smiles at her and looks back into the face of the child he's holding.

He weeps.

sixty-one
All the Hidden Things

On the night the man died in the chapel of their funeral home, Cohen sat for a long time by the upstairs window, staring out at the sycamore trees, watching the snow fade and the cars trickle by one at a time. He opened the window an inch and the cold air poured in, and he could hear the cars then, the endless shushing sound their tires made as they drove south, as if trying to convince him not to tell the secret.

Because of everything that had happened and everything that had come to an end, he felt like his life was beginning again. A life without Than and Hippie, a life without the Beast. A life without Ava, who had seen what he had done. He put his head down on the windowsill and stared up through the tree branches, and as the morning sifted down toward him he fell asleep.

When he woke, he didn't move, because he felt someone staring at him. It was like when they had first moved there and he always felt the eyes of the dead following him through the apartment. He cycled through all that had happened the night before, all that he had lost, and only after he got his bearings on the world did he raise his head, turn, and look toward his father's bedroom.

There stood Calvin, staring back at him. Cohen waited for it—the anger, the judgment, the shouting. But his father didn't move from where he stood, and soon Cohen realized why. His dad didn't know if he was real.

"Hi," Cohen said, trying to break through the curtain of silence between them, trying to reassure his father that he was flesh and blood.

"Cohen," his father said, but that was all.

Cohen.

"I'm sorry," Cohen said, apologizing without meaning to. In all the plans he had formed regarding the next time he saw his father, in all the ways he had considered things playing out, offering an apology had never entered his imagination. The words simply spilled out.

But his father shook his head. "Please don't leave like that again." Calvin walked slowly across the room to where Cohen sat. He cupped his hand around the back of Cohen's neck, and with his other hand he stroked Cohen's hair back out of his eyes. "Please don't disappear."

Twice in two sentences his father used that word. *Please.* Cohen caught a sob, somehow kept the tears from falling, but a little hiccup still escaped. He leaned into the weight of his father's hand and closed his eyes. His father sighed but didn't say anything, just kept pushing Cohen's hair out of his eyes.

"Dad," he said, determined to say the words before he lost the will, "there's a dead man in the chapel. The man you warned me about."

His father's fingers froze somewhere around his temple, and a few strands of his hair fell back in place on his forehead. Again Cohen waited. When his father didn't move, Cohen stood, the weight of his father's hands heavy on his neck and head until they fell away, listless. Cohen didn't say anything. Without looking, he reached back and took his father's large hand, then walked through the door and down the stairs.

Cohen paused outside the chapel door. He pursed his lips, pushed the door open, and walked to the front of the chapel to where the one small spotlight shone down on the pulpit. His father followed him silently all the way to the front of the chapel, where the dead man sprawled out on the floor, his head still propped against the wall. The bleeding had stopped, his skin a pale white in the dim light.

Cohen and his father stood there. Cohen waited for whatever was to come. He did not look at his father, though Calvin had drawn up beside him. He could feel his presence. He wanted him to say something.

"I shot him, Dad. I killed him."

Calvin didn't say a thing. And he wouldn't

say a word to Cohen again, not that whole long day. He turned and walked out of the chapel, and Cohen wondered where his father had gone. Back up to his room to drink this problem away like he did every other one? Up to the living room to call the police? The emptiness in the chapel, the loneliness, nearly drove Cohen to run again, out the glass doors, up the pre-dawn street, far away this time, never to return.

But a loud bump sounded against the chapel door, and Cohen looked over his shoulder in time to see a coffin coming in, the least expensive one they had. His father pushed it through on a cart, banged into a few of the chapel chairs as he made a wide turn, and moved it toward the front.

He still didn't say a word to Cohen, but he went to work. He opened the coffin, picked up the dead man under the shoulders, and somehow wrestled him into the coffin, a grappling that had him grunting and breathing hard. Afterward there was blood on Calvin's shirt, so he unbuttoned it, balled it up, and placed it at the feet of the corpse. He pulled a utility knife out of his pocket and cut a large square patch out of the chapel carpet, the section that had blood on it. He turned it into a tight roll and wedged it into the coffin beside the man.

Last, he saw the gun. He picked it up, stared at it for a moment, and slipped it into his pants pocket. He pushed the coffin into the display area, and Cohen followed him, unable to speak. His father locked the coffin and parked it beside the glass doors before returning upstairs. When he came down, he had a bucket of soapy water, and he cleaned off the door frame, the chapel wall, and the area outside the glass doors.

Cohen watched the entire time. He didn't know what to say. He didn't know what to do. His legs were so tired. He realized he was hungry. He couldn't remember the last time he had eaten, or what it had been.

His father went upstairs again. Light was creeping into the city, coming up over the buildings, lining the leaves. What Cohen could see of the sky in the east was clear and emerged slowly from black to navy to blue. He heard his father upstairs talking on the phone, only a few sentences, and when he came down ten minutes later he was dressed in his funeral clothes—black suit, shined shoes, black tie. The only thing that was different was that his head wasn't freshly shaven, as it always was on mornings he went to work.

Calvin looked at Cohen and still didn't speak. They stood there in the light of dawn, a father and a son. Cohen felt like he knew this man even less than he ever had before.

His father's gaze left his eyes and swept down over his clothes. He turned and unlocked the coffin, then came over and took Cohen's jacket from him. He lifted Cohen's shirt up over his head, took his shoes and his socks and his jeans, and put it all in the coffin. Cohen stood there in his underwear, cold and uncertain.

His father took in a breath to speak, stopped, shook his head. He put his hand on Cohen's cold shoulder, and he squeezed it once before going outside and pulling the hearse to the front of the funeral home. He propped open the glass doors, pushed the coffin onto the sidewalk, and loaded it into the hearse.

He drove away, Cohen went upstairs, and they never spoke of that night again.

One week later, on the front page of the local newspaper, Cohen read an article that listed the man as missing and reviewed his alleged offenses. One month later, a smaller article, embedded deep in the paper so that Cohen almost didn't see it, asked again for any information related to his disappearance.

After that, nothing.

sixty-two

"Though Vile as He"

The police call for nurses, who sweep in and take Kaye away on a stretcher. Her skin is a gray-white color. Her mouth is the horizon, flat and empty.

Cohen stands in the hospital hallway, still holding the baby girl, answering questions. Thatcher's mother is beside him, and Thatcher too, holding the first baby. Minutes pass. They give their information to the police.

Ava intervenes on their behalf, pulling them away, making assurances. "Where do you want to go?" she asks Cohen in a concerned voice.

"C'mon," Cohen says quietly, and they all follow him to his father's hospital room. Thatcher doesn't look away from the baby he is still holding. His mother walks quietly beside him, her arm situated protectively around his shoulders. Ava can't stop staring at Cohen and the baby girl he carries.

As the small, weary group approaches Calvin's hospital room, the sound of his mother's voice comes out to where they are.

> "The dying thief rejoiced to see
> That fountain in his day;

And there have I, though vile as he,
Washed all my sins away.
Washed all my sins away,
Washed all my sins away;
And there have I, though vile as he,
Washed all my sins away."

Cohen leads them all into the room. Cohen's mother looks up, sees the twins, and stops singing.

"Here," Cohen says, handing her the baby girl, the one with the green eyes mixed with flecks of brown. "The nurses are going to take them down to the obstetrics ward in a minute. It's chaos out there—when they take them, please go along and make sure everything is okay. I need to go check on Kaye."

His mother does not say a word. She takes the child into her arms and stares into those new eyes now closing, and Cohen wonders what she sees.

He turns and walks into the hallway, into the chaos of police blocking off the hall and doctors and nurses evacuating patients to other floors. Ava follows him. Fear and relief are thick there in the midst of gurneys being pushed and IV carts maneuvered. The sun is shining brightly through the glass at the end of the hall.

Cohen stops outside his father's room. "Ava?"

She looks at him with wide eyes.

"I know you were there. I know you saw what

happened in the funeral home when we were kids."

Her nod is barely perceptible. Cohen wonders if he imagined it.

"You never told anyone, did you," he says, and it is more a statement than a question.

She shakes her head.

"No one ever found out." He says this to no one in particular before looking up at Ava again. "Do you have a minute? I'd like to tell you the story."

She nods, and this time he's sure of it. She gives a barely noticeable smile, and they head for the elevator in single file, winding their way through the chaos. Through the police, the nurses, the people being escorted from the building.

"Isn't today the first day of spring?" Cohen asks quietly over his shoulder, but Ava doesn't hear him. The hallway is loud and words are easily lost. The two of them walk unnoticed, one in front of the other, the crowd unconsciously clearing a path for them.

Cohen reaches back and offers Ava his hand, and she takes it.

sixty-three

An End

It's late on Friday night, the cold front has passed, and a warm breeze blows through the chapel door, which is propped open. Cohen takes in a deep breath, smells the warmth, the wet sidewalks, the dark sky. A gust of wind sends whatever remains of the rain and snow falling from the trees. He can hear the drops pattering in waves that match the breeze.

"Bless me, Father, for I have sinned." The words slip from his lips, soothing. There is no more anxiety as to what he must confess, what he must keep secret. If he's learned anything this week, it's that relief and light lie on the other side of confession.

Father James's warm voice comes through the screen, and it brings Cohen the same feelings as the wind outside the door, of life and fresh starts. "The Lord be in your heart and mind, Cohen, and upon your lips, that you may truly and humbly confess your sins: In the Name of the Father, and of the Son, and of the Holy Spirit. Amen."

It is as if he's hearing those words for the first time.

In your heart and mind.

Upon your lips.

"Amen."

Cohen glances back up at the image of the crucified Christ, and there they are: those deep green eyes with brown flecks. He envisions again the eyes of his niece. How could he have seen such a different painting before?

"I confess to the Almighty God, to his Church, and to you, that I have sinned by my own fault in thought, word, and deed, in things done and left undone, but especially in regards to this week. I have hated my mother and father. I have not been straightforward. I have not always told the truth."

Cohen pauses.

"Father, the more often I come to confession, the more I have to confess. I don't know where to begin or end."

Cohen can tell the priest is smiling on the other side of the screen, not because he can clearly see Father James's face but because of the sound of his voice.

"Then you have learned the true practice of confession and why it is a sacrament of the Church. Our recognition of our helplessness is the beginning of true dependence."

"I killed my father."

Father James remains silent, waiting.

"I once did something that revealed a secret about him, and that ruined his life. I convinced my sister that taking him off life support was the right thing to do. I confess for that."

Cohen looks down at his hands, clenches his fists, and marvels at the elasticity of his skin, the structure of his bones, the visibility of his veins. He swallows hard.

"You know, this week I spent a lot of time thinking back over all the ways my father failed me, but then I remembered something." He looks up at the painting. "I remembered the one time in my life when my dad was there for me. I was terrified. My dad came out to where I was sitting beside the window, and he put his hand on the back of my neck and stroked my hair."

"That was your father," the priest whispers.

"What?"

"That was your father. Of all the images he presented you with, of all the different fathers, the one who came to you in the dark and comforted you, held you up, loved you, that was your true father."

Cohen feels that old familiar lump in his throat, the stinging in his eyes. "For all these years, I waited for the dad of my childhood to return, the dad from before my parents' divorce. But he never did, and I hated him for that. But I've finally remembered how for one day he was there for me. For one day he was the father I wanted. The father I needed. I don't know if what we did in those moments was right. Maybe my father should have told someone about what I had done, what had happened. Maybe he shouldn't have hidden it away. I don't know. But he was there for me." He stares hard at the eyes in the painting.

Father James speaks quietly. "Sometimes people don't have the power to be what we need them to be for us."

Cohen nods, glancing back at the screen. "I know that now. I think of my dad differently now that I think about that night when he came out to the living room and stayed there with me." He pauses, swallows. "I wish I would have remembered that before now. Why do we forget these things? Why do we forget the most important things?"

Another burst of spring air flows through the chapel, cooler this time but still overflowing with life. The pages of an open Bible rustle, first one way, then back again.

"I should go," Cohen says. "Thank you for listening. Thank you for being here this week."

Father James does not say anything, but Cohen sees the outline of him nodding behind the screen. Cohen begins the final line of the confession, but for the first time all week the priest interrupts him.

"Your father loved you, Cohen. I hope you know that. Your father loves you. As does God. I think you've been waiting for the God of your childhood to return as well, but God is not in the past. God is always here. You must only open your eyes to see."

Cohen sighs, takes a deep breath as if to speak, but lets it all out in another sigh. He slouches down in the chair, all the wind taken out of him. A kind of lightness fills his being, an ease and a peace that he has not felt for a long time. The words come slowly, and he means them with all of his heart.

"It is for these and all my other sins which I cannot now remember that I am truly sorry. I pray God to have mercy on me. I firmly intend amendment of life, and I humbly beg forgiveness of God and his Church, and ask you for counsel, direction, and absolution."

"Our Lord Jesus Christ who has left power to his Church to absolve all sinners who truly repent and believe in him, of his great mercy forgive you all your offenses; and by his authority committed to me, I absolve you from all your sins: In the Name of the Father, and of the Son, and of the Holy Spirit. Amen."

"Amen," Cohen whispers.

"The Lord has put away all your sins," the priest says.

"Thanks be to God," Cohen says.

"Go in peace," the priest says, "and pray for me, a sinner."

PART SIX

Saturday,
March 21, 2015

*Let us make man
in our image.*

Genesis 1:26

sixty-four

These Are the Same Hands

Spring arrives finally, completely. The sycamore trees reach out into the air, and a constant breeze sweeps through the city, tickling the tiny buds that unfold like hands relieved of pain. A bright sun coats everything in a thin layer of honey-colored warmth.

Cohen stands beside the bed of his father. Calvin is dead, his death declared accidental. Only Cohen's mother was in the room with him when he died, and afterward she finally agreed to eat, walking to the cafeteria with Ava and Thatcher, still humming hymns to herself.

Cohen stares down at his father's body. A shiver of sadness passes through him, and for a moment he feels unbelievably cold. A nurse comes in, asks him to sign a few things.

"Do you mind if I wash my father's body?" he asks suddenly, and the words surprise him nearly as much as they surprise the nurse.

"No," she says. "I don't mind."

"Do you have a container I can put some hot water in?"

She returns with a small white bucket, and the

water in it steams. She backs out of the room, closing the door, and everything goes quiet.

Cohen begins with his father's head, gently wiping the stubble that has formed during the week. It is rough and coarse, like a short-bristle brush. It springs back after the cloth passes, spraying a fine mist.

He moves down to his father's face, sliding the cloth in the hollows of his eyes, the dimple under his nose, the roundness of his chin. Calvin's jaw is stiff and unyielding, and this more than anything breaks Cohen's heart. He's crying now, the tears washing his own cheeks, dripping from his own nose, gathering under his own chin.

He peels back the sheets and undresses his father as if he's a child, untying the gown and pulling it gently off his arms, stripping it away. The cloth has grown cold again, and he dips it in the hot water, the steam rising. Cohen washes his father's body slowly, wondering what a father-and-son relationship would be like if the son would wash his father while he was still alive. Would they love each other more? Would that kind of a washing break down the usual barriers? Would a different kind of life, a different kind of knowing, push up through the rubble? Washing his father, he feels like he knows him in a way he never knew him before. He feels a kind of tenderness toward this old body.

Cohen washes his father's feet, remembering

the stories from his childhood, stories told to him by Miss Flynne about the time Jesus washed his disciples' feet. The flannel-board Jesus wearing only a kind of loose-fitting toga over one shoulder, bent at the knee over a stone bowl, his disciples looking on in astonishment. The shock! The impropriety!

His mother comes into the hospital room, but Cohen doesn't look up, doesn't say anything, and for once he feels no judgment from her—only a kind of curiosity. She watches as he finishes, saving his father's arms and hands for last.

His father's hands. The same hands that wore a baseball glove and threw the ball to him over and over, back and forth, under a blue sky. Now so old. So utterly and completely finished. Cohen gently moves the hot cloth through his father's fingers. They, too, are already stiffening.

Cohen puts the cloth back in the white bucket. He covers his father's naked body with the white bedsheet and takes a step back from the bed as if to survey his work.

This is it, he thinks.

His mother comes around the bed and stands beside him. They remain there together like two pillars, and Cohen doesn't want to leave. His mother reaches over, takes his hand with both of hers, and turns toward him. When he doesn't look at her, she puts her forehead on his shoulder and cries.

sixty-five

A Beginning

Cohen turns his car into the VFW parking lot later that afternoon, drives around to the back, and then follows the narrow road down the hill to the baseball field.

"C'mon!" Johnny shouts, dashing from the car.

Cohen smiles. "I'm coming, I'm coming."

He follows Johnny, holding his father's old baseball glove. He found it buried in the back of a closet, the leather stiff and cracking. It scratches his fingers when he puts it on, and he stops and stands there for a moment under that blue sky, flexing his hand, opening and closing the glove, trying to work the leather loose.

"I don't know," he says to Johnny, who is already thirty feet away and itching to throw the baseball clutched in his hand. "I don't know. This glove is in rough shape."

"No excuses, Uncle." Johnny laughs and throws the ball, its red seams twisting like strands of DNA.

Cohen reaches up, and the feel of the ball nestling in the web of his glove is almost enough to bring up the tears. He laughs because he must do something, he must make some sound through the unexpected emotion.

"Nice throw, Johnny!" he shouts. He throws the ball back into his own glove a few times, trying to loosen the leather. The smacking sound of the ball, the sting on his palm and index finger, the scratching of the baseball's seams on his throwing hand—all of it is a time machine. He raises the glove to his face, closes his eyes, and takes in a deep breath. It all brings his childhood racing back, those summer ball games, before everything fell apart.

"Uncle!" Johnny shouts. "C'mon!"

Cohen holds the ball again, the seams like small tracks against his fingers. As he throws it, he feels the old movement, the rotation, the release. The ball sails through the air and makes that satisfying *smack* in his nephew's glove.

"Nice catch!" he shouts. "Nice one, Johnny. How does it feel to be a big brother?"

Johnny throws the ball back. "Great," he says, and his voice sinks into reflection. "Do you think Mom's going to be okay?"

Cohen pauses the game of catch, keeping the ball in his glove. "She's going to be fine, Johnny. They've got her resting. She'll be out of that place in no time." He throws the ball back. "What?" he asks, pretending to be offended. "Don't you like staying with your Uncle Cohen?"

Johnny laughs. "I'd live with you if I could," he says.

"Whatever," Cohen says, but a warmth fills his chest. "You're a good kid. You know that?"

Johnny laughs again.

They throw the ball back and forth between them, back and forth. Cohen smiles at the simplicity of it, the repetition, the ease that it causes him to feel.

"Attaboy," he says. "You've got quite an arm."

The sun is bright in the sky above them, and the warm spring breeze sweeps through the farmers' fields. A train whistle screams somewhere far off, so far away that it is almost unrecognizable.

For a moment Cohen envisions himself and Johnny throwing the ball back and forth, but he is looking down at them from a great height. The two of them, he and Johnny, are two small specks in the middle of the dusty infield, which is a small brown fleck in the middle of all that green expanse of country, and there's nothing else left in the whole wide world to be afraid of, nothing to run from.

There are only the two of them, alive in the green and the brown.

Acknowledgments

Each book I've written has given me a different sort of joy, and this one has been no exception. There is much that the writing of this specific story has brought to the surface in me, things I will be contemplating for years to come. Thank you for joining me on yet another journey.

The following is my attempt to thank some of those who were most crucial in the coming to life of this book.

Thank you, Ruth, for being a wonderful agent. The crossing of our paths was such a blessing to me, the time we worked together was enjoyable, and I wish you all the best in your future endeavors.

Thank you, Kelsey, for continuing to believe in me and my writing.

Thank you, Jessica, for your fine-tuning. By the time you and Kelsey finish with my books, I wonder if you should both have a byline. The time and care you have put into my writing, and this book specifically, means so much to me.

A huge thanks to Gayle and the design crew at Revell for putting together such a compelling cover. I hope the words I have written live up to the promise of your creation.

Karen, Michele, and Hannah, I am so thankful

for all that you do to spread the word about what we're up to. I love working with you. Here's to many more books.

To Caleb, for answering my funeral director questions and for text threads the FBI almost certainly remains very concerned about. Thanks, my friend.

To all of you writing friends who travel the same difficult and rewarding road but still take the time to encourage me, share my work, and inspire me with your own beautiful words and dedication to the craft. Thank you.

Thanks, Mom and Dad, for being so much better at parenting than Calvin and Rachel.

Thank you, Maile, for always reading what I write, for your honest feedback, and for traveling with me through this life. You give me the courage I need to keep writing.

And to Cade, Lucy, Abra, Sam, Leo, and Poppy. Everything I do is for you. You're the best kids a dad could want. Keep looking up at the stars. Keep considering the light.

Shawn Smucker is the author of the award-winning young adult novels *The Day the Angels Fell* and *The Edge of Over There*, as well as the memoir *Once We Were Strangers*. He lives with his wife and six children in Lancaster, Pennsylvania. You can find him online at www.shawnsmucker.com.

Books are produced in the United States using U.S.-based materials

Books are printed using a revolutionary new process called THINKtech™ that lowers energy usage by 70% and increases overall quality

Books are durable and flexible because of Smyth-sewing

Paper is sourced using environmentally responsible foresting methods and the paper is acid-free

Center Point Large Print
600 Brooks Road / PO Box 1
Thorndike, ME 04986-0001 USA

(207) 568-3717

US & Canada:
1 800 929-9108
www.centerpointlargeprint.com